Plain Jane's Secret Admirer

Plain Jane's Secret Admirer

ANNE BLACKBURNE

YOU are the reason we do what we do here at Barbour Publishing. We promise that we will always use our God-given talents to produce content with you in mind—and that we will remain biblically faithful, no matter what.

Thank you for being the heart of our business.

Print ISBN 979-8-89151-257-3
Adobe Digital Edition (.epub) 979-8-89151-258-0

All scripture quotations are taken from the King James Version of the Bible.

Cover Design: Kirk DouPonce, DogEared Design

Published by Barbour Publishing, Inc., 1810 Barbour Drive, Uhrichsville, Ohio 44683, www.barbourbooks.com

Our mission is to inspire the world with the life-changing message of the Bible.

Printed in the United States of America.

Dedication

For Jennifer, always the better grammarian!
I know that you're drinking Everlasting Love
from the Flowing Fountain that is Jesus.

I'll see you later, little sister.

CHAPTER ONE

"I see you trying not to roll your eyes at me, Jane! Is that any way to treat a friend on the verge of a nervous breakdown?"

With a mighty effort, Jane Bontrager managed not to actually roll her eyes, but she couldn't hold back a laugh as her lifelong best friend and brand-new sister-in-law, Lizzie, stood wringing her hands as she glanced around the seating area of her business, The Plain Beignet. Lizzie and Jane's brother, John, were preparing to leave on their long-anticipated wedding trip, and Lizzie was experiencing last-minute jitters at the thought of leaving her business in other hands, even hands as capable as her good friends'.

"Are you sure you're all right with us leaving now?" Lizzie fretted, chewing on her bottom lip as she turned to look earnestly at Jane. "We don't have to go today. I'm sure John would understand. After all, we've only been married a couple weeks, and we could put off our wedding trip if you need me to stay."

Jane smiled at Lizzie, who almost looked like she hoped Jane would give her an excuse not to leave her beloved bakery. *Not going to happen, my friend.* "We'll be fine, right, Eliza?" Jane asked their younger friend who worked with them in Lizzie's New Orleans-style French/Amish bakery, located in the heart of Ohio's Amish Country in the town of Willow Creek.

Eliza King gave an emphatic nod, causing the strings of her translucent white prayer *kapp*, which was heart shaped in the Lancaster, Pennsylvania, style rather than the more cone-shaped, flat-topped ones found in Ohio, to swing about.

"*Ja*, of course we will. Don't you trust us, Lizzie?" Eliza batted her eyes at their friend just as a horn tooted out front, signaling that their ride to the train station in Akron had arrived.

Jane's older brother John came up and captured his bride's hand. He had clearly overheard Lizzie's nervous offer, and he gave her a reassuring smile she couldn't help but respond to. He lifted her hand and pressed a tender kiss on her knuckles, causing Lizzie to blush and Jane to sigh wistfully as she thought of another young man she wished and prayed would someday cherish her the way John obviously cherished her friend.

John smiled into Lizzie's eyes as if she were the only thing he could see. "Lizzie, you know you can trust Jane and Eliza to watch over the business while we're gone. They've both been with you since before you opened." He bent and picked up her backpack/purse and handed it to her before picking up the two suitcases sitting nearby on the wide plank pine floor of the bakery and turning toward the front door. Raising an eyebrow at his wife, he said, "The van is here. If we don't hurry, we'll miss our train."

Lizzie, normally a perfectly rational woman as well as a gifted businesswoman, cast a glance out the front door at the waiting vehicle then took a deep breath and visibly got hold of herself. "Of course I know you'll take *gut* care of The Plain Beignet. It's just that it's been a while since I went anywhere farther than Berlin, and I feel as if I'm abandoning you guys." She gave a sheepish smile and turned to walk toward the door.

John, who was holding the front door open, stood aside to let her pass, but she suddenly spun back, holding up a hand. "Remember the standing pastry order for Rebekkah's Country Kitchen. She picks up every morning by eight. Oh! And don't forget to deposit the money every evening. We don't want it sitting around in the safe, except for the starter cash." She paused to think for a moment, gave a nod, and started to turn—but then spun back. "I almost forgot! Remember Simon Yoder's birthday cake. Mary said she'd pick it up tomorrow afternoon." She stood frowning as if trying to think of something else, and Jane stepped forward and turned her friend toward the door, which John was still holding open.

"It's all written down, Lizzie. We'll check the calendar every morning and every night. And we'll remember to write down any new orders that come in. I promise not to run you out of business in the next few weeks. Now go! Enjoy your trip, and say hi to Ruth's folks in Beeville for me.

And give my love to our cousins in Wisconsin!"

John and Lizzie were traveling to Beeville, Texas, by train to visit several former members of their Amish community who had relocated to the Amish community in the Texas hills. They would also stop in an Amish community in Wisconsin to visit cousins of John and Jane's who hadn't been able to make it to their wedding.

Lizzie stood irresolutely by the door, an arrested look on her face as she tried to remember if there were any other vital instructions she needed to dispense.

"We'll remember everything," Jane said with a grin for her friend's nervousness. "And if you think of anything else, you can call us from Beeville. Now go! You're starting to make me think you don't trust us!"

"Of course I trust you!" She nibbled on her lower lip, then her eyes popped wide. "Remember to take good care of Little Mouse! She's going to think I'm abandoning her!" From the way she peered toward the stairs that led up to the residential floors of the building, Jane could tell that Lizzie was within an inch of running back up to kiss her pretty gray kitty goodbye once more—for what would amount to the fourth time that morning.

"Lizzie," Jane said gently, laying a hand on her friend's arm. "Little Mouse will be fine. She's got Secret to hang out with, and they're best buds, you know that. What could possibly happen to her? We'll all be fine. Go. Enjoy yourself."

"Go on, Lizzie, before you make us think you don't trust us!" Eliza King added with a smile to let Lizzie know she was joking.

After a moment Lizzie smiled tremulously at her two friends and hurried forward to give her bestie since childhood a strong hug, followed by a hug for Eliza. "I know you'll do fine. I love you guys! See you in a couple weeks! Hug Little Mouse for me! I'll check in once a week."

John did roll his eyes over his wife's head, and then he and Lizzie were out the door. Jane and Eliza stepped forward and waved as John stowed their luggage in the back of the large white van, and then they helped Lizzie climb up into the passenger area. They kept waving as the van pulled away and drove off down the street.

Jane closed the door, turned the lock since they wouldn't be opening for another hour, and grinned at Eliza. "Well, they're off!"

"Finally!" Eliza laughed. "I know she's worried about leaving the business for the first time since it opened. But actually, I think she's more worried about leaving Little Mouse. You know how she dotes on that cat!"

Jane grinned. "I think it's a draw."

"You're probably right. But I believe she'll end up having a great time."

Jane nodded. "Of course she will! And goodness, it's time she took a break. It's been over a year since we opened. You went to Lancaster to see your folks at Christmas, and again this summer, and I went up to Kelleys Island with my family for a few days this summer. Lizzie hasn't taken any time off. I was starting to worry she'd burn out. So it's very gut she's taking a few weeks off now. When she gets back she'll be fresh as a daisy and ready to get back to work!"

"Speaking of work, we'd better get back to it. It's Monday, so the ladies from the bank will be in for their doughnuts," Eliza said, waggling her eyebrows at the standing order the women from a local bank always placed for two dozen chocolate-covered chocolate cake doughnuts.

They looked at each other and simultaneously said, "Chocolate overload!" It was an old joke. The bankers, all in their fifties and sixties, had been eating the same kind of chocolate-on-chocolate doughnuts for more than twenty years. They wouldn't even consider trying any other type.

Chuckling, Jane said, "And the Realtors meeting is today, so they'll want a few dozen assorted pastries."

Eliza and Jane made their way to the back to get ready for the day ahead. Since they'd been baking for a couple of hours, they were both wearing white aprons over their dresses and hairnets under their kapps.

Jane pulled a sheet of croissants from an oven and set it on a stainless-steel counter before sliding a pan of beignets in and closing the oven door and setting a timer.

Eliza picked up a tray of cake doughnuts and headed up front to set them out in the display case. "I'll start putting out the pastries and make coffee."

Jane nodded. "Sounds gut. And I'll get started on the chicken and ham salads we're offering for lunch today."

Eliza disappeared through the swinging door into the front of the bakery, and Jane got to work on the lunch salads.

As she worked, Jane thought about the circle of close friends she'd known since childhood, some her age and some older or younger. She was blessed to have friends who really cared about each other. And beyond them, a wider community of friends, relatives, neighbors, and associates in the *gmay*, their church community, who watched out for one another the way she figured *Gott* had intended when He created people in the first place.

She stirred mayonnaise into the chicken salad and pondered the day her elderly friend Lydia Coblentz had gifted her and each of her seven best friends, all single Amish women, with a kitten from her cat Hepzibah's final litter.

"Four years ago," she murmured as she added pecans and dried cranberries to the chicken salad. "And three of us—Ruth, Mary, and Lizzie—are all married now!"

Finishing up the chicken salad, she stored it in the walk-in fridge and started on the ham salad. It was hard to believe how much had changed since that day in Ruth Helmuth's kitchen. Three of the eight married, and two of them with *kinner* already!

"And I'm still alone, pining foolishly after a man who acts like he doesn't even know I exist. Pathetic." She put the ham salad into the walk-in fridge and stood in the kitchen, hands on her slim hips, looking around as she decided what to do next.

A flicker of white at the corner of her eye caused her to turn toward the back door, which led into the alley behind the bakery and other buildings on Willow Creek's Main Street. "What on earth?"

She walked over to the door and peered out into the dawning day. A white envelope was taped to the glass. Frowning, she opened the door and peered down the alley in each direction. Seeing no one, she carefully pulled the envelope from the glass, turning it in her hands, and gave a small gasp.

"Why, it's addressed to me!" She was about to pull the door closed when she happened to glance down at the stoop, where she saw a small bowl containing a half dozen eggs in various shades of blue and green.

"How pretty!" she exclaimed, bending to retrieve the bowl, which she noted was made from brown pottery—plain but very pretty.

Closing the door, she walked over to the counter and put down the bowl of eggs, which she had to guess were fresh farm eggs, although who locally had chickens that laid such pretty eggs she didn't know.

Then she looked at the envelope again and, curious, grabbed a knife and slit it open. She withdrew a plain piece of white stationary, upon which was written a simple message:

> *I hope you like these eggs. They're as pretty as you are. And the bowl is both pretty and useful, so I figured you'd like it too.*

It was signed, *An Admirer.*

"Oh my goodness! Eliza!" she cried, "Come quick! You won't believe it!"

She turned toward the swinging door, but Eliza hurried through before she took a step. "Jane? Are you okay? I heard you yell. What's going on?"

"Eliza, look at this!" She stood aside and pointed at the bowl of eggs and waved the note at her friend. Eliza frowned and came forward, peering down at the pretty eggs before looking at Jane.

"What is this? I don't remember having colorful eggs. . .and I don't recognize this bowl. Did Lizzie leave it here as some weird surprise?"

Jane shook her head and thrust the note into Eliza's hands. "Not Lizzie, but someone did! Read the note!"

Eliza glanced at the note then looked back at Jane in disbelief. "Where did you find this?"

"I saw the envelope taped to the window on the back door, and the bowl of eggs was on the stoop!"

Eliza glanced doubtfully at the eggs. "I mean, they're pretty, but what kind of gift is this? Eggs and a bowl?"

Jane's face fell. "I don't know, I kind of like them. And look how pretty the bowl is! It looks hand fired to me. The glaze is beautiful. Plain and useful, sure, but also lovely."

A look of chagrin on her face, Eliza said, "I don't mean to ruin your enjoyment, I'm sorry, Jane." Eliza cast another doubtful glance at the eggs. "But you have to admit it's an odd gift for a secret admirer to leave at the door."

Then her eyes widened as she realized what she'd said. "Jane! You have a secret admirer! Who could it be?"

Jane stared at Eliza, who stared back. Blinking, she shook her head slowly. "I have no idea."

Samuel Mast grimaced as he fitted the final wheel onto the carriage of a two-seater buggy he was making for a family in a neighboring town. The wheel didn't want to go on properly, and after several minutes of attempting to bend it to his will, Samuel grunted in disgust and sat back on his haunches, staring absently at the stubborn contraption. He shoved a lock of chestnut-brown hair out of his eyes, thinking it was past time for a haircut. "I'm going to need help with this wheel."

A minute later he shook his head and pushed to his feet. "It's not the wheel's fault you're distracted, man," he muttered to himself. Turning away from the someday buggy, he stalked over to a window and stood looking outside at the field where his growing herd of Tunis sheep grazed contentedly, his hazel eyes unfocused as he gazed not on the scene outside the window, but inwardly on something that was troubling him.

With a groan of embarrassment, he saw himself carefully placing a bowl of colorful eggs on the back stoop of The Plain Beignet early that morning and then taping an envelope to the window of the shop. He'd peeked inside, where he'd seen two women, Eliza King and Jane Bontrager, talking as they took trays of baked goods out of ovens.

Suddenly aware he was acting like a Peeping Tom, he'd stepped away from the back door of the business and hurried down the alley to where he'd left his buggy and his patient standardbred gelding, Ralph.

Now leaning his forehead against the window glass, he rolled his head back and forth in disgust. "*Ach!* What was I thinking? Jane Bontrager would never look at me. She's so vital and fun, and I'm just. . .boring. And now I've started something I don't know how to finish. Secret admirer?" He smacked himself smartly on the forehead. "I'm a *dummkopf*! What kind of gift is a bowl of eggs? Eggs to a baker! It's as if I'd brought straw to Ephraim."

He closed his eyes. He knew that he was avoiding the most important fact of all—a fact that, if Jane knew it, would ensure that she would never, ever give Samuel a second glance. Not that she'd given him a first one yet, as far as he knew.

He recalled with anguish the day he'd bestowed on her the nickname of Plain Jane—a nickname that had, unfortunately, stuck with the young

Amish girl through her teen years.

It didn't matter that it had been unwittingly done. The fact was that the carelessly bestowed nickname had hurt her. He'd seen the pain in her expressive brown eyes, filled with tears the day she'd heard some of their schoolmates laughing and calling her Plain Jane.

Ironically, she was anything but plain, especially in his eyes! She was beautiful, and he'd made her doubt it, all because he was a coward.

He shuddered to think what would have happened if she had run around the corner of the one-room Amish schoolhouse in time to overhear him oh-so-cleverly calling her Plain Jane to prove to some foolish school chum that he didn't have a crush on her because the other boys had been teasing him about her.

Except, of course, he did have a crush on her, even back then when she'd been twelve and he'd been fourteen, almost done with school and old enough to know better than to call an innocent girl names.

She hadn't overheard him, but the nickname had quickly caught on, and the damage had been done. He hadn't known how to confess or apologize, and somehow nobody had remembered or told her that he was the one who'd come up with the mean name.

So instead of having the terrible thing come out then and there, and being able to own his guilt and apologize. . .he'd spent the next twelve years regretting what he'd done.

And pining for Jane Bontrager from afar.

A woman who didn't know he existed and who, if she knew what he'd done, would be more likely to shun him than to give him the chance he craved to be her man.

Samuel stared at the sheep and brooded.

"Pathetic," he muttered. "Okay, Samuel, get it together."

"Talking to yourself again, Sam?"

Samuel pulled himself away from the window, plastered a smile on his face, and turned to see who had come into his buggy workshop.

"Oh, it's you, Benuel."

Samuel's longtime best friend, Benuel Fisher, studied Sam then shook his head. "Okay, Sam, out with it. What's eating you?"

Samuel fought off the urge to tell Benuel to take a hike. It wasn't Ben's fault Sam had succumbed to some kind of insanity—hopefully the temporary kind—when he'd dreamed up the idea of becoming Jane's secret admirer.

He took a deep breath and blew it out before meeting his friend's perceptive gaze. "It's really nothing, Ben. I'm just having a broody day, that's all."

"Nuh-uh, I'm not buying that. The only time you get like this is when you're thinking too much about you-know-who."

"That's ridiculous," Sam said, spinning from the window and stalking back to the buggy in progress. "Help me get this wheel on, will you? It's giving me trouble."

Ben sauntered over and helped Samuel wrest the wheel onto the axle, holding it while his friend fitted it securely into place before stepping back and giving Samuel a knowing look. "Oh no, it isn't ridiculous. How long have we been friends?"

Samuel refused to meet Ben's eyes, just shrugging and wiping his hands off on a handkerchief he then stuffed back into his pocket.

"Come on, Sam. How long?"

"Well, since we're both twenty-six, I guess it would be twenty-six years, give or take a few months," Samuel muttered.

Ben grinned smugly. "That's right. And who knows you best in the world?"

"My *maem*?"

"Other than your folks, I mean. And other than your siblings," he added before Samuel could throw them in.

"Fine. That would be you. Satisfied?"

The smile melted off Ben's handsome, beardless face as he studied his friend's miserable aspect. "No, I'm not satisfied when you're obviously so unhappy. What happened?" He held up a hand. "Wait. You're about done here, aren't you? Let's go get some pie and coffee, and you can tell me then."

Samuel thought about it and shrugged. Pie and coffee were kind of a no-brainer, after all. "Sure, why not? It's not like I can make things worse."

He followed his friend out of the buggy shop, locking the door behind him. He'd have a little pie, coffee, and conversation. Maybe Ben, who had always had an easy way with girls, would have some useful advice for him. He could only hope!

CHAPTER TWO

Samuel sat across from Ben at a table at Ginger House Coffee in downtown Berlin, a spiced caramel latte warming his hands.

Ben plopped into the chair across from him, a whipped cream mustache on his upper lip, and took an appreciative sip of his own coffee before popping a doughnut hole into his mouth. "Mmm, hits the spot. I was starving."

Samuel continued studying his coffee, saying nothing. After a minute, Ben sighed. "Samuel, I overheard your comment about taking straw to Ephraim." When Sam's head snapped up at that, Ben shrugged. "Sorry. I wasn't exactly sneaking around. You were too lost in thought to hear me. So. Who did you take something they already have plenty of, if you don't mind me asking?"

When Sam just glared at him, unwilling to confess his embarrassing actions, a small grin stole across Ben's lips. "Okay, let's play a guessing game." He pointed to himself. "I'll guess, and you tell me if I'm right."

"This is silly."

"My first guess is that you took something to a certain pretty baker in Willow Creek. Am I right?" He tossed another doughnut hole into his mouth.

Sam grunted and took a sip of his latte, and Ben laughed and pointed a finger at him. "I'm right! I am, aren't I?" He popped two more doughnut holes, one after the other. "Come on, Sam, spill!"

"Don't talk with your mouth full. What, are you eight?"

Ben made a production of chewing with his mouth closed,

finishing with a big swallow of coffee. "There. So, am I right?" Sam puffed air from his cheeks and gave in. "Fine! Yes, I took a stupid gift to Jane and left it, along with a lame note, at the back door of the bakery."

"This is getting interesting." Ben leaned toward Sam, arms crossed on the table. "How stupid a gift? And how lame a note?"

"Pretty stupid and pretty lame."

When Ben just waited, Sam sighed again and then told his friend what he'd done. When he was finished, he sat back and waited to see what the man who knew all his hopes, dreams, and frustrations—as much as any guy knew such things about his best friend—would say.

For a moment, Ben said nothing. He bit the inside of his cheeks and covered his mouth with a fist, and Sam groaned, knowing this was going to hurt.

Ben held up a hand. "Okay, I'm not going to laugh. It was touch-and-go for a minute, but I've got it under control." He made a downward, calming gesture with both hands, smiling beatifically at his friend.

Sam blinked at him, and said, deadpan, "I'm so glad."

"Don't be sarcastic. I'm trying to help you. At least now I understand the straw to Ephraim comment. A baker probably has plenty of eggs." He held up a finger. "But! Maybe not fancy blue and green ones, so that's possibly not a total disaster." Apparently realizing he had icing from his last doughnut hole on his finger, he licked it like a kid. "Mmm."

Sam's eyes lit up a bit. "Do you really think so?"

Ben nodded earnestly. "Sure. And the brown pottery bowl sounds gut." He held up his hands, palms up, and raised one while lowering the other, and then reversed the process, as if weighing options. "Plain but pretty, and undeniably useful. So also not a terrible gift."

Sam allowed himself a small smile and sigh of relief. "So you don't think the whole thing was lame?"

Ben scratched the back of his neck. "Well, maybe not the bowl of eggs. But the note, man. What were you thinking?"

Sam groaned. "I don't know! I've been asking myself all afternoon. I compared a woman to a bowl of eggs. Eggs!" He smacked himself on the forehead. "Thank Gott I didn't sign my name. Maybe I can just pretend it never happened, and the whole unfortunate thing will just"—he wiggled his fingers in the air—"go away."

Ben snickered. "I don't think so. You've told a single woman she has a secret admirer. She'll be on this like a bloodhound on a scent trail. And the trail will lead back to you, my friend."

"But how? I haven't told anyone else. She couldn't figure it out, I'm sure."

"Question—which horse did you use this morning?"

Sam blinked. "Millie. Why?"

Ben ticked off the points on his fingers. "You went to Willow Creek early this morning, parked your buggy, with your very identifiable black-and-white paint horse, on the street—your first mistake. You should have taken her into the alley."

"I thought Jane might hear the hooves and come see who was back there."

"People drive through alleys all the time, Sam. She wouldn't have thought anything of it."

Deflated, Sam sank back into his chair. "Oh."

"That's done, so no point worrying over it. Your next mistake was giving her something so unusual. Not many people around here breed chickens that give colorful eggs. I don't even know what kind of chicken that would be. They weren't dyed, were they?"

Sam shook his head glumly. "Easter Egger chickens. A woman I know in Sugarcreek has a flock."

Ben gave him a lopsided grin. "Of course you know someone with chickens that lay Easter eggs. Moving on, you had to get that pottery bowl somewhere—I'm guessing a gift shop here in Berlin?"

"No, I got it over at Holmes County Pottery in Big Prairie a few weeks ago." He looked hopeful. "Maybe she won't figure it out?"

Ben shrugged. "Maybe. But the note, Sam. The note is the thing that will lead her to you."

"I don't see how. It's on plain white paper in a plain white envelope."

"Sure, but you said pretty things to a single young Amish woman and signed it as her secret admirer."

"Not secret. Just admirer."

Ben waved that away. "Same thing. She's what, twenty-four, twenty-five now? Probably wants to get married, and for some reason hasn't found the right man in the local Amish community. So she'll be feeling a bit desperate, probably. She'll come looking for you."

Samuel was insulted by his friend's reasoning. "Jane Bontrager has no reason to feel desperate about finding a man or getting married! She's a beautiful, interesting young woman, and when she decides to get married, she'll have no trouble." He stopped his tirade when he saw that Ben was sitting there grinning at him. "What?"

"You." He pointed at his friend, clearly delighted. "You're in love with this woman. You've been in love with her since school. Sam! Why don't you just ask her out before some other man notices how pretty and interesting she is?"

Samuel pursed his lips and looked away. "It's not that easy."

Ben looked truly puzzled by this. "Not easy to ask a woman out? Why not?"

"It's complicated, Ben. Have you forgotten what I did to her?"

Ben frowned for a few moments then raised his eyebrows in amazement. "Are you talking about the nickname?"

Soberly, Samuel nodded, his eyes full of misery. Surely now Ben would understand how impossible his situation was.

But it seemed Ben did not see things in that light. He opened his mouth then closed it, as if thinking better of whatever he'd been about to say. After a few moments, he spoke slowly, as if to a child. "Sam. . .we've talked about this before. And before that. And before that. I thought you'd let this go. Nobody has referred to Jane Bontrager as. . .what was it?"

"Plain Jane," Sam whispered shamefacedly.

"Right. Plain Jane." He chuckled. "It was pretty clever when you think about it." Obviously seeing that his friend didn't see the humor, he gestured with his half-eaten doughnut hole. "She's Plain, as in Amish, and her name is Jane. It rhymes and plays on her cultural identity." He shrugged. "Clever." He polished off the pastry then licked the icing off his fingers.

Samuel, panicked at the thought of anyone overhearing, looked wildly around the coffee shop. Nobody was paying attention, thank goodness. "Ben, not so loud!" he hissed. "It wasn't clever, it was mean. I did it because I was young and stupid, and didn't want the other fellows to know how I felt about her. Now I've lost her forever, all because I was *dumm* as a *youngie*! You'd have heard me yourself if you hadn't been out with chicken pox. Who gets chicken pox when they're fourteen? You should have been there to stop me from ruining my life!" He dropped his face into his hands.

Ben sighed. "Sam, you are a lost cause. I guarantee that if you walked up to Jane"—at Sam's renewed glare, he lowered his voice and leaned closer—"and told her you were the one who accidentally bestowed that nickname on her, told her exactly what you just told me, she would probably either have no idea what nickname you were talking about, or she would laugh and say she hadn't thought about it in years."

Sam frowned. "You think so?"

Ben sat back and gave a breezy wave. "I know so. Nobody holds a grudge that long, Sam. So, why not try?"

Sam thought about it, trying to picture himself walking up to Jane Bontrager and confessing the sin he'd been agonizing over for more than ten years. It was terrifying. He bit his lips, and Ben shook his head.

"Sam, you have to get over this shyness around women, or you'll be a bachelor forever."

"Says my friend the bachelor."

Ben slapped a hand to his chest. "I'm a bachelor because I haven't met the right woman yet. You've known who the right woman for you was since you were what, six?"

"Eight. She's two years younger."

"Right. Pathetic."

Sam sighed. "I know. I've told myself exactly that. It doesn't help."

Ben folded his arms across his chest. "So, what if I help you?"

"Help me? How?"

"Let me think about it for a few days. I'll come up with something." He stood and stretched. "Come on. I have to get home and do the chores before dinner. Maem is making meat loaf! Good thing I had the doughnut holes, or I never would have made it."

Samuel followed his friend out of the shop, second thoughts already assailing him. "Ben, you have to promise you won't do anything without talking to me about it first, okay?"

Ben cast a sideways look at Sam. "What would I do?"

"I don't know, but I need that promise, Ben. I'm serious."

"Fine. I won't do anything without discussing it with you first."

They climbed into Sam's one-seat buggy and turned toward his home, where Ben had left his own horse and buggy. After a few minutes of companionable silence, Sam said, "Or say anything."

"What?"

"You can't say anything to anyone without talking to me first, either. Don't do or say anything to anyone about this without first talking to me."

"Wow, Sam, you're a mess."

"Don't you think I know that? Just promise, Ben. I'm a desperate man, here!"

"Okay, okay, I promise." They pulled into Samuel's driveway, and he parked the buggy and jumped out. He began unhitching Ralph, his brown standardbred ex-racehorse, whom he'd taken to the coffee shop since Millie had gotten to go out that morning, while Ben led his own mare, Cupid, back to his buggy and hitched her up.

They finished at about the same time, Sam having stowed the tack and turned Ralph into the pasture after giving him a quick rubdown, and Ben climbing into his own one-seat conveyance. Sam walked over to wave his friend off and couldn't stop himself from extracting one final promise from Ben.

"I won't say anything, Sam. I already promised. Besides, I have a plan."

"A plan?" Sam was a bit worried. "What kind of plan?"

"I'm not ready to tell you yet. It's not completely formed, but don't worry, my plans always work out!"

"What? No! They don't!"

Ben pointed at his ears and pretended he couldn't hear Sam.

"Remember the pie when we were fifteen? That didn't work out very well!" But Ben was already driving down the long driveway. Sam thought he might have heard his friend's laughter trailing behind but couldn't be certain.

Sam watched him go, feeling an odd combination of hope and dread. He wasn't sure which emotion had the upper hand. "Sometimes Ben's crazy plans work out," he reminded himself. "But that pie plan did not go well."

He sent up a silent prayer to his heavenly Father for courage.

Gott, please help me. Ben's right. I'm a mess. This has gone on for far too long. You know how I feel about Jane. Please help me find a way to tell her what I did. And please, if it is Your will, let her understand and forgive. And maybe return my feelings, if that isn't asking too much. Your will be done, Vader.

He paused, then added out loud, "And Vader, please, whatever idea Ben's cooking up, don't let it turn out like the pie thing. Amen."

He stared down the empty driveway then shook off his uneasy mood. "I've got time to put another hour into the buggy before dinner. It's not going to build itself."

He walked back into his workshop, wondering what he'd gotten himself into and knowing that whatever happened he couldn't blame all of it—or even most of it—on Ben.

"A secret admirer? But Jane, that's *wunderbar*!" Jane's elderly friend Lydia Coblentz clapped her hands in delight. "Don't you think so, Abram?"

Abram Troyer, the bishop of their Amish district, looked less thrilled. "I don't know, Lydia. It's rather unorthodox, don't you think?"

Lydia frowned at her longtime friend Abram, who was seated at the table in the bakery's kitchen, reading the note Jane had found taped to the back door of the bakery that morning. "What's unorthodox about a young woman having an admirer?"

"It's fine for her to have an admirer. It's the secret part I don't like. A proper Amish man should not be afraid to step forward and express his interest in a young woman. It feels off somehow."

Jane felt a new uncertainty creep in at the bishop's words. "Off? How do you mean, Abram? Do you think whoever sent that note could be. . .I don't know, dangerous somehow?"

Abram's gaze softened when he looked at Jane. "Now, Jane, I didn't mean to imply that. I'm sure he's just not ready to show his hand yet, whoever he is."

"Right! It could be for any number of completely understandable reasons," Eliza tossed in from over by the sink, where she was washing up the latest pots, pans, baking sheets, and dishes.

Jane cast her friend a skeptical look. "Oh? Can you name one?"

Eliza frowned and turned back to the sink. "Hmmm. I'll think on that. Washing dishes is a great way to let go and allow your mind to ponder things you don't have time to think about at other times, because you're too busy!"

"I've always thought the same thing." Lydia smiled. "Some of my best ideas have come to me while I washed dishes and let my mind wander."

"Hmph, if you have nothing to think about, you should turn your mind to prayer," Abram said. "That's a much better use of your brain than daydreaming!"

Lydia patted Abram on the arm. "Oh, Abram, don't be a grump." Turning her attention back to Jane, she waved the note at her. "Now, Jane, you just let this simmer. Wait and see what he does next. Personally, I can't wait to find out what that will be!"

"Just so it's nothing too fancy," Abram grumbled.

"Eggs in a brown pottery bowl are not my idea of fancy. Are they yours?"

"Well, no. Eggs are a sensible gift," he allowed.

A corner of Jane's mouth quirked up at that. In fact, the old proverbial expression about taking straw to Ephraim (referencing a place mentioned in the Bible that was rich in wheat) had occurred to her when she realized she'd been gifted eggs. . .which she placed in the bakery refrigerator beside dozens of eggs they used in their baking every day.

But she knew she would be keeping these particular eggs for her own personal use. They were not going into a baked good to be sold in the bakery. They felt special.

"He's shy!" Eliza exclaimed.

"Huh?" Jane asked, pulled from her thoughts of how to use the pretty eggs.

"Your admirer must be shy, so he can't tell you to your face how he feels," Eliza explained, drying her hands on a dish towel.

"That could well be," Lydia said, pushing to her feet. "Time will tell. Come, Abram, we still need to stop at the market so I can pick up a few things for supper."

"*Denki* for stopping in, and for your opinion on this matter," Jane said, giving Lydia a hug. "Come back soon."

Jane saw Lydia and Abram to the front door then returned to help Eliza put the bakery to rights in preparation for the following day.

"Do you think there's something brewing between those two?" Eliza asked as she cleaned out the display cases, making certain to leave no crumbs that might attract critters.

Jane smiled. "I've thought so for a while, but until they decide to do something about it, we'll just have to wait and see."

"They should marry," Eliza mused aloud. "It would make their lives easier."

"They might enjoy their lives just as they are," Jane pointed out. "They've both been married before, and perhaps they like their own space. They seem to be together nearly every day as it is."

"Mmm," Eliza hummed, closing the final display case with a decisive snick of the latch. "I suppose. Well, that's it for today. I guess I'll head home. Any plans for this evening?"

Jane saw Eliza to the front door, standing inside as Eliza walked out onto the sidewalk. "*Nee*. Little Mouse, Secret, and I will probably have a quiet evening at home. I'm in the middle of a good book, and honestly, with Lizzie and John on their wedding trip, I think I'm going to enjoy the alone time."

"You won't feel odd, being in this big place all by yourself?"

"Nee, I like it. Besides, the cats will let me know if they hear anything out of the ordinary. Remember how fierce Little Mouse was when she was protecting Lizzie from the man who wanted to put the bakery out of business last year?"

The small gray kitty had caterwauled deafeningly and leaped upon the villain's head, incapacitating him until the police could grab him. It had been something to behold!

Eliza looked up at the three-story, historic brick building and gave a small shudder. "Well, I'd find it creepy being in there all alone at night. But that's just me. I'll see you tomorrow, bright and early!"

She turned and headed down the sidewalk toward the upstairs apartment she shared with Jane's younger sister, Susan. The apartment was just a couple of blocks away above the local doctor's office. The doctor, Reuben King, was Amish, and married to their friend Mary. He was also Eliza's big brother, which was how she'd gotten the nice apartment situated within an easy walk of the bakery.

Jane closed the door and locked it, then turned and surveyed the empty space that made up the public area of her friend Lizzie's bakery. She supposed some might find being alone in the big old building uncomfortable, especially since they'd found out the previous year that a murder had taken place in the building about a hundred years earlier, back when it was an inn. But Jane wasn't the fanciful type, and ancient history didn't bother her.

To her, the building was home for her and her little cat, Secret, as well as her big brother John, her friend Lizzie, and their cat, Little Mouse. That was all. It helped being Amish, she mused. They didn't believe in ghosts. Why would Gott leave someone's soul behind on earth? It made things easier when one was alone in a big, old building to remember that!

She thought she might just make her dinner and eat it in the cozy area, which was filled with tables and chairs as well as comfy groups of armchairs and a sofa or two.

"I'll sit in front of the gas fireplace. Secret and Little Mouse can come downstairs and lounge on the hearth."

Wandering back to the kitchen, she opened the door of the staircase that led up to the second and third floors; the third floor was all hers. Leaning in, she called, "Secret! Little Mouse! Come on down and hang out with me. Everyone is gone for the day!" She heard a little *prrrpt!* and knew her friends would be down in a few moments. Pleased with her plans for a quiet evening, she set about preparing supper for herself and for the cats.

"Life," she murmured to herself, "is good."

CHAPTER THREE

"Ah! That's all of them," Jane said with satisfaction as the contents of the last blue egg dripped into the mixing bowl on the table where she was seated. She was up early and had gotten the idea while putting the first of the day's baking in the ovens to blow the contents out of the pretty eggs from her secret admirer without breaking the shells, thus preserving them. She'd learned the trick from her mother when she was a little girl.

"*Guder mariye*!" Eliza's cheerful voice caused Jane to bobble the egg in her hand, but she juggled it a moment, catching it and breathing a sigh of relief.

"Don't sneak up on me that way!"

"I didn't; I came in the same as always, but you weren't out front. So I called, but you didn't answer until I came in here."

"I must have been too engrossed with my little project. Look, I've blown all the eggs, and now I can keep them forever!"

Eliza looked doubtfully at the colorful green and blue eggshells that were sitting on a paper towel on the counter, drying off. "Really? That's a thing?"

"Ja. My *mudder* taught me years ago. You wash the eggs with soap and water, then you poke little holes in both ends, and use a needle to break the yolk. Then you blow into the hole in the top of the egg, and the yolk and white come out the bottom. Then you soak the egg in soapy water to clean out the inside, and dry it. And you've got a perfect, empty eggshell! We used to dye them for Easter."

Eliza's brows rose. "That's really neat! We'll have to try that this

Easter!" She bent down and studied Jane's eggs. "So, what do you do with them now?"

Jane smiled fondly at the pretty eggs. "I'm going to display them in the little pottery bowl they came in." She frowned. "Hopefully the cats won't think they're toys."

Eliza laughed. "Good luck with that." She put on an apron and put her hairnet on under her prayer kapp. "So, you've got the first round in the ovens? Am I late?" She glanced at the clock on the kitchen wall.

"No, I was up early. The cats woke me up with the zoomies."

"The what?"

"The zoomies. That's when they just run back and forth for no apparent reason, like they've lost their minds. They zoom around—get it?"

"Ach, ja. Maybe Susan and I should rethink the kitties we're getting next weekend. I'm not sure I'd like being awakened early. I get up early enough as it is!"

"Oh, Eliza! You found kittens?" Jane clapped her hands in delight. She knew Eliza and Jane's little sister, Susan, with whom she shared her apartment above Dr. King's office a few blocks away, were looking for two kittens, but they weren't that common in November.

"Well, sort of. Not kittens, actually. We decided to rescue two cats from the shelter instead of getting kittens, since older cats are harder to place. So we went down there last weekend, and there was a bonded pair of brothers they wanted to adopt out together. We put in an application and a down payment, and we heard last evening; we're approved! We can pick them up this weekend!"

"That is so exciting," Jane enthused. "I think it's lovely that you girls are adopting older cats. How old are they?"

"Six or seven. The elderly *Englisch* woman who owned them passed away, and nobody in her family wanted them. So they ended up at the shelter. They weren't neutered, so that's happening tomorrow, and Saturday they'll be ready to come home with us!"

"Wunderbar! Lydia will be thrilled. She'll probably come by with kitty housewarming gifts."

"I wouldn't be surprised."

"What do they look like?"

"Mine is all black with tuxedo markings. His name is Little John.

And his *bruder* is all white, with four black paws and a black tail, and a little black mustache! He's darling. That one is Susan's. His name is Friar Tuck! I guess their former owner was a Robin Hood fan."

"Little John and Little Mouse!" Jane chuckled. "And Friar Tuck and Secret. They'll probably become good friends. We'll have to have kitty playdates. I can't wait to meet them." She glanced at the clock. "And now it's time for me to clean up this mess and get the first baking out of the oven. We open in an hour."

"I'll get the baking. You deal with the eggs." Looking at the bowl of eggs, Eliza asked, "What are you going to do with that? Seems a shame to waste it."

Jane considered the stainless steel bowl of egg yolks and whites. "I had my mouth on the eggs, so we can't use them to bake. But I hate to waste them. How about I whip up omelets for our breakfast while you get the second baking in?"

"Mmm, sounds good! I'm on it!" Eliza bustled about, switching out the pans of baking and then stocking the display cases up front while Jane made them a big omelet with veggies and cheese from their personal refrigerator. While the second baking cooked, they enjoyed the tasty omelets with fresh cups of coffee.

"These eggs are really fresh and delicious!" Eliza scooped up another bite, which she ate with enthusiasm. "I hope your secret admirer brings you more. I could get used to this."

"They're certainly a healthier choice than pastries, for sure and certain. I think I've got enough blue and green eggshells, though."

Eliza shrugged as she shoveled another forkful of omelet into her mouth. "If you get more, I'll take them."

Jane rested her chin on her hand and smiled at her younger friend. "Do you mind swallowing before you talk? I don't want to wear the eggs, denki."

Eliza grinned and washed the omelet down with a gulp of milk. She picked up her napkin and blotted daintily at her lips. "Sorry. It was so gut, I forgot all my manners! It really beats my usual bowl of cereal with a cut-up banana that's either too green or ready to become bread."

Jane thought about her usual, rushed breakfast routine upstairs in her personal kitchen. She grimaced as she considered the slapdash choices she often made. "You know, there's no reason we couldn't make a healthy breakfast every morning. We could take turns. When Lizzie gets back, there will be three of us," Jane suggested.

Eliza nodded enthusiastically. "Great idea! Besides, John will expect a gut breakfast every morning, and I doubt he'll be getting it upstairs in their apartment, even though they have that nice kitchen."

Jane snickered. "Nee, not with Jane needing to get started on the baking at four thirty. I know the furniture shop doesn't open until seven. Let's do it! Today is a gut start!" She rose from the table and carried her dishes to the sink, where she washed them up. The oven timer went off as she finished, and Eliza pulled the baking trays out of the oven and stacked them on cooling racks.

"I'll make the lunch salads," Eliza said, turning to pull the makings for ham, chicken, tuna, and egg salad from the fridge, but she stopped short, looking at a spot on the floor. "What's that?"

"What?"

"There's water on the floor over here."

Jane groaned. "Of course. Lizzie and John haven't been gone a full day, and stuff is breaking. It probably came from one of the refrigeration units." She walked over to have a look and felt a plop of water hit her forehead and trickle down her nose. "Ach! *Sis yuscht*! The water is dripping from the ceiling!"

Both women stared at the ceiling, where a drop of water could be seen forming before dropping with a plop onto the floor, joining the growing puddle there.

"This can't be good," Eliza said.

Jane shook her head. "Nee. Okay, please make the salads, and I'll go see if I can figure out what's happening upstairs. Oh! And please get Rebekkah's order boxed up. She'll be here at eight."

"Will do," Eliza said. "And I'll get the orders ready for the bank ladies and the Realtors too. Busy morning!"

Jane opened the door to the back stairs and hurried up, starting with the second-floor apartment belonging to John and Lizzie. It was currently unoccupied, as Little Mouse was staying on the third floor with Jane and her brown tabby cat, Secret. As soon as she entered the hallway, she knew they had a problem. She could hear water dripping. Following the sound, she entered the bathroom and cried out, "Ach, *du lieva*! What is this?"

Water was pooling on the floor of the bathroom, but she couldn't discern a source for it, until once again she felt a water drop hit her face. Looking up with a feeling of dread, she saw water trickling through a hole in the ceiling plaster from the room above—her bathroom.

"Oh no!" She ran for the stairs, which she took two at a time to the third floor. Bursting into the hallway, she found water flowing slowly across the wood floor from her bathroom—and she could hear running water. "What? I didn't leave the water running!"

Hurrying toward the bathroom, she stopped abruptly to remove her shoes and stockings. She waded barefoot through the growing flood coming from her bathroom and then stepped into the doorway and beheld the culprits that had caused the minor disaster. Little Mouse and Secret had somehow managed to turn the bathtub faucet on full force. They'd also managed to depress the lever to close the drain, probably by stepping on it while playing in the water. The tub was full and overflowing onto the floor. Fortunately it must have only run over a short time prior, as there wasn't as much water as there might have been. The cats were having a grand time playing. Both were drenched, and they were currently batting at a floating bar of Ivory soap that they'd knocked into the tub.

Jane took a deep breath to calm herself before wading over to turn off the water. Secret yowled her displeasure at her game being summarily ended.

"You'd better disappear, Missy. You and your pal here are not in my good graces right at the moment!"

Little Mouse trotted over to the toilet, which was closed, and leaped up to sit on the lid where she began taking a thorough bath. Secret yowled again and waded through the flood into the hall, scurrying out of sight.

"Oh my goodness!" Eliza gasped as she stepped into the doorway, her own feet bare. "What a mess! A piece of the ceiling has fallen into the bathtub down on the second floor." She looked around. "How did this happen?"

Jane silently pointed at Little Mouse, innocently cleaning her face on the commode. "That little villain and her fuzzy little friend did it. They turned on the water and plugged the drain! They were playing with a floating bar of soap when I got here!"

Little Mouse gave a small meow, as if protesting her innocence. Eliza snickered. "Where's Secret?"

"She took off when I got here, the little scamp." At Eliza's giggle, Jane gave her a sharp look. "What's funny? We've got a big mess to clean up now, and we open in twenty minutes!"

"It's just the idea of the cats turning on the water and blocking the drain until it all ran over!" She snickered again and then covered her mouth at Jane's glare. "Oh, come on, Jane, you've got to admit it's pretty funny."

Jane tried to keep a straight face, but with Eliza giggling from behind her hand, her own sense of the ridiculous got the better of her, and she snorted out a laugh. "You should have seen them! Both sitting on the rim of the tub, batting at the bar of Ivory!"

They looked at each other and were suddenly laughing so hard they had to hold their sides. With a grumpy growl Little Mouse jumped down into the water. Shaking each foot as she set it into the flood, she daintily exited the room, making the girls laugh even harder.

"Oh! Oh! We have to stop. We need mops, and we need to clean this up. Then we need someone to fix the ceiling downstairs!" Jane gasped.

"What on earth is going on?" A deep voice from the hallway caused both women to stop laughing and look at one another in alarm.

"Who's there?" Eliza called. "We aren't open yet! You shouldn't be up here!"

To Jane's utter astonishment, the last face she ever expected to see in her home peered around the edge of the door.

"Samuel! What are you doing here?" Jane gasped.

"I'm here too," came another voice, and Sam's friend Benuel Fisher stuck his face around the doorframe next to Sam's. He looked around, eyebrows nearly touching his bangs, and whistled. "Wow, you ladies have sure made a mess!"

At that, both women looked at each other, and they started laughing again.

Sam looked at Ben and asked, "What are they saying?"

Ben shrugged. "Something about the cats doing it?"

Jane got herself under control and, a hand on her aching stomach, waded out of the bathroom. "Excuse me, I need to get a mop."

The men stepped aside, and Jane saw that they were both wearing sturdy work boots. The water wasn't deep enough to be a problem for them. She opened the hallway utility closet doorway and pulled out a mop bucket, which she pushed toward the bathroom.

"Ach, what time is it? We're going to be late opening!"

Samuel pulled a pocket watch from his pants and looked at it. "It's about time for you to open. Why don't you both go on down. Ben and I can clean this up."

Stunned at the generous offer, Jane looked from one man to the other. "Are you sure? Don't you need to get to work?"

"We've got time. We had to be in Willow Creek this morning. I was delivering a buggy, and Ben followed me in to give me a ride home," Sam explained. "So of course, we decided we needed coffee and beignets."

Jane smiled. "Of course. Who wouldn't?"

Sam smiled at her, and she reflected that it was possibly the first easy interaction they'd enjoyed since they'd been kinner.

"You can be sure you'll be getting all the coffee and beignets you can eat this morning! But I'm still confused as to how you guys got in? I thought the door was locked," Jane mused.

"I opened it to check the mail," Eliza admitted. "I must have forgotten to relock it."

Jane cleared her throat. "That explains it. Okay, then, thanks, guys. Um, the bathroom below this one needs mopped up too. And a piece of the ceiling fell in from the water."

"I'll take a look at that," Ben said, giving Eliza a friendly grin. "I'm Ben Fisher, Sam's friend. Do you want to show me the second-floor bathroom, Eliza?"

She looked at Jane, who shrugged. "Go ahead and show him, Eliza. And get him the mop from the second-floor hall closet if you don't mind. I'll get downstairs and open up. You join me in a minute, ja?"

Eliza nodded. "Sure! Come on, Ben, back the way we came." She paused to grab her shoes and stockings and led the way down the steps.

Jane glanced back at Samuel, who was already mopping up water and squeezing the water into the bathtub, which she had drained a few minutes earlier. He glanced up at her and gave her a shy smile. She returned it and gestured back toward the closet. "There are paper towels in there if you need any. And. . .denki. You didn't have to do this."

He nodded, and she left, hurrying down the stairs to the first floor, wondering why Gott had delivered the literal man of her dreams into her presence when her hair was a mess, her kapp askew, her dress wet, and her feet bare. As she hurried into the kitchen and grabbed a towel to dry off her feet, she stifled a leftover giggle. "Ach! Sam Mast is cleaning my bathroom. Sam Mast smiled at me! Will wonders never cease?"

With a disbelieving shake of her head, she mopped up the water on the floor of the kitchen and put a bucket below the still-dripping ceiling. She ducked into the kitchen washroom to put her shoes and stockings back on, then she proceeded to open the bakery and get the workday started.

Sam's heart raced as he cleaned up the third-floor bathroom, and not from the mopping. "I can't believe I'm here, in Jane Bontrager's home, cleaning her bathroom! I'm in her bathroom!" He paused, frowning. "Okay, that really sounded weird and creepy."

Weirder was the fact that her bedroom was just down the hall. He thought about that as he finished up and replaced the mop and other cleaning supplies into the hallway closet. Surveying the bathroom, he was satisfied that all was as it should be—sparkling clean. Sam liked things to be in good order, and as a bachelor who lived alone, he was used to cleaning, cooking, and other chores generally thought of as falling into the woman's domain in the Amish world. A guy alone couldn't be fussy unless he wanted to eat nothing but sandwiches and canned soup and didn't mind living in a dirty house.

Since Sam's parents had died when he was young, leaving him to be raised by an elderly uncle who taught him the buggy building trade, he'd learned early to be handy around the house. His uncle wasn't much of a cook, so Sam had learned to fend for them both. And he'd gotten to be a pretty good cook too. They'd lived above the buggy shop in town, really a redesigned loft above a good-sized barn, and it had been a gut life. And when his uncle died at a ripe old age, he'd left it all to Sam.

After a few years, Sam had wanted to expand to a larger building for the buggy business, and he had a longing to have a farm where he could raise animals, plant a few crops, and raise a family—things he'd missed out on growing up.

So he'd sold the barn in town when the right property had come up for sale and moved in a few years earlier. And now he was living his dream—except for the family part. He was still cooking and cleaning for himself. He didn't mind, except that sometimes it was lonely.

And he knew who he'd like to ask to share everything he was building, if only he could find a way to atone for the past and win her love.

He stood in the hall next to the closed utility closet and looked toward the front of the building, where he figured the living room and kitchen were. Along the hallway were open doorways, sunshine pouring through the doors invitingly, that he assumed were the bedrooms. "Jane allowed me to clean her bathroom," he muttered. "She did not invite me to snoop around her apartment. Go downstairs, Sam—now."

Obeying himself reluctantly, because he would have loved nothing more than a peek into Jane's private world—but not in a creepy way, and taking a peek without permission seemed creepy—he headed down the stairs, stopping on the second floor to check on Ben's progress.

His friend had also finished cleaning up, but Sam found him standing in the bathroom doorway, hat in hand, staring up at the wet, gaping hole in the ceiling where water had poured through from above.

"Well, that's a mess," Sam said. "Gotta let it dry before we can patch it."

"Ja. Gonna be a few days." He slanted a look at Sam. "You're a better drywaller than I am, especially on ceilings."

"What are you talking about? You did it for a living for a couple of years."

Ben shook his head. "But you're quite competent at it." He cast his eyes back to the hole in the ceiling. "I'm pretty sure I'm busy the day we need to patch this."

"So we'll do it another day," Sam said cluelessly.

Ben shot an exasperated look at his friend. "Sam, I'm trying to help you out here. This is a golden opportunity to get closer to Jane. And it fell into your lap—maybe dropped there by Gott, did you think of that?"

"What do you mean?"

"No wonder you're still single."

"Says my single friend."

"Right. Pay attention. We tell the ladies I'm busy, but you can come patch the ceiling when it dries in a few days. Then you get to come back. Here. To Jane's place of residence. And do something nice for her out of the goodness of your heart. Is the light dawning, friend?"

Sam blinked at Ben, and the light dawned. His eyes widened. "Oh."

Ben grinned. "For a smart man, you can be very slow."

Sam smiled sheepishly back at Ben. "I guess so." He looked around. "Gut job here. So, we're done for now."

"For now. I figure you'll be able to patch that on Wednesday." He glanced around.

"What are you looking for?"

"A fan. It would speed things up. We want to make certain it's really dry before you patch it."

Ben left the bathroom and walked up front to the living area, followed by Sam. The living room was wide and deep. Spanning the width of the historic building, it had huge windows across the front that let in an amazing amount of natural light. The room was furnished comfortably, with a mixture of styles reflecting the residents, and from what Sam understood, that of the people Lizzie had purchased the building from.

"This is very nice," Sam said.

Ben spotted a battery-powered fan and walked over to grab it. "Here we go." He tested it. "The battery is still gut. I'll put this in the bathroom. C'mon."

Sam followed and watched Ben place the fan in the bathroom, perched on the wide marble windowsill, tilted slightly upward toward the ceiling.

"That should help." Ben dusted off his hands. Then he looked at Sam. "Is the upstairs apartment just like this one?"

Sam shook his head. "I don't know. I didn't look around. No reason to."

Ben shook his head. "How could you resist?"

"I didn't have permission. It would have been crossing a line."

"Did I just cross a line by finding the fan in the living room?"

"Nee, but that's different." When Ben just looked at him, Sam rolled his eyes. "Because this isn't Jane's apartment. Okay, I admit it. I was dying to look around, but it seemed weird, you know?"

Ben grinned wickedly. "Totally. But I would have done it. In fact, I'm going up there now to see if I can find another fan." He waited a moment. "Coming with me?"

Sam glared at his friend. "No. I'll go downstairs. I'll tell Jane and Eliza what we're doing, and that I'll be back in a few days when the ceiling is dry."

Ben headed up to the third floor to look for another fan, and Sam trotted down the back stairs into the kitchen. The door to the kitchen was standing open, as was the door out into the dining area. He looked around, but neither woman was in the kitchen. A glance at the clock showed there were still a few minutes before opening time, and he saw a full pot of coffee on the counter, with a tree of mugs standing invitingly next to it.

"Help yourself. You've earned it."

He looked over and saw that Jane had come into the kitchen, an empty tray in her hands. He smiled tentatively. "Denki. Um, Ben went up to the third floor to look for a fan. We found one on the second floor in the living room. We can't patch the hole until the ceiling plaster dries."

Looking surprised, Jane said, "You're going to patch the hole?"

He nodded. "If you'll let me. I'd like to help."

She glanced up at the kitchen ceiling, where the water had been dripping, but there was no hole there. A small bubble showed where a bit of water remained, but Sam didn't think it would show damage once it dried. If it did, he would offer to deal with it.

"Have you worked with drywall and plaster before?"

He nodded. "Ja, from time to time. It's drywall in the upstairs bathroom." Studying the ceiling, he gave a firm nod. "Here too. They must have replaced the plaster at some point during remodels, or following other unfortunate accidents."

She chuckled. "Which happen regularly in all homes. I know. Denki, Sam. I really appreciate your help. It's very nice of you. I'm glad you and Ben happened by today. You've both been a big help."

He felt a dopey smile overtaking his face and tried to school his muscles into a look of polite interest. She gave him an odd look, which made him think he hadn't quite succeeded, and probably looked like he had a stomachache or something. But before either of them could say more, Eliza popped through the open doorway between the dining room and kitchen. "Okay, we're all set to open and just in time! It's eight on the nose!"

Sam looked at the clock on the kitchen wall and was surprised to see how the time had flown since he and Ben had arrived. "Ach, Ben needs to get to work. I'd better let him know what time it is."

He walked over to the open stairway door and called up. "Ben! It's eight o'clock! We need to get going."

A call of, "I'll be right down!" drifted down the steps, and Sam turned back toward the women.

"Sam, you and Ben are welcome to come in anytime, but please be careful to close the front door behind you," Eliza said. "It's been sticking a bit, and doesn't always latch. It was ajar just now."

"Oh, I'm sorry! I came in last, so that's my fault. I'll be more careful in the future."

Jane was gazing at the open doorway to the dining room with a look of dawning concern on her face.

"What is it, Jane?" Sam asked, looking around to see what could be causing her unease.

"It's just. . .has the door between the kitchen and the dining room been open all morning?"

Sam thought a moment. "It was open when we came in. We checked the kitchen, and when we didn't find you in there we wondered where you could be. Then we saw the water on the floor in here and realized there was a problem, so we headed upstairs to see if we could help."

Rather than reassuring her, Sam's explanation seemed to upset Jane further, and now Eliza looked alarmed too.

"Oh nee!" Eliza gasped.

He looked from one to the other. "What's going on?"

Eliza looked at Jane and cried, "The cats! They could have gotten outside!"

"When did you last see them?" Jane asked, heading for the stairs.

"When they left the bathroom on the third floor." Eliza's hands flew to cover her mouth. "They wouldn't have gone outside, right? They've got to be upstairs somewhere. I'm sure they went into one of the bedrooms to clean up and nap. Why would it even occur to them to go outside? They wouldn't know that today all the doors were open, giving them a clear path." She was right behind Jane climbing the stairs, taking them two at a time despite her dress. Sam followed on their heels.

"What's this about cats?"

They burst out one after another into the second-floor hallway, nearly mowing Ben, who was about to descend to the first floor, down in his tracks. "Whoa! What's going on?" He caught Jane by her shoulders to steady her, and Eliza ran into her back. Sam managed to stop short of barging into them all, windmilling his arms to catch his balance.

"Have you seen the cats?" Jane gasped, looking past Ben toward the living room.

Ben looked lost. "Cats? No. . .oh, you did mention them earlier. But I haven't seen any. Have you, Sam?"

Sam shook his head. Jane pushed past Ben and hurried to the living room, while Eliza ran and checked the three bedrooms on that level. They emerged at the same time and looked at each other, rising alarm evident in their faces and body language.

"Anything?" Jane gasped.

"Nee!" Eliza said. She yanked the door to the utility closet open and peered inside before slamming the door shut. "Upstairs!" She darted back into the stairwell and headed up to the third floor, followed by Jane.

Sam and Ben looked at each other, and Sam said, "This can't be good. We'd better follow them." He headed up the steps, followed by Ben.

Upstairs they found the two women searching through all the rooms, calling, "Secret! Little Mouse! Where are you?"

But no cats emerged from clever hiding places, and after a few minutes the women had to admit they weren't on the third floor.

"Maybe they're in the dining room!" Eliza said. "Why didn't we start there?" She burst back into the stairwell and thundered down the steps, followed by Ben. Jane, looking like she was ready to cry, started after them, but Sam caught her hand. "Wait, Jane. Be careful. Those stairs are steep. Ben and Eliza are already downstairs. They're looking. Please don't rush down the stairs."

She stared at their joined hands and then raised tear-soaked eyes to his. "Sam, Secret and Little Mouse are precious to us." Her breath hitched. "And Lizzie trusted m–me to watch her c–cat while she and John went on their w–wedding trip!" She swiped impatiently at a stray tear that escaped and rolled down her cheek, and Sam itched to reach out and comfort her. But he didn't have that right. She still didn't know about the nickname.

"I'm sure we'll find them," he said. "Come, let's go down and see. Maybe Ben and Eliza have already got them."

She nodded and ran the edge of a hand under her nose then followed him down the steps at a more reasonable pace than their friends had taken.

After emerging into the kitchen, they hurried up front. A couple of customers had entered and were standing around looking bemused at finding everyone in a tizzy instead of serving up pastries and coffee like usual. Rebekkah was there for her standing order, and Anita Frederickson, the Willow Creek tourism director, was standing in front of the counter, her little dog peeking out from where it was tucked into her purse as always, drumming her beautifully manicured nails—were those little turkeys appliqued onto her nails?—on the display countertop.

"Excuse me, Jane," Anita started, "I have a meeting. . ."

"What?" Jane popped up from peering beneath a table to stare uncomprehendingly at Anita. "Oh, I'm sorry, Anita! Help yourself to whatever you need. We've got an emergency on our hands. Rebekkah, here's your order. I'm sorry we're running late." Jane rushed around, checking all the seats in the dining room. "They aren't here! Lizzie's going to be crushed if anything happens to Little Mouse!"

"Lizzie's gonna kill us if anything happens to Little Mouse," Eliza amended, looking at Jane, and Sam thought the two of them had run out of ideas.

"Your cats are missing?" Anita looked horrified. "Oh, I don't know what I would do if my little Mitzi got lost!" She rubbed the ears of her tiny toy poodle, and Mitzi gave a high-pitched yip of reassurance. The weenie apricot dog was not going anywhere. She knew where her biscuits were buttered.

"Is there a basement?" Ben asked.

Eliza perked up. "Oh, ja! Of course! I'll bet that's where they are, Jane. You know they're always trying to get down there. I think they may hear mice and want to investigate." She rushed into the kitchen, followed by Ben. "I'll go down with her," he called. "You help Jane look outside, Sam."

Jane's eyes widened. "Outside. That's what I'm afraid of." She put her hands over her mouth. "If they did go outside, they could be anywhere!" She rushed out the front door followed by Sam, who glanced back to see Anita and the other customers shrugging and moving behind the counter to help themselves to pastries. Rebekkah picked up her order and followed them out.

Outside, Jane stood on the sidewalk, looking up and down the street. Sam followed her gaze but couldn't see any cats anywhere.

"I wish I could help you look for your cats, but I've got to open up my restaurant," Rebekkah said. "I'll pray you find them fast."

"Denki, Rebekkah," Jane said, still searching the street visually.

"Have they ever been out before?" Sam asked, going over to look down into the window well looking into the basement.

"Once, last summer, Little Mouse chased an intruder out and across the street, through that park." She pointed. "The police found her and brought her back. She'd given the intruder a good scratch before he got away."

"Wow, that's a brave cat."

Her eyes filled again. "I know! Lydia Coblentz, an elderly friend in our community, gave kittens from her cat's last litter to Lizzie and me and several of our friends. Her one stipulation was that they had to be inside cats." Her voice caught on a sob. "And now we've let them out! Oh, Sam, we've got to find them before something terrible happens!"

Sam felt just awful about leaving the door ajar when he and Ben went into the bakery earlier. He told Jane as much, and she shook her head. "I know you didn't mean to. Besides, it sounds like Eliza left it open first. They might have gotten out before you and Ben got here. There's no use casting blame. It could have been any of us. I need to get that door fixed! Later. Come on, let's look around back." She strode off around the building, her sage-green dress fluttering around her legs. Sam hurried after her, and soon they rounded the side of the big structure and turned into the alley that ran behind all the buildings on this side of the street.

"Maybe they're at your back door." Sam walked quickly that way, hoping to see a cat. But no cat jumped out from behind the dumpster or called from any of the stoops leading up to the back doors of the commercial buildings along the alley.

"How did you know we had a back door?" Jane asked absently, her eyes and attention focused on any nook or cranny where a cat might hide.

With a jolt of dread Sam realized he'd just given away a clue to the fact that he was the one who had left the bowl of eggs on the back stoop, along with that note. What had he been thinking? "Um, well, I figure all the buildings must have back doors into the alley. And they do!"

And now he was lying to Jane—again! Ach, this was not gut!

"Oh, right, of course," she murmured. Stopping, she turned in a circle. "They've just disappeared. What am I going to do?"

He stepped toward her and placed a comforting hand on her arm. "Let's pray. Gott knows where your cats are. He'll help get them home safely."

She looked up into his eyes and nodded. "Ja, gut idea. You say the prayer, okay? I'm too upset."

Sam drew in a deep breath, searching for the right words. Then he closed his eyes and spoke from his heart. "Vader, Your daughter, Jane, has need of Your help. You know her need, to find her two cats that may have gotten outside from the bakery today. Please keep them safe, and bring them back where they belong. Denki, Vader. Your will be done."

He opened his eyes and found Jane standing with her eyes still squeezed shut, as if offering up her own silent prayer for the safety of the cats. His eyes moved to her lips, and he longed to bend over and press a comforting kiss onto them. Her eyes opened, and she smiled up at him. "That was a very gut prayer. Denki."

"I hope it helps to bring Secret and Little Mouse back."

She opened her mouth as if to answer, but a tiny meow interrupted her. Snapping her mouth closed, she looked around frantically. "Did you hear that? A meow! Where did it come from?"

A second meow, closer, drew their attention to the far end of the alley, where a lone brown tabby cat trotted in their direction. "Secret! It's Secret!" Jane rushed toward the cat and scooped her up into her arms, where she cradled her, kissing her head as the cat purred and rubbed her cheek.

Sam looked around. "Where's the other one?"

Jane looked up from Secret. "Oh no. We've got to find Little Mouse!" She started down the alley, but Sam put a hand on her arm. "Why don't you take her inside? I'll go look for Little Mouse."

Jane looked torn, but then she nodded. "Ja, I'll get her back where she belongs, and then I'll come help you. Little Mouse just has to be close by, if Secret was!"

Sam opened the back door, which was unlocked, and Jane went up the steps into the kitchen. Eliza and Ben were there.

"There you are!" Eliza cried. "And you found Secret! Yay!" She looked around and saw Sam, his arms empty. "But where's Little Mouse?"

"She wasn't in the basement?" Sam asked.

Ben shook his head. "Nee. They must have both gone out the front door." He looked at the girls. "I'm really sorry, Jane, Eliza. I should have made certain it was closed."

"I'm the one who didn't close it properly," Sam said.

"I'm the one who didn't close it properly before you," Eliza pointed out sadly.

"I'm going back out to look for the other cat," Sam said. "What does she look like?"

"She's gray, with amber eyes," Eliza said.

"I'd like to help, Sam, but I really need to get to work. I can come back tonight if you still haven't found her," Ben offered, looking genuinely regretful. He glanced at the clock. "I can just make it if I leave now."

"Go. I'll let you know if we find her," Sam said.

"Okay. I'll talk to you later. See you ladies later." Ben waved as he walked out the back door. Sam followed, looking back at Jane and Eliza. "You go ahead and help your customers. Hopefully you haven't lost any sales."

"Oh, no problem," Eliza said. "The money for the pastries and coffees was all left neatly on the counter. Plus generous tips! Everyone hopes we find the cats." She glanced at Secret, held securely in Jane's arms. "Well, the cat. Okay, I'll go cover the front, Jane. You take Secret back upstairs. I'll see you in a few minutes."

"I'll look for Little Mouse. I'm sure I'll find her quickly. She couldn't have gone far," Sam said.

With a last look at Jane, who smiled at him and mouthed the word *denki*, he nodded and pulled the door closed.

Ben was standing in the alley waiting on him. They walked together around front to where Ben's buggy was parked. "Good luck, Sam. Can you get a ride later if you find the cat before I come back?"

"Sure, no worries. We delivered the buggy, so I was actually planning on spending today just doing errands and working around the farm." He shrugged. "But I really want to stick around a while and help them find the cat."

Ben gave his friend a level look. "You know, you already helped find Jane's cat. That makes you a hero."

Sam rolled his eyes. "We don't do heroes."

"I'm just saying. This would be the perfect time for you to tell her about you-know-what, when she's feeling kindly toward you."

Sam wasn't quite so sure about that. "I don't know, Ben. I have no idea how she feels about me."

"Well, I noticed something that should give you hope, my friend."

Sam studied Ben's smug smile. After a few moments, his curiosity got the better of him. "Okay, so tell me. What did you notice?"

Ben studied his nails for a moment then looked up at Sam with a grin. "Only a little brown bowl of colorful eggs on the counter in the kitchen. She poked holes in all the eggshells and blew out the contents, washed up the shells, and she's keeping them. Eliza told me she loves them."

Sam blinked. "Really? She's keeping them?"

"Yep. As a decoration." He slapped Sam on the back. "You really got that right, my friend. So capitalize on it and tell the woman what you did when you were a foolish boy. Then apologize and ask for her forgiveness. My guess is, she'll forgive you."

Sam frowned. He just couldn't believe it could be that easy. Not after all these years of dreading her ever finding out. And if it was, then how foolish would he feel for having wasted all this time—time they could have shared together? He cringed at either possibility.

"I'll think about it, Ben. Maybe, if I find the other cat."

"You're a hopeless case, Sam." Ben climbed into the buggy and waved as he drove off.

"Maybe I am." He looked down the street, hoping to see a little gray cat coming his way. But there wasn't even a bird or a squirrel. "But I need to remember that with Gott, nothing is hopeless. Not finding a lost cat. And maybe not even my chances with Jane Bontrager." He set off toward the end of the street that led to the alley where Secret had come from, determined not to return without the other cat.

CHAPTER FOUR

By that afternoon Sam knew it wasn't going to be an easy thing to locate Little Mouse and return her to The Plain Beignet.

He'd looked all over town, stopping into shops, both Englisch and Amish, and asking whether anyone had seen a small gray cat with amber eyes.

As the early November evening began to fall, he trudged dejectedly back toward the bakery building, empty handed.

The cat seemed to have vanished without a trace. When the bakery came into sight, windows alight and welcoming in the growing dusk, he sent up a silent prayer for help.

Vader, I know she's only a cat, but a cat is one of Your creatures, after all, and considerably bigger than a sparrow. And this particular cat, as You know, is important to Your daughters Lizzie and Jane. For those reasons, and also because I carelessly left the front door open and let her out, I need Your help bringing her home where she belongs.

Please let no harm befall her. And please guide me in my search tomorrow, for I'll have to keep looking until she is found. Oh, and if You could help me figure out a way to talk to Jane about the unfortunate nickname, I could really use help with that too. I'm sorry to bother You with such trivialities. Denki, Vader. Your will be done.

As Sam walked up to the front door of the bakery, Ben's buggy pulled up to the curb, and Sam walked over and secured the horse's reins to a hitching post. Ben hopped down and walked around to where Sam waited on the street, stroking the soft nose of Ben's mare, Cupid, another former racehorse. Cupid's outstanding feature was that she possessed one blue eye and one green.

"Any luck?" Ben asked, reaching up to scratch Cupid between her ears, which pricked in his direction as if eager to hear Sam's reply.

Sam heaved a sigh of defeat. "Nee. And I looked everywhere—except wherever she is."

Ben looked concerned. "Huh. I wouldn't think it would have been so hard to find one little cat. It's not as if Willow Creek has a big stray cat problem."

"Believe me, I've learned a lot about stray cats in Willow Creek today. I guess they catch strays and have them neutered or spayed before releasing them where they were caught. They've been doing it for long enough that it's really made a difference in the stray cat population."

"Interesting. Okay, did you ask around?"

"Of course. I stopped at every business downtown. Nobody's seen her." He pulled off his wool hat and scratched his head. "How could one small cat disappear so completely?"

"Somebody must have her."

Sam looked sharply at his friend. "What? What do you mean?"

Ben shrugged. "It's common sense. If you looked everywhere and asked everyone, and nobody has seen her and she didn't come home with her sister, then the logical assumption is that someone picked her up very early on, before she had a chance to wander far."

Sam pondered that. "That would explain why we found Secret headed home down the alley, but Little Mouse wasn't with her."

Ben nodded. "Ja, it would. Now we have to hope whoever picked her up is local."

Sam's eyebrows shot upward. "I hadn't even considered that someone from out of town might have picked her up. That would be terrible! We'd never get her back!"

"It's unlikely that she would have allowed a stranger to pick her up, right?"

"How would I know? Maybe she's the trusting type."

Ben frowned. "I guess we better go inside and report to Eliza and Jane. They're not going to be happy."

Sam sighed. "Right. I wonder how long Lizzie and John are going to be gone. It would be gut to find the cat before they return."

"Let's ask."

They pushed through the front door, setting the bells jingling. Eliza popped up from behind the display cases where she was cleaning up for the day, and Jane came through the kitchen door, hope etched on her face until she saw that their arms were empty.

"Oh, sis yuscht. You didn't find her," Jane moaned, walking over to plop onto a chair in the dining area.

Sam walked over and took another chair at the table. "I'm sorry, Jane. I looked everywhere, and I stopped in every shop and asked about her."

"What are we going to do?" Jane looked truly lost. "I don't know what to do next. It was so hard working today, knowing she was out there somewhere and not being able to help search for her."

"We could make a poster and hang it up," Eliza suggested.

"Gut idea!" Ben said enthusiastically. "If you'll make it, I could take it over to the newspaper. They make copies."

"I'm not much of an artist," Eliza said.

"You're better than I am," Jane said.

Eliza sat down beside Jane, and Ben joined them, pulling a chair up to the table.

Eliza brightened. "You know who is a gut artist?"

At their blank looks, she said, "Susan! Your sister, Jane. She's a very gut artist! And she knows Little Mouse. We can get her to draw the poster."

"Great idea!" Jane said, hope dawning on her drawn face. "But we'll have to caution her not to tell Maem and *Dat* that Little Mouse is missing, in case they tell Lizzie and John when they call to check in."

"That's a good point," Eliza said, face sobering. She jumped up. "I'll go home now and ask her to draw it tonight. We have colored pencils, so she can make it realistic. I'll bring it back tomorrow, and Ben can take it to the newspaper!"

Ben stood as well. "It's getting dark. I'll drive you home, and then I'll come back for you, Sam."

Sam frowned. "I could just go with you now. It seems silly to have to backtrack."

Ben gave him a pointed look. "Nee, Sam. You need to fill Jane in on your search, so she knows where you've looked and who you talked to. I'll be back in a half hour or less."

"Denki, Ben!" Eliza said. "Let me just get my bonnet, cape, and purse. I'll be right back." She disappeared into the kitchen and was soon back with her things. She and Ben headed for the front door. "I'll see you tomorrow, Jane! Don't lose faith. We'll find her! You'll see!"

Then Eliza stopped, as if struck by a thought. "Hey, Mary King hasn't come for her bruder's birthday cake yet." She glanced at the clock in the wall. "Wasn't she supposed to be here earlier?"

Jane frowned. "Ja. That isn't like her. I hope everything is okay with her and Reuben and the *boppli.*"

Ben held the door for her, and she gave him a lovely smile as she slipped out past him. It was Ben's look of dopey happiness that gave Sam pause, making him wonder whether perhaps his old friend was the one finding romance—something Ben had always said he was in no hurry to do.

The door closed behind them, but then it creaked open a few inches. "Ach!" Jane cried. "That's what happened this morning!" She jumped up and hurried over, pulling the door closed and latching it firmly. "I need to fix that."

Thinking maybe he could make a little restitution for his mistake, Sam stood. "Where's the toolbox? I'll fix it while I wait for Ben."

When she started to demur, he gave her a look of supplication. "Please let me do something to make up just a little bit for letting the cats out. It'll make me feel better."

She studied him for a moment then smiled softly. "Well, okay then. If you insist." She stood and smoothed her black apron over her green dress then headed into the kitchen, Sam following closely behind.

"We keep the tools in the broom closet," she said, opening the door and going inside. A moment later she emerged with a pink toolbox. Sam snorted when she handed it to him, and she raised an eyebrow. "What? Pink tools do the job same as boring ones."

He chuckled. "I suppose so. Is this Lizzie's?"

"It is now. The previous owner, Mrs. Petersheim, left it behind when they sold Lizzie the building and the business." Her lips quirked. "I admit I was surprised to find such a fancy thing here too. But as I said, the tools are gut quality."

"That's all that matters." He carried the pink box up front, fervently hoping Ben wouldn't return and catch him using a pink screwdriver on the front door.

While he adjusted the hinges on the old door, he told Jane about his day spent searching the town for the missing cat.

"It really sounds as if you asked everywhere. Ach, where could she be?"

He tested the door several times, and when he was satisfied it would close properly, at least until the hinges loosened again, he returned the toolbox to the broom closet. When he returned to the dining room Jane handed him a cup of cocoa and invited him to take a seat at one of the tables, and she set out a plate of cookies she'd baked the day before. With a sigh, she picked up a cookie and murmured, "Where could that cat be?"

"Ben and I were thinking that maybe someone picked her up, to keep her from getting hit by a car or something," Sam said. He sipped his cocoa and chose a cookie from the plate, eating half of it in one bite. He polished it off and reached for a second as Jane watched.

"Are you hungry, Sam?"

"I guess I forgot to eat lunch. And breakfast," he admitted. "I was too caught up searching for the cat."

She jumped up. "I'll make you a couple of sandwiches. Do you prefer chicken salad, tuna salad, or egg salad?"

He smiled. "I like all three."

"Then I'll make you three sandwiches. Hold on, it'll only take a minute."

Before she could go back into the kitchen, there was a knock on the front door, and Jane and Sam turned and saw Mary King, with her one-year-old baby on her hip, waving at them.

"Oh, she brought the boppli!" Jane cried, hurrying to open the door for her friend.

"I'm so sorry I'm late," Mary said, smiling warmly at Jane. Her gaze moved past her friend, and her eyes widened when she recognized Samuel Mast standing behind her. Like all Jane's girlfriends, Mary knew that Jane had been crushing on Sam since she was a girl.

"Hi, Sam. I didn't expect to find you here," Mary said brightly, looking at Jane and wiggling her eyebrows.

Sam wondered what that was about.

Jane frowned and drew her friend inside and closed the door against the cold evening. "Oh, Mary, it's just awful! Wait until you hear."

She explained about the water leak, about the cats getting out, and about only recovering Secret so far. Then she looked at Sam and said, "Did you know that Lydia also gave one of her kittens to Mary? She's a sweet little calico called Hope."

Sam shook his head. "Nee, I didn't know that."

"Oh, ja. So I know how much Little Mouse means to Lizzie," Mary said. "Ach, Jane, would you take this sweet girl for a minute? Holding her too long while I stand hurts my back."

"You don't have to ask twice. Come to *Aenti* Jane, *liebchen*." She took the pretty child, tiny with blond curls peeking out from under her adorable baby-sized prayer kapp and bundled up in a pink fleece snowsuit and little pink knitted mittens, and snuggled her in her arms. Sam thought the child looked natural in Jane's arms, and he was filled with longing to build a family with his secret childhood crush.

"Sam, do you mind going behind the counter and grabbing the big cake box marked King? If you could just carry it out to Mary's buggy, that would be such a help."

"Ja, sure!" He hurried behind the counter, glad to have his mind engaged by something more productive than how he could win Jane's trust and love. He found the box and carried it out to the buggy by the curb while Mary settled her bill with Jane. Then the two women, Jane still carrying the baby, came outside. Mary was using a cane to walk, and Sam remembered that she'd been injured in a terrible buggy accident as a child, that had taken the life of her father and left her with chronic pain and difficulty walking. She'd relied on two crutches for most of her life for mobility. A daring surgery a couple of years ago had improved her mobility and day-to-day pain, but she still needed the cane. Still, he mused, looking at the relative ease with which she now moved and at her beautiful little girl, things had turned out well for Mary and for her husband Reuben King, the good Amish family doctor.

"Denki, Sam! It was so gut to see you again. I hope you find Little Mouse soon. I'll pray." Mary reached out for her daughter, but Jane said, "Oh, let me put her in her car seat, Mary."

Mary smiled. "Sure! It's gut practice for the future, ja?"

Sam thought it was interesting that Mary's teasing words made Jane blush as she lifted the little girl into her car seat and buckled her in. But she ignored her friend and patted the child's leg. "There you go, darling Annie. Tell your maem to bring you around here more often!" She gave the child a kiss on her soft, rosy cheek and stepped back. Mary checked the fastening on the car seat then, with a satisfied nod, closed the door and made her way around to the driver's side. She climbed up and blew a kiss at Jane. "See you soon, my friend!"

Jane waved while Mary guided her buggy down the street toward home. Then she and Sam went back inside, and she made the promised sandwiches. Soon Sam was munching hungrily while he and Jane discussed different possible scenarios regarding where a missing cat could be.

"Hopefully once the posters go up, whoever took her will see one and know where she belongs," he said.

"But, what if someone passing through town, a tourist maybe, saw her. She didn't have a collar on. They could have thought she was a stray!"

"If she was as well fed and healthy looking as your cat, nobody could mistake her for a stray. They have to know someone is looking for her."

"We just have to hope it's someone who cares," she whispered. Her eyes met his, and he found himself caught up in their luminescent brown depths. "Sam, I'm so worried. How will I tell Lizzie if we don't find her?"

He dared to reach out and cover her hands with one of his, and he gave a little squeeze.

"Let's pray together, Jane. Gott will watch over her, and if we don't find her, He will comfort Lizzie."

She nodded, and they both closed their eyes and silently offered up their prayers.

If Sam's held a little extra request, one involving finding courage to do the right thing and then forgiveness where it perhaps wasn't merited, then that was his secret.

Jane's dreams that night were filled with lost kitties plaintively crying in the dark. She jumped out of bed more than once and hurried downstairs to see if she'd really heard Little Mouse calling at the front or back doors for admittance, only to find nothing more than a startled family of raccoons searching the dumpster in the alley for scraps.

In the morning, Jane read from her Bible while snuggling with Secret and enjoying a restorative cup of lavender-chamomile tea and a few gingersnaps in her living room. She gave her kitty her daily brushing and filled her bowl of kibbles and her water bowl before firmly closing the door of her apartment and heading downstairs to get the baking started.

She opened the back door to the fresh, cold morning air and called softly for Little Mouse, listening hopefully for an answer and gaining only more disappointment.

She peered out the front door as well, calling again, but no answering meow could be heard.

With a despondent sigh, she started the morning baking, putting the first trays into the oven as she heard the front door open. Eliza called out a cheerful greeting and then popped into the kitchen.

"Did she come home last night?"

Jane shook her head. "Nee. Sam and I prayed before Ben picked him up last night. At this point, we have to put our trust in Gott, Eliza."

"Of course!" And Eliza held up a well-drawn flyer of a cat with contact information should anyone find her. "But Gott helps those who help themselves, so I asked Susan to make this up. I think she did a really gut job! What do you think?"

She handed the flyer to Jane, who perused it and nodded. "Ja, this is excellent. It's amazing how much it looks like Little Mouse! Susan really captured her spirit. She always was the best artist in the family."

"I agree, it looks just like Little Mouse." Eliza set the flyer carefully on the kitchen table and washed her hands before beginning the prep for the second baking. "Ben said he'd come by before work and take the flyer to the *Examiner*." She started a batch of dough for doughnuts, as they offered a selection of traditional bakery goods along with the New Orleans–style French patisserie fare, before suggesting offhandedly, "I could go with him, just to be sure we get the right sort of flyers. We wouldn't be gone long, I imagine."

Jane felt amused at Eliza's attempt to seem cool and disinterested, as if it didn't really matter what Jane said about her accompanying the handsome young single Amish man to the newspaper office. Jane suspected that it actually mattered quite a bit and that Eliza might have her first serious crush on a man. She supposed she could do worse, but then, she didn't really know much about Sam's friend Ben. Maybe she should mention him to Eliza's older brother, Dr. Reuben King, Mary's husband, and let him decide whether Ben was a suitable potential match for his little sister.

On the other hand, if someone did that to her she'd be furious. She frowned. What a quandary!

Eliza misconstrued her frown. "I don't have to go with him if you need me here. It was just a thought."

"Oh no, I don't mind. I was thinking about something else." She stole a sidelong glance at the younger woman. "So, do you fancy Ben?"

Eliza looked at Jane, a blush staining her cheeks. "Fancy? That's an old-fashioned word!"

Jane shrugged. "It's a gut word. Gets the meaning across. So, do you?"

"I mean, he's a nice man. And he was very helpful yesterday, wasn't he? And he's coming all the way back here this morning to help us before going to work. I'd say his character is gut, wouldn't you? Plus, he's a friend of Sam's, which speaks well of him, I'd say."

Jane supposed these were good points. "All true. But you haven't answered the question. Don't think I didn't notice." She grinned at her friend, who wrinkled her nose and shook her head.

"Okay, fine. Ja, I like him. But I only met the guy yesterday, so it's a little early to play matchmaker." Turning the tables, she sent a sly look at Jane. "What about you? I believe you and Sam actually exchanged more than two words yesterday! And he spent all day trying to help you. That says he's interested, in my book."

"Do you really think so?"

"Ja, Jane, I do. You have to talk to him, get to know him. Just be yourself. You're a pretty neat lady."

Jane smiled. "Now you're just trying to butter me up so you can go to the newspaper with Ben. Fine, go. And you might as well hang up a few flyers while you're out, if he has time. There's tape in the drawer. Take it with you."

"Denki! I'll ask him." The bells on the front door jingled as someone entered.

"I left the door unlocked because I knew Ben was coming. That's probably him now." Eliza jumped up and was nearly to the door when it swung open and Ben smiled at them both.

"Guder mariye! You both look bright-eyed and bushy-tailed this morning!"

"Guder mariye, Ben!" Eliza gushed, grinning at him. "Would you like a coffee? Jane said I can go with you to the newspaper office. It's still a little early, so you might as well sit down and make yourself comfortable."

"Denki, I wouldn't mind some coffee. And are those fresh baked glazed doughnuts?"

"Would you like one?" Jane asked, "Or possibly two?"

"I wouldn't say no."

Eliza used tongs to take the still-warm doughnuts from the cooling rack and place them on a plate, which she set before Ben along with a mug of fresh coffee. "There you go!"

The front door bells jingled again, and all three of them turned to see who could be coming in so early.

"It's me, Sam! Guder mariye!" He came into the kitchen and looked at the three of them. "Well, I see I'm just in time for some fresh doughnuts!"

Jane smiled naturally at him and invited him to sit. She was surprised at how easy it was. Eliza got him a couple of doughnuts and some coffee, and soon he and Ben were contentedly munching the pastries and chatting about their plans for the day.

"The paper opens soon," Ben said. "Eliza and I are going to take the flyer Susan made and get copies made, and hang some around town." He stood up. "In fact, we'd better be going, Eliza, if we're going to have time to get all that done before I have to head to work." He paused and looked at the brown pottery bowl sitting on the counter, holding the lovely blown green and blue eggs. "My, those are pretty eggs!" he exclaimed, slanting a glance at Sam. "Where did you get them?"

Jane blushed. "Um, I'm not sure where they came from, to be honest."

"Her secret admirer left them here!" Eliza said. "With a note and everything! She likes them so much, she blew out the eggs so now she can keep them forever in the pretty bowl that came with them!"

"Eliza!" Jane was horrified at her friend's oversharing. "Sam and Ben don't care about that. You'd better get going, so you can be back before we get busy."

"Huh, I wonder what kind of a guy leaves anonymous gifts and notes for a woman to find," Ben mused aloud. "What kind of a guy do you think would do that, Sam?"

"A desperate one, I'm thinking," Sam muttered. He stood. "I'd like to check the ceiling in the second-floor bathroom, if you don't mind, Jane? The fans may need recharging too."

She nodded, embarrassed that he'd heard she had a secret admirer. Would it hurt her chances of catching his attention? Would he think she preferred whoever had left the gifts to him? Did he even care?

"Sure, go on up. The door to the third floor is closed so Secret can't get out. She's not allowed down here when we're cooking, or during business hours."

"Why not?" Ben asked. "You guys could have a cat cafe."

Jane laughed. "We have all we can do to run a New Orleans–style Amish bakery, thanks. I'd hate to think what additional rules and regulations we'd run into if we added cats to the space."

"I've been to one," Eliza said. "In Lancaster, the last time I visited home. It's called the LanCATster Cat Cafe." She giggled. "It was fun." Then she cast a look at Jane. "But I wouldn't want to add cats to our bakery either. Too much added work."

Jane nodded. "I'll bet! So, Sam, please just don't let Secret out of the third floor, if you need to go up there."

"I won't go up there," he promised. Looking at Ben, he said, "I'll see you later, Benuel."

Ben gave him a grin and opened the door for Eliza to pass through. She grabbed her outerwear and the flyer and, with a wave to Jane, left with Ben on their errand.

"I wonder if we should consider putting an ad in the paper too," Jane said to Sam, who was about to head upstairs. "It's another way to reach people. We could even have them print the picture Susan drew of Little Mouse."

"That's a gut idea. If you hurry, you could ask Eliza and Ben to take care of that while they're there."

"I think I will." Jane got up and hurried through the bakery and out the front door, where Ben was just about to pull away from the curb. "Wait! I have an idea!" she called.

Eliza rolled down her window, and Jane told her and Ben her idea about running an ad with the cat's picture in the paper. "Use the bakery phone number for people to call, same as the flyer," she said.

"Gut idea!" Eliza said. "That will reach a lot of people."

"Just so none of them tell Lizzie," Jane muttered. She waved them on their way again and went back inside, shivering against the early morning cold. She hadn't paused to grab her wool cape, and it was chilly out!

Sam was just coming into the dining area as she went back inside. "The ceiling is almost dry, but it needs another day or two. Then I'll be able to patch it," he said.

"You really don't have to do all that," she protested.

But he shook his head. "It's my pleasure to help out, really." He stood awkwardly for a moment then blurted out, "Don't you think it's kind of weird, someone giving you gifts and notes anonymously? Aren't you afraid he's some kind of creep or something?"

"Um, I hadn't really considered him being a creep," she said slowly. "Although Bishop Abram suggested the same possibility. I just thought maybe he was someone shy, who was afraid to approach me openly. The note was sweet, and I like the gifts." She frowned. "You don't think I should be worried that he's someone dangerous or deranged, do you?"

She bit her lip. "Maybe I shouldn't keep the things he gave me. I wouldn't want to encourage someone unbalanced."

"Oh no, I didn't mean to imply that you should be afraid. I only wondered what you thought of the whole thing, that's all," he finished rather lamely. Jane wondered whether he was jealous of the unknown gift giver. But that would imply that he liked her, and he'd certainly never given her any indication that that was so!

"What if he gives you something else? What will you do?"

"Hmm? Oh! I don't know. I guess I hope he'll get up the courage to tell me who he is at some point. Anonymous gifts are nice, but that can't go on for long. What would be the point?"

"I guess you're right. Well, it's none of my business. I guess I was just intrigued with the idea of a secret admirer. Not something you hear about every day."

Jane nodded. "It was certainly a first for me. But it's been a few days, and there hasn't been anything else. Maybe he's done. Decided he really isn't interested after all." She laughed. "Who knows? Well, enough about that. What are you doing today?"

"I need to start a new buggy this afternoon, but this morning I thought I'd look around again for Little Mouse. Maybe I'll hang some flyers too, once we have them."

She smiled at him. "You really care about getting her back home again, don't you?" She blinked back tears. "Denki, Sam. That really means a lot. It's gut to know you and Ben and Eliza are all helping to bring Lizzie's kitty home."

He held up his hands in dismay. "Well, don't cry. I'm just doing what any decent person would, especially if they were part of the reason the cat got out in the first place!"

She gave him a watery smile and nodded. "Denki anyway. Now, I'd better get ready to open. I'll see you later, maybe?"

He nodded and left through the front door, and she felt a surge of gladness as she watched him walk off down the sidewalk to search once again for Little Mouse. She'd been pining for this man most of her life, and here he was, helping her solve not one but two problems—figuring out what had happened to the cat and patching the soggy bathroom ceiling. Maybe, just maybe, Gott had a plan for the two of them.

If Sam didn't shy away because he thought she preferred some silly secret admirer, that is!

"Enough! Time to open Lizzie's business. There's no point messing that up, along with losing her cat. Some friend I'm turning out to be!"

With that, she put worries and wonders out of her mind and got down to the business of the day. Later would take care of later.

CHAPTER FIVE

"Hello? Am I too late to get a beignet?"

Jane popped out of the kitchen, wondering where Eliza was, and was delighted to see her old friend Miriam Zook standing at the counter. Miriam was one of the eight young Amish women who had received a kitten from Lydia Coblentz's cat's last litter, along with Jane, Lizzie, their friends Mary Yoder and Ruth Helmuth, and several others.

"Miriam, it's so gut to see you! It's been far too long. How are you?"

Miriam put her mittened hands on the counter and grinned at Jane. "I'm just fine! I delivered a few new paintings to the gallery down the street, and I realized I couldn't possibly leave town without saying hello to you and Lizzie, and buying a beignet. Or a dozen."

"How about a baker's dozen? No charge for the thirteenth."

"What a deal. I'll take it!" She looked around, a small smile on her lips. "What a nice atmosphere you've all created here. I just love it. Where's Lizzie?"

"She left on her wedding trip a couple days ago. She and John won't be back for a few weeks. Eliza and I are holding down the fort."

"Oh, I should have remembered that." Miriam looked nonplussed for a moment before regaining her customary easygoing manner.

Jane felt a strong need to confide in her old friend that they'd misplaced Little Mouse. She bit her lip, wondering whether she should tell. The more people who knew, the more likely it was that Lizzie would hear about it, ruining her trip. But then again, they had hung posters up all over town, so Miriam was bound to find out sooner or later.

"Miriam, can you sit for a few minutes? It's nearly closing, and I can take a break before I clean up. I—I really need to tell you about something that's bothering me."

Her old friend's arched black brows rose curiously above her emerald-green eyes. "Of course I can sit, especially when an old friend needs to talk."

Jane felt a rush of affection for her friend, along with relief that she could share her burden. "Denki! Here, take this coffee, and go sit down. I'll bring some pastries—something besides beignets, since you've already bought all of those we had left!"

Miriam chuckled. "You don't have to ask me twice." Taking the coffee, she wandered over to sit in a cozy armchair in front of the gas fireplace. Jane put a few pastries on a plate, poured herself some coffee, and walked over to sit on the small sofa next to Miriam's chair. She placed the plate of pastries on the small table between them, toed off her sensible black shoes, and propped her stocking feet up on the brick hearth. "Ach, the heat feels so gut on my feet. They do get a bit achy after a long day."

"Great idea," Miriam said, toeing off her own shoes and propping her feet on the hearth next to Jane's. "Now, tell me what's on your mind. You seem troubled."

Jane stared into the fire, seeking the courage to tell Miriam what had happened. She silently asked Gott for guidance and launched into the tale.

When she finished, Miriam shook her head, her jet-black hair gleaming in the firelight around the edges of her prayer kapp. "Oh, Jane, I'm so sorry you have this burden on your heart! Is Secret all right after her little adventure?"

Jane nodded. "Ja, she seems just fine." She shuddered. "But when I think of how I would feel if it were Secret who was missing instead of Little Mouse, I almost can't stand it."

Miriam nodded in understanding. "I do know just what you mean. My little gentleman is such a comfort to me, I don't know what I'd do without him. I often thank Gott for the trust Lydia placed in me when she gave him to me."

Jane winced. "A trust I've broken now. Oh, Miriam, what am I going to do if we don't find her? How will I tell Lizzie? Or Lydia!"

Miriam reached over and took Jane's hand. "Why don't we pray about this? Not only about Little Mouse getting home safely but also for your peace of mind."

Jane nodded gratefully, and the two women bowed their heads and asked for Gott's blessing and help. Afterward, Jane did feel a little bit lighter, as if giving some of her worries to Gott had actually removed them from her shoulders.

They sat back and spoke of other things for a few minutes while finishing their coffee and pastries.

Just when Jane thought Miriam must be ready to leave, the pretty young woman, who was a couple of years older than Jane, sighed and said, "Jane, I wanted to ask you something."

"Sure, go ahead."

"I heard a rumor that David Miller was coming back to Willow Creek. To stay."

Jane sat back and looked at her old friend, who was gazing back at her expectantly. "I hadn't heard that. He wasn't able to make it to Lizzie and John's wedding. He was on a mission trip to Costa Rica with the Mennonite church he attends. But I imagine you know that."

Miriam gave a crooked, wistful smile. "Ja, I knew. I was hoping he'd come for the wedding, but when he didn't, I told myself it was for the better. After all these years, I've never had a word from him. And why would I?"

She stared into the fire, blinking rapidly, and Jane suspected she was getting a few tears under control. She knew that Miriam had been in love with Lizzie's cousin David Miller ever since she could remember. She could sure relate to that! But the handsome carpenter had decided not to be baptized into the Amish faith. Instead, he had moved to a small town outside of Indianapolis and joined a Mennonite church and community. Although she knew from Lizzie that David wrote to his parents frequently, he hadn't been back very often. And she knew that Miriam had had no better luck moving on in her feelings about David than she, Jane, had had getting over her feelings for Sam.

"Miriam, I've always wondered. Before he left, did the two of you ever talk about your feelings? Did he know you cared for him?"

Miriam shrugged and laughed. "Sort of, but it was already too late. I got up the nerve to tell him the night before he left, and he'd already purchased his bus ticket and packed his bags. He'd sold his buggy and horse, and broken his parents' hearts—and mine. When I confessed I had feelings for him, he looked a bit shocked and sorry—which was mortifying! He was very kind and told me he liked me a lot, but he had to go. He had nothing to offer me at the time. And the next day he was gone. I haven't seen him since. It's been seven years."

"Wow, I didn't realize it had been that long. And now you say he's coming back?"

Miriam nodded, still staring into the flames. "That's what I heard. I was hoping to ask Lizzie. But I guess I'll have to wait on that. I just hope he doesn't appear in church one Sunday with no warning. I might pass out." She glanced at Jane and cracked a smile. "That would get his attention, don't you think?"

Jane laughed. "Oh, for sure and certain! Especially if you broke your head. Oh, Miriam, just pray. And if he comes back, see what happens. He's not married, as far as I've heard, and if he's coming back maybe he's ready to be baptized into our faith!"

"He's not married. I would have heard. So would you." She gave a humorless laugh. "You would probably have been invited to the wedding."

"Okay, so if he's still single and decides to become Amish again, there's still hope."

"I don't know why he left in the first place. What would have changed in the last seven years?"

"Only he can answer that, my friend. If he does come back, don't be like me—go see him right away and make it clear that you still have feelings for him. He needs to know what his options are. Otherwise, you can be sure and certain some other single *maedel* will snap him up."

Miriam stood, the crooked smile back on her pretty face. "Right. Well, denki for the chat and the snack. It's really gut to catch up. I'll come sooner next time, or you come visit me out on the farm!"

Understanding that her friend was talked out on the subject of unrequited love, Jane stood and gave Miriam a hug. "I'll go admire your paintings down the street tomorrow."

Miriam blushed. "Oh! Denki. If you have time." She smiled sweetly and tucked a stray ebony lock back into her prayer kapp before donning her black bonnet and putting on her wool cape. "Good night, Jane. I hope you find Little Mouse! I'll keep my eyes and ears open."

Jane walked her friend to the door and saw that she had an Englisch driver waiting for her outside. That made sense, since she was taking her art to the gallery in town that sold it to tourists. Miriam did beautiful acrylic paintings of Amish life that appealed greatly to Englisch tourists. Truthfully, Jane wouldn't mind having one of the colorful scenes depicting barn raisings, quilting bees, wedding lunches, harvest days, laundry day, or other Amish scenes herself. They were all uplifting and had something godly about them that she couldn't really put her finger on. But Miriam was gaining in popularity as an artist, and the paintings were getting more expensive each year.

With a last wave, she pulled the door closed and locked it, turning the sign from OPEN to CLOSED.

"Ach, I'm sorry I've left you to finish up without me!" Eliza bustled into the room from the back, a handful of flyers in her hands. "I just took a few flyers to our neighboring businesses. Everyone let me hang one in their windows! Isn't that nice?"

Jane smiled. "Ja, very nice. You missed Miriam Zook. She just left."

"Oh! That's too bad. Was she taking paintings to the art gallery down the street?"

"Ja. I want to go look at them tomorrow. I really like her work."

Eliza wiggled her eyebrows. "I hear a certain young man who is related to our Lizzie is returning to town after a long absence, and plans to be baptized and open his own carpentry business!"

Jane crossed her arms and regarded her friend with amazement. "Eliza, you are better than that Google thing the *Englischers* use for information on their computers. Where did you hear that?"

Eliza shrugged and began wiping down the counters. "Here and there. I don't know that it's all true, but I guess we'll see. What did she want?"

"To ask Lizzie whether she'd heard that same rumor."

"Aha! Well, here's hoping it's true, and he'll soon be back. I hear he's a handsome one." Finished with the counters, Eliza tossed the cloth into a laundry bag and looked around as if to see if anything else needed to be done.

Jane carried the coffee creamers into the kitchen and stowed them in the fridge before returning to the dining room and continuing their conversation. "Ja, but Miriam has been pining for David Miller for years."

"Uh-huh, just like you and you-know-who."

"Eliza!"

Before Jane could chastise her friend, a knock came at the front door, and Jane turned to see Sam smiling in at her. She was mortified at the thought that he might have overheard Eliza's comment.

Ach! Nee, the door is closed. He couldn't have overheard. Could he?

From the look of her impish grin, Eliza found this timing to be quite amusing. "Speak of the devil, and you'll hear the flap of his wings!"

"You hush!" Shaking her head, Jane unlocked the door and let Sam in.

"Denki." He stood looking down at her for a few moments, and she felt caught in his gaze, before he cleared his throat and looked away, only then noticing Eliza standing nearby. "Oh! Eliza. I didn't see you there."

"I could tell." She held up her handful of flyers. "I hung up a lot of these today. But we still have more. Tomorrow I'd like to take some a bit farther away, in case someone picked Little Mouse up and might see the flyers at the Amish market or something."

"Gut idea. How will you get there?"

"Ben said he'd take me, if you can spare me for an hour or two, Jane?"

Jane nodded. "For a gut cause."

"I've got to get some hours in on the buggy I just started," Sam said. "But I can come by in the afternoon, around closing? I'll look at the bathroom ceiling, and then if you think of anywhere else to hang the flyers, I could drive you."

Behind his back, Eliza waggled her eyebrows again, giving a big double thumbs-up, and Jane bit her lips so Sam wouldn't see her exasperation at her friend's antics. "Denki, Sam, that would be very nice of you."

Eliza put on her black bonnet and swung her cape around her shoulders. "Well, I need to get home. Susan and I are setting up our litter boxes and cat beds and such tonight. We're getting our cats this weekend!"

"That's so exciting!" Jane exclaimed, truly happy for her sister and Eliza. "You know, it's been too long since I spent time with Susan. Why don't you both come by for supper Friday night?"

"Denki, I'll accept for both of us." Eliza looked at Sam, and Jane knew the twinkle in her friend's eyes meant trouble even before she spoke. "Sam, why don't you and Ben join us? There will be plenty of food. Susan and I will make something to pitch in."

Sam looked at Jane as if to check her reaction to the invitation, and when she just cocked an eyebrow, he smiled and nodded. "Denki. I'll check with Ben, but I think we should be able to make it. Maybe after supper I'll get started on the bathroom ceiling. It should be dry by then."

"Perfect. Well, I'd better be getting home," Eliza said.

"Can I drop you off? I need to head home too."

"But you just got here," Eliza said. "Didn't you want to hang out for a while? Have you had supper?"

"Well, I. . . No, actually, I haven't." He looked at Jane. "What about you? Have you eaten?"

Caught unprepared, Jane could only shake her head. "Nee, I haven't. We just finished for the day."

"Hmm. Well, you've got to eat, and so do I. Do you want to go over to Rebekkah's and see if she's got any baked steak left?"

Jane blinked at him, unsure what to say. This was Sam. Asking her out. To eat. In real life—not a dream.

"Jane, tell the nice man yes, you'll go eat with him," Eliza prompted.

Jane blushed and nodded. "Denki, Sam, yes, I'd like that. I'm a big fan of Rebekkah's baked steak, as a matter of fact."

"Gut. So am I. We can drop you off on the way, Eliza," Sam offered.

Jane got her cape and bonnet and called up the back stairs to Secret that she wouldn't be gone long. Then she followed Sam and Eliza out the front door, locking up the bakery so she could enjoy the unusual treat of dinner out.

Dinner out with Samuel Mast! Like a date. Would she wake up soon and find it had all been a dream? Eliza's smug grin behind Sam's back as they climbed into his buggy suggested it was real, all right.

She pinched herself on the arm to be sure.

Yep. Real.

They waved good night to Eliza and watched her unlock the front door of the building that housed her older brother Reuben's medical practice, which was located in a large old home in Willow Creek, with an apartment upstairs where Reuben had formerly lived, and which was now inhabited by Eliza, and Jane's sister, Susan.

Eliza closed and locked the door behind her and waved at them through the glass panes in the doorway before turning and rapidly climbing the stairs up to the apartment, disappearing from sight.

Sam turned and looked at Jane seated beside him in the front of his buggy, and he found himself at a loss for words. Eliza's chatter had carried them this far, but now he was sitting in a buggy with the woman he'd longed for since. . .forever.

What now?

He didn't want to mess it all up. And he was ever conscious that she still didn't know his terrible secret.

Jane broke the silence, raising an eyebrow and laughing at Eliza's ability to completely fill any silence. "She's a gut one to have around when you need the ice broken."

He nodded and forced a smile. "I'll bet. She's a nice girl. I think Ben may be smitten by her."

He cast a sideways glance at Jane to see what she thought about that. She was nodding thoughtfully. "I think you may be right. She's twenty, so old enough to court. He could do worse, for sure and certain. I count her as a gut friend."

Satisfied, he nodded. "I know you do. I'll tell you that she could do worse as well. Ben is loyal as the day is long, and honest." He winced. "I'm making him sound like a good dog."

She laughed. "Not at all. Loyalty and honesty are nothing to be taken lightly in a potential spouse. I hold both very high in my regard."

His wince was internal this time, as he considered several ways he had been less than loyal and honest to this woman. Should he pull over and confess all right now? At least if she was going to send him packing, it would be over.

But his chance was lost when she said, "Ah, we're there already! I didn't realize how hungry I was. Denki for suggesting this." He returned her smile and pulled into the parking lot, heading for the area reserved for horses and buggies to tie up.

Inside they saw several people they knew and, after exchanging greetings and brief small talk, were seated in a booth too close to other diners for anything other than superficial dinner conversation. And before he knew it, they were enjoying dessert and decaf coffee, and their time together was nearly over for the evening.

Back in his buggy, Jane leaned back, a hand on her belly, and sighed with utter contentment. "That Rebekkah sure as certain knows her baked steak! I couldn't eat another bite. I'm a little afraid I may burst."

Feeling pleasantly replete himself, Sam steered his American paint horse, Millie, toward the bakery.

"This isn't your usual horse, but she sure is pretty," Jane observed, watching Millie's smooth movement through the front windshield of the enclosed buggy. "Where did you get her?"

Looking fondly at his beautiful black-and-white mare, Sam was happy to share his enthusiasm for the breed. "I saw her at an auction a few years ago. She's a registered American paint horse, and at the time she was just a filly, eighteen months old. I have no idea how she ended up at that auction, but I knew she had to be mine as soon as I saw her."

Jane looked at him fully, as if amazed at his passion for the horse that was currently pulling them down the road. He gave her a wry smile. "Sorry. I tend to overshare."

"That's all right. I like learning new things. I really don't know anything about paint horses."

He gave her a careful look and decided she was being sincere. "Well," he began slowly, "they have to be either registered quarter horses, Thoroughbreds, or American paint horses to be in the American paint registry. Other breeds can have spots and patches, and they're often called pintos. But to be American paints, they have to be registered to one of those three breed associations."

"So, they're all pintos?"

"Ja, but all pintos aren't American paints, *fashtay*?"

"Nope, but I'm willing to learn."

Taking her at her word, he spent the rest of the drive telling her about his favorite horses. Pulling up in front of The Plain Beignet, he reined in Millie, who Jane had been informed was a registered American quarter horse and a registered American paint horse.

"It's amazing that she was there, with her papers, and at an affordable price," Jane commented.

"Don't I know it. I was blessed that day, more than even usual! Old

Ralph is a gut boy, for sure and certain," he said, referring to his patient standardbred ex-racehorse. "But he's getting on in years now, and I thought it would be gut to have a second horse." He smiled fondly at Millie, who stood patiently waiting to be directed as to what was expected of her next. "And that gave me the perfect excuse to buy Millie."

"I can't blame you. Like I said, she's just beautiful. Well, I'd better get in. Secret will be miffed that her dinner is late, and as always, I have to be up early."

He smiled. "Denki for having supper with me. I really enjoyed our conversation."

Jane suddenly looked shy, a rosy blush stealing over her lovely features. She pushed her door open and stepped down before turning to answer him. "I enjoyed it too. Denki."

She closed the buggy door quietly and, with a wave, let herself into the bakery and closed the door behind her. A moment later, the inside lights went out, and yet Sam sat there for several more minutes, until he saw the third-floor lights come on, letting him know she was safely in her own apartment for the night.

With a wistful sigh, he jiggled the reins, letting Millie know it was time to go home.

If he'd glanced up again, he'd have seen Jane looking down at the horse and buggy as they made a U-turn and headed back up the street, taking Sam homeward. But his thoughts were full of whether he should confess to being her secret admirer. Whether to tell her about the nickname debacle. Whether, perhaps, the secret admirer should leave another gift. Whether, perhaps, he should check into a psychiatric ward.

"Ach, Sam, go home. Work on the buggy. Do your farm chores. Read a book. Read your Bible. Get a gut night's sleep. Stop stop *stop* obsessing over Jane Bontrager. At least for tonight."

He chuckled as Millie pulled him into the darkening evening. That would be easier said than done, for sure and certain!

CHAPTER SIX

In the wee hours of the following morning, Sam walked his brown gelding, Ralph, as quietly as possible through the alley behind The Plain Beignet. He'd taken Ben's advice on the matter—not that Ben had intended for Sam to make another trip to the bakery as Jane's secret admirer—and hitched up his less identifiable horse to the buggy that morning. And he was boldly driving right to the back door of the bakery building, rather than parking on the street and skulking around like a thief. Still, it wouldn't be easy to explain what he was doing back there if Jane, or the Willow Creek police, noticed him and asked questions.

Pulling up on the reins at the back door of the bakery, he was relieved to find the windows still dark. Jane wasn't downstairs yet.

Breathing a sigh of relief on that count, he climbed quietly out of the buggy, leaving the door open. He stroked Ralph's nose, whispered to him to keep quiet, and stealthily crept up the back steps of the bakery. He taped an envelope with Jane's name on it to the window and placed a wrapped parcel on the stoop. He stared down at the package, which contained something he'd thought would be perfect. "Ach," he whispered, "I hope I'm not making a mistake."

A noise from the dumpsters a short distance down the alley caused him to spin around and peer nervously into the dark, but when he spotted a pair of raccoon eyes peering back at him, he closed his eyes, counted to ten, and walked back to his buggy. "Get ahold of yourself, man. It's just a raccoon. You were about five seconds away from running down the alley in a panic."

Shivering in the predawn dark of late autumn, he climbed into his buggy and gave his horse the signal to walk on.

He was relieved to turn out of the alley into the road and steer Ralph back toward his farm.

He'd second-, third-, and fourth-guessed himself about leaving another "secret admirer" gift, but Jane's obvious enjoyment of the first one encouraged him to go ahead and leave the gift he'd already purchased and prepared the previous weekend.

"I hope she likes it," he mused. Then after a few moments quietly listening to Ralph's hooves beating a tattoo on the blacktop as he trotted toward home and breakfast, he laughed at himself. "Of course, it's sort of *narrish* that I'm basically creating a rival for myself with this secret admirer thing. Now that Jane and I are actually talking to each other, I should probably let him—me. . .ach! the secret admirer—fade away into the sunset. Jane's unsolved mystery."

He continued homeward for a few more minutes, then shrugged. "Oh well, too late now, unless I want to do a U-turn and zoom back there and try and beat Jane to the gift." He bit his lip, actively considering the pros and cons of the idea, before giving a firm shake of his head. "Nee, Samuel! It's done, for better or worse. And tonight you'll get to hear all about it from Jane. For better or worse."

At four in the afternoon., having put in a good day's work on the new buggy in his shop, Sam pulled Millie up to the hitching post in front of The Plain Beignet then sat and stared into the windows of the bakery. He could see Eliza and Jane bustling around inside, taking care of the routine chores involved in closing up for the day. Feeling resigned and also aware that he'd made his own bed and now he'd have to sleep in it, he jumped down from the buggy and secured Millie to the hitching post, giving her a feed bag to keep her happy. "Gut girl," he told her, scratching the place behind her ears he knew she liked. "I'll be back out soon."

Before he could open the front door of the bakery, he heard his name called. Turning, he saw Ben guiding Cupid into the diagonal parking space next to Millie. The horses nickered a greeting to one another, and Ben hopped out, secured his own mare, and gave her a feed bag like Millie's.

Jogging up to Sam, Ben grinned and slapped him on the back. "So! How was your day? Get much done on the buggy?"

Sam regarded his friend narrowly. "Ja, I did. You seem pretty chipper this afternoon."

"Oh, I am! I'm looking forward to finding out more about the new offering from Jane's secret admirer." His lips quirked as he observed his best friend, who found himself squirming a bit under Ben's regard.

"What?" Sam asked irritably.

"I thought you were going to let this go, friend. You've created a rival for yourself, you know. Why would you do that? I can understand the first time, before you and she actually started speaking to each other. But now?" He shook his head in bewilderment. "Now you're just making your own life harder."

Ignoring the fact that he'd had the same thoughts on the matter himself earlier that day, Sam snarked, "Well, if I'd known you were such an expert on dating and women, I would have asked your opinion. It actually did occur to me, what you just said, about how I'm competing against myself now." He shook his head in disgust. "But not until after I'd already crept up on the back door of the bakery like a thief at 3:00 a.m. and was halfway home."

He cast his friend a miserable glance. "Now I have to go in there and listen to her either disparage my gift or rave about something she thinks came from another man. I really am an idiot."

Ben clapped him on the back again. "Nee, you're not an idiot, Sam. You've just been pining after the girl for half your life, which is kind of pathetic—not the pining part, the not doing anything about it part—and you've got yourself tangled up in knots. Let's go on in and take a look at the bathroom ceiling. And we'll see if that cat showed up after I dropped Eliza off this morning. We hung flyers out at the Amish market and at businesses between here and there."

"Denki, Ben. You're a gut friend."

"I am. Remember that the next time you get gut advice from your gut friend—and maybe heed it!"

"Ja, okay." Sam sighed. "Well, here we go." He opened the door and was greeted by Eliza, who waved from where she was wiping down the counters and cases. "Sam! Ben!" Sam thought she blushed a bit when she greeted his friend, but he couldn't be certain as she immediately ducked her head and scrubbed industriously at an invisible spot in the display case.

Jane poked her head through the door from the kitchen and smiled at the men. "Good afternoon! We're about done here, then we can go up and look at the bathroom."

"Or, if you don't mind, Ben and I will just head up now and check it out. No need for you to go up. Unless you wanted to, of course."

"No, that's fine. You know the way!"

"Did Little Mouse come home this afternoon?" Ben asked hopefully. Eliza and Jane shook their heads sadly. "Nee. She's been gone three days now. I just hope she's somewhere warm, with food and shelter, and that whoever has her sees our flyers and returns her!"

Eliza rubbed Jane's back. "It's not as if she's a valuable breed or anything someone would steal. I think she's probably staying with someone who is trying to find out where she belongs. I've been praying for that to be the case, and for a gut outcome. Gott hears our prayers, Jane, you know He does."

"I know. I'm just worried sick. If it were Secret missing, I don't know what I'd do! Poor Lizzie is off on her wedding trip thinking everything is peachy here, and in reality we're basically lying to her by omission." She nibbled on her thumbnail, something Sam had noticed she did when nervous. "Maybe we should call and tell her."

Three voices cried, "Nee!" at the same time, and Jane looked at them all in surprise. "Well, okay! I just hate this whole situation."

Ben, Sam, and Eliza exchanged looks, and Eliza said, "Jane, why worry Lizzie for nothing? She can't search for Little Mouse from Texas. You'll just ruin her fun, and she'll want to come home early. Let's not do that to her."

Jane looked at Sam and Ben, who nodded slowly in agreement.

"It's not really lying," Ben pointed out. "If she calls and asks how Little Mouse is, you'll have to tell her the truth. But until then"—he shrugged—"let it ride, is my advice."

"His favorite advice," Sam muttered.

"What's that, Sam?" Eliza asked. He glanced up and found Ben frowning at him, and he looked at Eliza and Jane, who were regarding him curiously. "Oh, nothing. Just an old inside joke."

He winced as the girls nodded and turned back toward the kitchen. "We'll get things ready for morning while you two check the bathroom ceiling." They all walked into the kitchen, and Sam immediately saw, in a place of honor in the center of the kitchen table, his early morning offering.

"What's this?" Ben, who'd also spotted the odd gift, walked over to the table and picked it up.

"Oooo," Jane cried, clapping her hands together. "It's such a neat gift from my secret admirer! It's a battery-powered automatic cat waterer! It's a little fountain! Cats love running water, which is how we got into our current mess with the bathroom ceiling, if you remember. So my secret admirer must have heard something about this somehow, because he got me this cunning little kitty water fountain! Secret and Little Mouse—when we get her back..." She tapered off, and Eliza chimed in, "Which we will!"

Jane smiled gratefully at her friend. "Which we will!" She continued, "They'll love this thing! I can't wait to set it up for Secret to try out later."

Sam gave Ben a smug glance and found his friend shaking his head. Okay, so maybe it would have been smarter to have given Jane the gift as himself, instead of making her think it was from some other guy. But at least she seemed to love it.

"That's pretty cool," he said disingenuously. Ben gave a snort, and Eliza glared at him. "What? Don't you think it's a perfect gift for Jane? Obviously her secret admirer is someone who knows her well." Her glance slid to Sam, and she winked.

She winked! Sam had to fight to keep from giving away the whole thing then and there. Somehow, Eliza had guessed that he was the secret admirer. He stared at her, praying she wouldn't give him away, and she smiled softly. "There was another poem too. Jane, read the guys the poem."

"Oh, I don't know," Jane said, frowning down at a piece of notebook paper lying on the table. "It's kind of silly."

Ouch, so much for my brilliant poetry. Oh well, the cat fountain is a hit, anyway.

"Well, okay. If you insist," Jane was saying, and Sam realized he'd missed Eliza cajoling her friend into reading the note aloud.

Sam braced himself, and good thing, because as Jane read, he could tell Ben was having a very hard time not bursting into laughter.

"Here's to the kitties, who turned on the water; playing as if they were a pair of happy otters. They'll love this little fountain, so you can forget about your dread; it will keep the ceiling from crashing down upon your head."

Jane finished and looked expectantly up at her friends, who were all trying to look serious and clueless—not, Sam reflected, as if everyone in the room except the person most involved knew exactly who had written that piece of drivel.

He let out a small groan, and Jane frowned.

"All right, so maybe it's not the most brilliant or sophisticated poem ever written, but you have to admit it is very appropriate to the situation." She frowned. "Except, how, exactly, did my secret admirer even find out about the situation? I haven't told anyone the exact details of what led to Little Mouse getting out. Have any of you?"

They all shook their heads. "Nee, at least, I don't think so," Eliza said. "Maybe one of us did mention it in passing, though, while we were hanging up flyers. Are you sure you didn't, Jane?"

Jane frowned. "Pretty sure. But I don't know. I could have, I suppose. I've been so distracted, I can't be certain whom I've talked to in the last couple of days, let alone exactly what was said. I feel like I'm losing my marbles."

Oh, great. Now I've gone and made her doubt her own sanity. I really need to confess. But. . .I can't do it here, with Ben and Eliza around. Maybe later, if I can talk Jane into getting supper again, I can find a way to tell her everything.

Ben poked him. "Wake up, Sam. Let's go up and check that ceiling."

"Oh, ja, coming."

They trooped up the stairs and down the second-floor hallway to the bathroom, where they found the ceiling was nearly dry.

"I think by Friday we can patch this," Ben said, gently poking the ceiling around the hole. "It's only a bit soft. Nearly dry now." He jumped down from the footstool he'd used to reach the ceiling. "Sam. This thing"—he gestured downward, toward the kitchen and the women—"it's getting out of hand. You have to tell the woman everything."

Sam felt miserable. "Ja, I know. I thought maybe I'd see if Jane would have dinner with me again tonight, and tell her then."

Ben nodded approvingly. "Gut! You can't keep letting some other man take credit for your clever gifts." He winked. "Even if he's you!"

Sam laughed weakly. "What a mess."

"Yup. Best fix it before she finds out some other way. That will really make her mad. Or worse, you could hurt her feelings if she misunderstands and thinks it's a game to you."

Sam nodded. "You're right. I know you're right. It's just, when I try to imagine telling her about what happened back then, I just freeze up."

Ben shrugged. "You'd better get some ice melt, then, buddy. Or you're not going to get the girl. She'll choose the mystery man instead."

"But he's me!"

"He won't be if she finds out all of this on her own. Trust me on this. Confess. It's gut for the soul. Just ask the bishop."

"I know, I know. Man, I wish I hadn't gotten myself in even deeper."

"Cheer up. You've still got time. Now, an idea just occurred to me. Let's go see if we can talk Eliza and Jane into dinner at Mose's. I could go for a cheeseburger and fair fries. And we'll take two buggies. You can talk to Jane when you drive her home after."

"That is a gut idea. Cheeseburgers and fair fries always cheer me up." Sam grinned.

"Let's go do some fast talking!"

On the way downstairs, Ben whispered, "A pair of happy otters? Where did you come up with that?"

"It rhymed!"

Ben's laughter trailed him down the stairs into the kitchen, where he and Sam didn't have to try too hard to convince Eliza and Jane to accompany them to Mose's Drive-In, a popular local Amish-owned restaurant that served excellent burgers, fries, onion rings, and other greasy food.

Everyone agreed it sounded perfect, and they piled into the two buggies and headed out to eat, forgetting their various problems for an hour or two on a crisp, clear November evening.

After ordering burgers, fries, and a big basket of onion rings to share, the group took their sodas and found a booth by a window. For a moment, they stood hesitantly, trying to figure out who would sit where. Then Ben stood aside and gestured for Eliza to scoot into one bench, which she did, moving over to make room for him. He joined her, and Jane shyly glanced at Sam, who was smiling at her softly, waiting for her to sit down on the other bench. She sat and slid over to the far side of the bench, making room for Sam.

He sat down, and she could feel the heat of his arm near hers, though they were both wearing long sleeves against the cold evening. After a few moments, she relaxed and tuned into the conversation between the others as they shared about their days, waiting for their food to be ready.

A couple of minutes later a bell dinged up front, and Ben and Sam stood up. "Food's ready!" Ben said. He and Sam headed up to get the food, and Jane leaned across the table toward Eliza. "This feels like a double date!"

Eliza wagged her eyebrows. "Ja! And not even planned. The best kind!"

Jane bit her lip. "I don't know, Eliza. I feel kind of weird."

"Jane! Will you for once relax and allow yourself to have a little uncomplicated fun? What could go wrong?"

"Uncomplicated? That shows what you know!"

The men returned with the food, cutting their debate short.

"I've been meaning to ask, did you two get the ad in the *Examiner* while you were making copies of the flyers?" Sam queried as he and Ben carried their food to the table and started sorting out who got which burgers, fries, onion rings, coleslaw, and sodas.

"Mm-hmm." Eliza nodded as she chewed a generous bite of her double cheeseburger. Swallowing, she grabbed her napkin and dabbed at her chin before answering. "Ja, we put an ad in. The paper comes out Monday, so we'll have to wait and see if it brings any results."

"Oh, I hope Little Mouse is home before Monday," Jane said, and Sam handed her a napkin and the ketchup.

"If so, the ad won't hurt anything. It was a gut idea," he reminded her.

Before anyone could comment further, a couple of young Amish men stepped up to their table. One was Abner Hochstetler, who worked at the sawmill with Ben. The other was a stranger Jane hadn't seen before.

"Ben! Sam!" Abner cried. "Trust the two of you to be out enjoying dinner with two of the prettiest maedels in the district!"

"Hello, Abner, *wie ghets*?" Ben asked. He turned to the others and said, "Everyone, you know Abner. This other fellow is Daniel Beechy, newly arrived from Wisconsin. He's working at the mill while he decides if Ohio is where he wants to settle down."

Did Jane detect a note of disapproval in Ben's tone? She glanced at him, and his face gave away no such thing. She decided she must be imagining things. She looked at the newcomer and noted his dark brown eyes and raven hair. His hat was just a little different from the black wool hats worn by the men in her community, marking him as an outsider.

He smiled at everyone, showing off even, white teeth and a dimple in one cheek. "Nice to meet you all," he said, his inscrutable eyes lingering a little bit longer on Jane than on the others.

She felt heat creeping up her neck and face at the stranger's bold regard. She looked down at the table. "Nice to meet you, Daniel," she murmured.

"Daniel is far from home and needs friends," Abner said, jovially clapping Daniel on his broad shoulders, clad in blue with black suspenders. "Ain't that right, Daniel?"

Daniel smiled easily at Abner. "Sure. Friends are always gut, nee?"

Jane thought that was an odd response, but what did she know? Maybe people talked that way in Wisconsin. She didn't think she'd met anyone from Wisconsin before, though Lizzie and John were stopping there to see distant relatives on their trip. She tried to recall what town, exactly, but for the moment it escaped her.

She glanced back up and found the stranger's eyes still on her face. He smiled a bit at her obvious discomfort, as if it somehow pleased him. Catching Eliza's eye, she found her normally easygoing friend looking a bit out of sorts. "Eliza, I need to freshen up. Would you like to come with me?"

Eliza nodded. "Sure."

Excusing themselves, the two women waited for Ben and Sam to stand up before scooching out of the narrow booth and then heading to the bathroom in the back of the restaurant.

Once the bathroom door closed behind them and they made sure there wasn't anyone in the stalls, Eliza turned to Jane, eyes wide. "Jane! That Daniel couldn't take his eyes off of you! Surely you noticed."

Jane shrugged. "He made me uneasy. He stared too much. It felt rude."

Eliza seemed to consider her response. "I can see what you mean." She frowned. "And I got the idea Ben doesn't like him much."

"Yes! I noticed that too. He seemed almost. . .disapproving when

Abner said Daniel was deciding whether he wanted to settle in Ohio. Did you catch that?"

Eliza nodded. "Exactly. I wonder why?"

"Maybe you can ask him when he drives you home."

Eliza straightened her kapp and checked to see whether she had food in her teeth. She looked at Jane. "Ready?"

Jane glanced at the stalls. "Actually, since I'm here. . ."

"Okay, I'll wait for you. Hurry up; I don't want my fries to get cold."

Soon they were back in their seats, enjoying their dinner. Abner and Daniel had picked up a carryout order and left, according to Ben, and the foursome discussed other matters for the remainder of the meal. As they were getting ready to leave, Jane thought to ask Eliza whether she and Susan had everything ready for their new cats.

"Oh, ja! We put together their climbing tower and set it in front of the living room window where they'll be able to watch the birds and squirrels in the maple tree out front. And we put two covered litter pans in the bathroom—there's plenty of room in there! And they each have their own darling little beds made of the softest fleece that Susan made at the quilt shop. And we got them matching food and water bowls, which are on the cutest mats in the kitchen." She paused, obviously trying to decide whether she'd forgotten anything, and snapped her fingers. "And we found such fun little toys! You should see the little fishing pole with a feather on the end. I can't wait to play with them!"

Jane couldn't help grinning at Eliza's delight, and she saw that Ben and Sam felt the same way.

"Wow, those are some lucky cats!" Sam exclaimed. "I'm sort of jealous, to tell the truth. I want a fishing pole with a little feather on the end."

They all laughed and headed outside. Darkness had fallen while they ate, and Jane was glad their bishop allowed battery-operated flashing lights on the rear of the buggies. They'd also added small pieces of white PVC pipe to their wheels, which, when hit by an approaching car's headlights, glowed like spinning lights. Their buggies also had battery-operated headlights, along with the standard reflective orange slow-moving-vehicle triangle. Staying separate was all well and good, Jane thought, but in safety matters, she preferred a greater level of protection from cars and trucks whose drivers were often in a hurry, or distracted, and might not notice a black buggy without such safety measures until it was too late. And in a contest between a buggy and an Englischer vehicle, the buggy seldom came out ahead.

Calling their good nights, Ben and Eliza climbed into Ben's buggy and headed down the road. Sam and Jane soon followed a little ways behind, and Jane noticed, not for the first time, how cool those pieces of white PVC pipe looked on the spinning wheels when hit by headlights. They created the illusion of a circle of white light and were very noticeable, with no technology at all!

"Look how cool those wheels look!"

Sam nodded, keeping his eyes on the road. "It's pretty neat. Whoever came up with that idea was a genius."

Before long, they passed Ben and Eliza, who had turned into the doctor's parking lot. And a couple of minutes later, they were back at the bakery. Sam pulled up out front, and they sat for a moment, not speaking.

Uncomfortable with the silence, Jane sought to fill it by telling Sam more about the new gift from her secret admirer.

"I just can't get over how perfect the kitty fountain is! How do you think he knew?" When there was no answer, Jane looked over at her companion, who was sitting with arms folded over his chest, staring out the front window of the buggy. He looked irritated.

"Sam? How do you think my secret admirer knew what a perfect gift that kitty water fountain would be?"

He snorted out a breath and grunted, "No idea. Maybe he's psychic."

Definitely irritated. Well, what does he expect? All these years, and he's never made a move, so now that some other man is, does he think I should ignore the attention?

She emitted an unladylike snort. *Not likely!*

"What was that for?"

"What?"

"That, I don't know—that snort you just did."

"I don't snort. Pigs snort."

"You definitely just snorted there," he insisted.

She rolled her eyes. "Fine. I snorted. I can't remember why now. Thanks for dinner. I have to be up early. Good night."

"Good night."

She opened the buggy door and jumped down, closing the door a tiny bit too hard before turning without another look for the infuriating Samuel Mast, marching to the door, unlocking it, and slamming it behind her. Turning around in the darkened front room of the bakery, she peeked out at Sam's buggy and found it still sitting there.

"Go, already!" she cried. "You had nothing to say before!"

Instead of leaving, she saw him climb down and stalk to the front door. He knocked on the glass, and she turned the lock and pulled the door open. "Ja?"

"I wanted to be sure you were safely inside."

She stared at him. "You saw me go in."

He pulled off his hat and scratched his head. "Well, ja, but the light was out, so I couldn't see that you were safe, ain't so?"

"Well, you can see now. Are you satisfied? Or would you like to search the building for intruders?"

He frowned. "I could if it would make you feel better."

She glanced behind her at the darkened room and thought she actually wouldn't mind. It was a big building, and except for a cat up on the third floor, she was alone. And she hadn't noticed when John and Lizzie were on the second floor, and there were two cats in residence, how empty the building was when it was just her. And Secret, of course.

But she couldn't very well admit any of that, so she shook her head. "Nee, denki. I'm used to being here alone. I'll be fine."

He looked skeptical. "You're used to being here with other people, not alone. Except for the last couple nights. Maybe you could get Eliza and Susan to stay here until Lizzie and John return."

Oh, that sounded like a sweet idea! Except they were getting their new cats and wouldn't want to leave them alone. So she shook her head. "Nee, I'll be fine. Denki, Sam."

When he didn't say anything else, she started to close the door. "Well, gut night."

He nodded, and she closed and locked the door. She waved at him, and he turned and walked back to his buggy and soon drove off down the street.

Feeling a tiny bit creeped out and wishing she'd swallowed her pride and allowed Sam to check the building, Jane walked into the kitchen, turned on the light inside the door, and brewed herself a cup of tea. When it was ready she grabbed a battery lantern and headed up to her apartment and her cat.

That was not how she had wanted the evening to end. *What went wrong? We've been doing so well.*

She thought about it as she climbed the stairs and grimaced when she recalled how she'd gone on and on about the gift from the secret admirer. Maybe—possibly? Sam could be jealous?

Well, if he is, why doesn't he DO something to win me for himself?

She sighed as she opened the door to her apartment and was greeted eagerly by Secret, who wound sinuously around her ankles, obviously demanding her own dinner.

"I'm sorry, *lieb*. I should have checked your bowl before going out. That was selfish of me." She poured kibble into Secret's empty bowl and changed her water before plopping onto one of her vintage light blue vinyl chairs and picking up her tea. After taking a thoughtful sip, she told her cat, "Well, maybe you could say paying for my dinner twice this week, and driving me around in his buggy, is doing something. Some would see it as courting, for sure and certain." She took another sip of tea. "The real question is, does Sam see it that way?"

Secret had no opinion, so Jane drained her cup and then headed to bed. She read from her Bible and spent some time in prayer, including a little extra request for wisdom when it came to dealing with men in general, and Samuel Mast in particular. Then she tossed and turned for a long while, trying to decide what to do—if anything—about Samuel Mast, Amish procrastinator extraordinaire. And she puzzled about why the newcomer from Wisconsin had troubled her so.

CHAPTER SEVEN

"Ach, these are wunderbar!" Jane breathed to herself as she wandered the art gallery down the street from the bakery, perusing the work Miriam Zook had dropped off earlier in the week.

With a quick glance over her shoulder, she leaned in to peer at the price discreetly printed on a small, tasteful white card tucked into a glass frame on the wall next to the painting, giving the name of the artist and the title of the work, *Quilting Bee*.

"Ach, goodness!" She couldn't help but exclaim when she saw what her friend's work was bringing. Easily as much as a good queen-size Amish quilt! She felt very pleased for her friend, while at the same time regretting that she would not be purchasing one of Miriam's paintings anytime soon.

"May I help you?" a refined voice asked from behind her, causing her to jump just a tad. She hadn't noticed anyone approaching, and she smiled at the man standing a few feet away, studying the painting she'd been admiring.

"This is a fine example of an American folklore style, depicting an Amish life scene. It's by a local artist, you know." He peered at her. "Are you interested in purchasing it?"

She gave a small laugh. "I wish, but no, denki. Actually, the artist is a gut friend of mine, and she mentioned when she stopped in at The Plain Beignet, where I work, that she was bringing you new paintings the other day. I told her I'd stop in and see them. So here I am."

He gave her a genuine smile at this. "Ah, I enjoy your strudel! What a good addition to Willow Creek your bakery is, Miss. . . ?"

"Oh! I'm Jane Bontrager. The bakery belongs to my friend Lizzie, and her husband, John. John's my bruder, actually."

"I see. Well, I adore your pastries, and I'm sure you have something to do with making them."

She blushed. "Denki, Mr. . . ?"

"Oh! Do excuse me. I'm Remington Jirles, the proprietor of Visions of Willow Creek."

"It's nice to meet you. You have a very nice shop."

"Thanks. It was my mother's originally. She was an artist and had an excellent eye for what would sell. She taught me everything she knew, then sent me off to learn more. When she passed, I came back to take over her legacy. I couldn't just let it die."

He looked around, seeing the shop through eyes Jane couldn't fathom, and she respected him for carrying on his mother's dream.

"So you're an artist too?"

He smiled. "Now and then, but honestly, I'm better at selling other artists' work. I'm afraid that despite my mother's faith and an excellent education, I never rose above what one might generously call adequate."

"Is any of your art displayed here?"

He peered at her through narrowed eyes as if trying to decide whether she was being kind or genuinely cared. Pursing his lips, he nodded. "Follow me."

He led her through the sunny, open-concept studio into a long hallway that Jane could see opened into several rooms. As they passed the first two, she saw that they were additional display areas.

"These rooms are where we house our collection of local art, including paintings, sculptures, textile art, and so on. We acquire more than we can display up front at any given time, and so we rotate things through."

He stepped into a darkened room and flipped a light switch, and Jane beheld several dozen paintings hanging on the outside walls, and more displayed on tall three-sided displays scattered around the room. "Most of these are the work of my mother, Marian Jirles. It's her legacy." He wandered the space, followed slowly by Jane, who took in the beautiful watercolor, acrylic, and oil paintings depicting everything from local scenes to beach and waterfront scenes to tropical jungles to street scenes—just everything!

"Why, these are breathtaking!" Jane wandered the room, awestruck by the beauty depicted there. She came to a final wall toward the back of the room holding a collection of lovely studies of people and animals and somehow knew that a different hand had created these. "These are just as beautiful," she softly said, "though I believe someone else painted them?" She turned to look at him, and he was regarding her with a peculiar smile on his mouth.

"Yes, those are mine. Mother insisted I display them here in the room with her work, although I objected on the basis that they're inferior and bring down the tone of the room."

Jane frowned and shook her head. "I can't agree with you, Mr. Jirles. To my eye they're just as lovely as your mother's work. It's true I'm no art connoisseur, but I know what I like."

His smile blossomed into something genuine. "Well, thank you, young woman. That's very kind."

He walked to the door, and Jane knew her private art viewing was at an end. She walked through into the hall, and he switched off the light.

"Well! I'll just let you browse. If you have any questions, do feel free to ask. I'll just be in my office, just here off the gallery." He pointed into a small, cluttered room and stopped there.

"I will, denki."

He entered his office, and Jane crossed the gallery and returned her attention to Miriam's extraordinary work. Peering closely at the piece titled *Quilting Bee*, she thought she could make out the tiny, even white stitches on the quilt that a group of Amish women wearing colorful cape dresses and black aprons were making. And looking more closely, she felt she was almost part of their lively conversation, humor gleaming from their eyes, tongues wagging. They were having a gut time, for sure and certain.

"It's a quaint piece of work, but personally, I'm tired of such scenes, invariably done by Englisch artists intent on exploiting our culture for profit. Aren't you?"

She was again pulled from her pleasant contemplation by a masculine voice, but when she turned to see who had uttered such an uninformed opinion, she was taken aback to see the man from the restaurant she'd met last night at dinner. Daniel. . .whatever his last name was.

He was apparently waiting for her to agree with him, so she gave him a frown. "This painting, and the others in the same style, are done by a friend of mine. An Amish friend. So no, I don't think she's exploiting our culture. She's attempting to make others understand it. And I think she's done a brilliant job of it."

He blinked. Probably, where he came from, proper Amish maedels didn't go around contradicting what Amish men told them. But really, he'd been so far off the mark she couldn't exactly agree with him. So what did he expect? All he had to do was look at the name of the artist to find out she was probably Amish. How many Englisch artists were named Miriam Zook?

He had the grace to look embarrassed. "Ah, I see. Well, that's what I get for trying to sound like I know something about art in order to impress you. Epic failure, I guess."

Her mouth dropped open for a moment until she caught herself. He was trying to impress her? That left her with basically nothing to say, so she just stared at him like a nincompoop until he smiled wryly. "Are you going to let me off the hook, Jane? I'm sorry for insulting your friend's work. It is very pretty; I can see that for myself. Other than that, I really don't know a thing about art."

"Then why would you say such a thing?"

"As I said, I was trying to impress you. I'll try to do better next time."

Next time? What did he mean by that?

"But why would you think that insulting an artist's work, no matter who he or she was, would impress me?"

He gave a noncommittal shrug and moved closer to the painting and took a look at the card on the wall. When he saw the price, his eyes widened and he gave a low whistle. "Goodness, who would have thought a pretty painting could go for a price like that?"

"Ja, about what you'd get for an Amish-made queen-size quilt."

"I don't know anything about quilts either. The only thing I know is lumber, I'm afraid. We have plenty of that in Wisconsin. So I was fortunate to find a job at a sawmill when I got here."

"When was that? I haven't seen you at Sunday services."

"I got here a little over a week ago, after the last church Sunday. I'll be joining you at services this coming Sunday, though."

Jane wasn't sure she was happy to hear that for some reason. The man rubbed her wrong. She had no idea why. But she decided to heed her instincts and remove herself from his presence.

"Well, it was nice seeing you again, Daniel, but I have to get back to work." She turned and headed for the door, and he hurried to open it for her and followed her out.

"Didn't you want to stay and look at the paintings?"

"Oh no—I'll confess, I was passing by, and I saw you through the window. I enjoyed meeting you last night, so I thought I'd come in and say hello."

He looked charmingly sheepish, as if she'd caught him doing something sort of silly but endearing. She was sure many maedels would find him adorable and irresistible. But she was not one of them.

"I see. Well, here's the bakery. Perhaps we'll run into each other again. Goodbye."

"I'll see you at services, for sure and certain! I'll be looking forward to it! What are you bringing? I'll be sure to get a serving of it, whatever it is. I'm sure you're a superior cook!"

Nonplussed, she shook her head. "I don't know yet. Well, good day, Daniel." She reached for the door, but again he beat her to it, opening it and standing back to let her go inside. Happily, he didn't follow her. After all, it was a public store and he could have claimed to have a hankering for a pastry. Or something.

Instead, he gave a little salute and turned and, whistling, sauntered off down the street. Eliza came to stand beside her, a broom in her hand. "Isn't that the guy from the restaurant last night? Daniel what's-his-name?"

Jane nodded. "Ja. He came into the gallery while I was looking at Miriam's new paintings and insulted her work, then tried to convince me he was trying to impress me with his nonexistent knowledge of art. It was very strange."

"Huh. He's very good looking."

"Ja, no denying that."

"Yet. . ." Eliza met Jane's eyes.

"Ja." Turning, she dusted off her hands. "Well, my break is over. Time for me to get to work. But you should go see Miriam's new work. It's wunderbar, Eliza. There's one painting I'd love to have, but it's out of my price range."

"Maybe you could trade her something for it."

"Interesting idea. I'll have to give it some thought." Glancing at the clock on the wall, she grunted. "Almost time for the lunch rush. I'll get the sandwiches ready. Will you make a pitcher of lemonade?"

"Two pitchers are already in the fridge, cooling off."

"You're the best!"

"Tell Lizzie that when it's time for raises."

Laughing, Jane started preparing for the onslaught of customers who would soon arrive for lunch to eat ham salad, egg salad, and chicken salad sandwiches, while also putting a serious dent in their supply of pastries. "I love my job," she murmured as she put on an apron and got to work.

"I love my job," Sam said to himself, humming a favorite hymn under his breath as he completed the frame for the new buggy he was building for a man who'd confided in him that he needed a larger conveyance as his wife was expecting their first boppli soon. "I make things for people who are moving on in their lives, achieving important goals, and reaching longed-for milestones. It's very satisfying!"

He sat back on his heels, hammer hanging loosely in his grip, as he pondered the irony of this. "And yet, here I am, my personal life stagnating and unable to move forward due to sheer cowardice."

Surging to his feet, Sam replaced the tool in its place on the pegboard on the wall of his shop. "I build buggies for people who are going courting. Or for people who are getting married. Or for people who are building families. And yet I could get by with a bicycle, because Sam Mast is a single guy, with no girlfriend, no wife, and no kinner. I don't even have a dog." He realized with a twinge of embarrassment that his voice had risen with each sentence, until he'd been fairly shouting at the end of his little tirade. He glanced around, but there was nobody to hear. He could yell all he wished—he was, as always, alone.

Walking outside, he surveyed his holdings. He had his large buggy shop, which was housed in a very nice, white clapboard-sided outbuilding on his farm. In fact, he'd purchased the spread a few years earlier specifically because of the building he knew would be perfect for his growing business. He recalled that Bishop Abram Troyer had initially attempted to convince him that Ruth Hershberger—then Ruth Helmuth—was thinking about selling the large farm she'd inherited from her grandparents and lived on with her late husband, Levi. But he heard from mutual friends that Ruth was absolutely not interested in selling, so he had looked until he found this place.

Turning, he regarded his big white traditional bank barn, with room for cows and horses and whatever else he might fancy owning on the lower level; the threshing floor on the main with the bank leading up from the farmyard, where he stored all his equipment; and a huge hayloft above. Turning again, he saw his house, a four-bedroom white farmhouse with room for a hoped-for yet still-nonexistent family. And surrounding these buildings were fields and pastures, gardens, farm fields, and orchards. He was a blessed man, for sure and certain. Except for one gaping, painful hole—the lack of the wife of his choosing. Namely, Jane Bontrager.

There was no use in all the free advice his friends and family were always tossing his way, to marry and fill his house with kinner, to come meet this maedel or that one, who might be the perfect woman for him. He knew that whoever she was, and whatever her accomplishments and personal charms, she couldn't be the right woman for him because that position had been filled long ago—by the woman who would doubtless shun him if she knew what he'd done, no matter how inadvertently.

"Ach! What am I going to do? Ben says I need to go talk to the woman and just come out with all of it and throw myself on her mercy. But what if she rejects me? What if she hates me?"

"What if she doesn't?"

Sam spun around and was chagrined to find the bishop of his Amish community, Abram Troyer, standing quietly a few feet away, a look of sympathetic concern on his aging visage.

"Abram!" Sam was aghast that the bishop had overheard his rant. "I'm sorry, I didn't know anyone was near. Why didn't you speak up sooner?"

Abram shrugged eloquently. "What, and interrupt what was really a marvelous bout of self-pity and angst? Not likely. It was obvious you needed to get all that out, kind of like when you lance a boil." He shuddered a bit at the thought. "If you keep it inside, it can't heal. Better to get it out, painful as the process might be."

Sam's shoulders slumped. "Well, I got it out all right. You must think I'm pathetic."

"Not at all. I have recent personal experience with being afraid to come to the point when it comes to courting a woman. I can't judge you, my boy."

"Lydia?"

Abram gave a fierce frown. "Maybe."

"Sorry. It's just, you're always together. It's kind of been a subject of conjecture around here for quite some time, to be honest."

Abram pursed his lips then nodded. "I see I'll have to lead by example. How can I convince you to go expose your heart to Jane if I won't do the same? Tell you what, Sam. Let's both promise to find the courage to act on what our hearts have been pushing us to do for years. In both of our cases."

Sam looked at the bishop, who was a good fifty years his senior. He'd been married, raised a family, lost his wife, and was now obviously in love with Lydia Coblentz, an elderly woman beloved by everyone in the community. Sam nodded slowly in agreement. If Abram could find it in his heart to confess his feelings to Lydia, how could he do less?

"I'll do it, Abram. Denki for showing me what I need to do."

"I think we showed each other."

"Why did you come by?"

Abram frowned. "Hmm. I'm not sure I remember." He pondered a moment. "Ach, ja! My buggy needs to be updated. I've got the flashing lights, but I want some of those PVC pipe wheel fixings. Can you do that?"

"Of course! Can you bring the buggy by next week?"

"Ja, that's fine." The old man smiled wryly. "Maybe by then, one of us at least will have gut news to share, ja?"

Sam chuckled. "Maybe so, Abram."

The bishop smiled and walked back to his buggy. Before climbing in, he turned back to Sam. "I understand there's another man who has taken a shine to our Jane, by the way."

Sam came to attention like a hound on a scent trail. "What? Who do you mean?"

"That newcomer, Daniel Beechy from Wisconsin. I hear he's been sniffing around the bakery. You'd better not waste any more time, young man. Daniel from Wisconsin might steal your thunder. And that would be a shame."

Sam blinked as the impact of the bishop's words registered fully. Then, feeling in a bit of a daze, he asked, "But, what if it is Gott's will that she end up with him? What if that's why I haven't been able to bring myself to tell her the truth about. . ."

Abram's eyebrows rose. "The truth about what, young Samuel? Do you need to clear your conscience of something?"

Sam gave Abram a miserable look. "Aw, it's really not that big a deal. But I've blown it up in my mind over the years until I can't get around it."

Abram cocked his head and waited patiently while Sam wrestled with his desire to unburden himself, in opposition with his embarrassment at admitting to the bishop what he'd done all those years ago.

Finally, Sam sighed. "When we were kinner, I was trying to convince some of the guys at school that I didn't like Jane—you know, like a girl."

Abram nodded his understanding. "What did you do to convince them?"

Sam cast his eyes at the ground then raised them to the bishop's and spilled out the whole sad tale about how he'd come up with the awful nickname of Plain Jane, which had stuck with Jane for years, to her misery.

When he finished, Abram pursed his lips and steepled his fingers while he thought about it.

"Well, Samuel, it's unfortunate that as a child you did this. But much, much more unfortunate is the fact that you've let her suffer with this all these years, not knowing who was responsible."

Sam felt the sting of tears in his eyes and blinked rapidly to clear them. Abram smiled sympathetically but clicked his tongue. "Samuel, I think you know that you have some amends to be making. I recommend you pray on this." He held up his hand. "I know, you've already prayed on it. You're a gut boy. But I suggest this time, pray for Gott to guide you in your actions for reparation, rather than praying for Him to forgive you and help you not to feel so bad about your actions. Until you fix this with the person you hurt, you won't find peace in your own heart. Fashtay?"

Sam nodded. "Denki, Abram. I honestly do appreciate your input. Do—do you think I'm a terrible person?"

The elderly bishop stared for a few moments at Sam then cuffed him on the shoulder. "Goodness, no, Samuel. You're a human. We all make mistakes." He shook his head. "Sometimes I forget what it's like to be young and full of passion. Goodbye, Samuel. I'll bring the buggy by next week."

Abram climbed into his buggy and waved at Sam before giving his standardbred mare, Spot, the signal and driving away down the road, leaving Sam feeling as if he'd been run over by a prize bull.

"I need to get over to the bakery. Ben and I are patching the ceiling tonight, and I'll get to talk to Jane. Daniel can just go back to Wisconsin if he thinks he's going to steal Jane Bontrager out from under my nose!"

But as he hurried inside to wash up before heading to the bakery, he felt a new worry gnawing at his stomach. And the worry rode on a cold wind blowing from the general direction of Wisconsin.

Pausing a moment, Sam took time to pray for help from his heavenly Father.

"Vader, please help me find the courage the bishop spoke of. People think I'm a confident, successful businessman. But You know the truth of my heart! I've been afraid for so long, I'm wasting my whole life! I need to talk to Jane. If she doesn't want me, I've lost nothing, because I have nothing to lose! Please, help Your foolish son to find the right words to express my feelings. If this is not the path You have in mind for me, I'll accept that. But if there is a chance I could make a life with Jane, please, please help me figure out how to do it. Your will be done."

"Eliza, the guys are nearly finished upstairs in the bathroom. Is the pot roast about ready? They'll be hungry, and we promised them a gut supper."

"Ja!" Eliza turned from the oven, hefting the heavy roasting pan containing a roast and vegetables and placing it on a couple of hot pads on the counter. "There!" She whisked the lid off, and fragrant steam rose from the meat, which was so tender it was falling apart.

"Ach, Eliza, you make the best pot roast!" Jane's mouth watered as she contemplated how delicious supper would be.

"It's my auntie Sherry's recipe," Eliza confessed. "My Englisch auntie Sherry Eddy!"

Jane was surprised. "I didn't know you had an Englisch aunt. What's the connection?"

Eliza explained as she plated up the meat and veggies. "Well, my father's sister back in Lancaster jumped the fence as a young woman, before she was baptized. She married a veterinarian she met when he came out to her father's farm to vaccinate their herd of Guernsey cows. Since she hadn't been baptized, she wasn't shunned, and she remained a close part of our family."

Jane smiled. "I like that she stayed a part of your family. Too many people drive away anyone who isn't the same as they are, who doesn't conform. As if they're afraid being around someone different might taint or tempt them."

Eliza nodded. "Ja. Some thought my parents were wrong. But Auntie Sherry and Uncle Andy are wunderbar people. Auntie Sherry even got her veterinary assistant certificate so she could assist Uncle Andy in his work."

"I imagine when the *bopplin* started coming, he had to find someone else?"

"Nee." Eliza looked sad. "They never had any. So instead they spoiled all of us, and we got to go on veterinary calls with them. I have a younger bruder who wants to be a vet in the worst way." She frowned thoughtfully. "He hasn't been baptized. I wouldn't be surprised if he finds a way, like our bruder Reuben found a way to be a doctor. Of course, our parents want him to stay and work in the family hardware store."

"Well, at least Reuben came back to the community, thankfully, so he and Mary could be together. And now you have a wunderbar sister-in-law and an adorable little niece!"

"Happy endings all around!" Eliza carried the platter of meat and veggies to the table. "Would you please make the gravy, Jane? Yours is better than mine. You have a knack I lack."

"You're a poet!" Jane chortled, moving over to the roasting pan to make the gravy. "You could get the rolls, butter, honey, jam, and whatever else you want and put it on the table," she suggested.

"On it."

They worked efficiently, and by the time they heard the stomp of work boots clomping down the back stairs, all was ready.

"The ceiling is patched! Tomorrow we'll sand it, and then we'll be able to paint it next week, and it'll be good as new," Ben explained as they entered the kitchen.

"Ach, what an amazing smell!" Ben rhapsodized as he entered the kitchen, eyes closed, nose in the air. "Is that pot roast?"

Eliza blushed and smiled. "Ja, with veggies."

Sam was right behind Ben, and his eyes widened when he saw the table. "Wow, you two have outdone yourselves. This looks amazing. Denki, Eliza. Denki, Jane."

Jane grinned at him. "Eliza did most of the cooking. Her pot roast is *appenditlich*. I just made the gravy."

She went to pour it into the gravy boat from the heavy roaster, but Sam nudged her aside. "Let me do that. It's heavy."

She stepped aside but gave him an impatient look. "Who do you think lifts such things when there are no big, strong men around?"

"Shh, don't disabuse him of thinking there's no possible way you could have transferred that gravy without him." Ben laughed. "He'll cry like a baby."

"I would not cry like a baby," Sam protested, carrying the gravy to the table. "I would cry in a dignified manner, like the strong man I am."

Everyone laughed, and then Jane said, "Let's wash up. It's time to eat."

Ben looked around. "Where's Susan? I thought she was joining us?"

Eliza grimaced. "She has a migraine. She said to tell you she's sorry, and she'll see you next time."

"Oh, that's too bad," Ben said, moving to help Eliza fill the water glasses.

Sam caught Jane's eye and stepped closer to her. "Jane, I need to talk to you."

She was surprised. "Now?" She looked at the table, where Ben and Eliza were talking quietly together. "But we're ready to eat. Can it wait?"

He frowned but nodded. "Ja, of course."

She smiled. "Gut, then we'll talk later. About the bathroom, I assume. Come, let's eat!"

Soon they were seated, and Jane looked at Ben and Sam. "Who would like to lead the prayer?"

Ben nodded at Sam. "You're the oldest, Sam. You do the honors."

With a small smile Sam bowed his head, followed by the others. After they'd all silently given thanks for the meal, they began passing the food around.

"Ach, Eliza, this is so gut!" Ben said, talking with his mouth full.

"Sorry, it is just so gut!"

Eliza blushed and smiled, meeting Jane's eyes; then she glanced back at Ben, who was busy demolishing his plate of food. Jane glanced at Sam and found him watching her, a serious, almost worried look in his eyes, and she gave him an inquiring look, wondering for the first time since he'd spoken what he'd wanted to talk about—but he dropped his eyes and addressed himself to his food.

What's that about?

She looked at Eliza, trying to catch her friend's eye, but Eliza was picking at her own food and sneaking glances at Ben, who seemed oblivious.

Unable to stand the strange tension that had invaded the room, Jane pushed back from the table and stood, picking up her dishes and whisking them to the sink. She filled the sink with hot soapy water and scraped the remains of her dinner into the trash before washing her plate and utensils. She turned and looked at the table, to find everyone staring at her, forks suspended in midair, surprise on all of their faces. She realized that she'd behaved oddly by jumping up in the middle of the meal and throwing out half her food.

But she couldn't help it. She couldn't sit there with Sam behaving oddly as well, not knowing what he thought about her.

"Jane?" Eliza said, rising halfway and reaching a hand toward her friend.

"I'm sorry," she gasped. "I suddenly don't feel very well. You all go on and enjoy the meal. I'm going on up to bed." She pointed at the stairs and then, with a jerky wave, rushed to leave the unbearable scene. She picked up the battery lantern from the counter, and at the door she stopped and forced herself to turn back and look at Eliza, who was clearly at a loss to understand Jane's behavior.

"Please lock up when you leave," she said to Eliza, who nodded, the compassion in her eyes acknowledging her grasp of what Jane was suffering.

Jane quietly pulled the door closed behind her. And she did what she rarely did—she turned the deadbolt in the door, ensuring her privacy.

With a heavy heart at the way the meal had ended, at least for her, she hurried upstairs to seek comfort from her cat, who never behaved in a way she couldn't understand.

And the thought of Secret reminded her that Little Mouse was still missing, and tears flooded her eyes.

As she entered her apartment, she pulled the door closed and deadbolted that as well. Secret greeted her, glad as always to see her, and she scooped the pretty brown tabby into her arms and stood in the hallway, crying bitter tears of confusion and disappointment, which she happily absorbed into her fluffy fur. "Oh, Secret," she whispered brokenly, "you're the only one who really gets me. I know what you want from me, and even if food is on the top of your list, I know that I'm not far behind."

Secret uttered a little chirp Jane chose to interpret as reassurance, and she gave a watery laugh and carried her cat into the kitchen, where she topped off her bowl of kibble and gave her a couple of kitty treats simply for being there.

Jane sat on the floor beside her as she gobbled her food, stroking her silken fur. In the distance, a siren wailed, and Jane whispered a prayer for the safety of whoever was involved. Then her mind turned back to Sam and his mercurial behavior toward her.

"Secret," she whispered, "I don't know what Sam thinks, or what Sam wants, or why he can't seem to make up his mind. One minute he's friendly, and I start to get my hopes up. The next he's distant and almost looks as if he's afraid to talk to me! What on earth could be the problem? I don't think I could be any clearer that I care for him." She heaved a frustrated sigh and pushed to her feet. "Oh well. Maybe he'll figure it out soon, and then I'll get a clue as to his feelings and intentions."

She glanced at the kitty water fountain sitting on the floor in the kitchen and contemplated her options. "If Sam doesn't decide he wants to court me, there's always my secret admirer. He seems to get me, Secret."

She nibbled a thumbnail as she stood looking at the fountain and then at the bowl of delicate, colorful eggshells in the brown pottery bowl on the table.

"Whoever he is."

Picking up the battery lantern, she went to get ready for bed.

CHAPTER EIGHT

Sam watched impatiently as Ben considered his options before at long last reaching for a slice of pecan pie to add to the plate of food he'd prepared for himself from the heaped tables that had been set up in the large basement family room where church services had been held that morning, in the home of Jonas and Ruth Hershberger.

Ruth, lovely in an eggplant-purple dress with an apron over it and a pristine white prayer kapp partly covering her glorious red hair, laughed at the sight of Ben's plate. "You know, you can take another plate, or even come back for seconds," she said with a friendly grin.

Ben grinned back. "But the best pieces of pie might be gone if I do! Too risky."

"I understand." She leaned toward him and whispered conspiratorially, "I already put aside the piece I want!"

"Wise move." He looked around at the crowded room. "These folks will go through this like termites in a woodpile!"

She turned to Sam. "Won't you have some lunch, Sam?"

He gave her a tight smile. "I'll eat in a bit. I need to talk to Ben, if he ever finishes choosing between the different kinds of desserts!"

Ruth shook her head and turned to help the next man in line, and Sam sighed deeply as Ben debated between lemon bars and gingersnaps.

"Hurry up, Ben! I've been standing here for five minutes while you pick and choose."

Ben ignored Sam as he settled on the lemon bar and placed it carefully onto his overloaded plate. But Sam wouldn't go away and let him eat in peace. "What, now? We'll miss lunch."

"Ja, now please. Besides, you've got enough food on that plate to satisfy two normal men."

With a last glance at the tables as if to be certain he hadn't missed anything important, Ben grabbed some cutlery and reluctantly followed Sam as he walked briskly away from the after-service lunch crowd and out through the sliding doors into the side yard of the house. "Okay but not for long. It's cold out here."

Sam led the way around to the back of the big barn housing Jonas' basket business, followed by Ben. Sam looked around to be certain no one was near enough to hear their conversation and then stepped closer to Ben. "I want your opinion on something, Ben."

"I figured, since you dragged me back here. What is it?" Ben shoveled some German potato salad into his mouth and regarded his friend, waiting.

Sam shoved his hands into his pockets and felt certain he looked as embarrassed as he felt. He was sure Ben would think he'd lost his wits, but he plowed ahead anyway.

"I've decided to talk to Jane and tell her about. . . Well, you know about what."

Ben looked pleased. "Excellent! You're finally going to do what you should have done years ago, and then you can finally get your life started." He bit into a thick ham and cheese sandwich, balancing his plate in one hand while he demolished the sandwich.

"That sounds pathetic, doesn't it?"

"Not at all." Ben spoke around a mouthful of barbecue potato chips. "It would be pathetic if you kept putting it off." He gestured at Sam with a chicken drumstick. "Actually doing what you need to do takes courage. So, when will you talk to her? Today?"

Sam took off his black wool hat and scratched his head then slapped the hat against his leg. "I'm not sure." He looked at Ben and plopped the hat back onto his head. "Look, Ben, what do you think about Jane's secret admirer sending one more gift?"

Ben's hand froze midway to his mouth, a forkful of baked beans dripping back onto his plate as he stared open mouthed at his friend. "Sam, what are you talking about? Why would you want to do that? You should leave well enough alone and just go to her and tell her the truth.

All of it." He ate the beans and finished up the rest before picking up a roll and mopping up his plate with it.

Sam walked away a few feet before turning and looking sheepishly at his friend. "I just thought maybe I could leave one more gift, with a note setting up a meeting, where I'd tell her I was her secret admirer all along—and sort of soften her up before confessing the rest."

He searched his friend's face for a clue as to his true opinion on the matter. Ben sighed. "While I don't understand why you'd need to do it that way, I suppose it won't hurt anything. But you've really got to tell her. You can't just keep procrastinating." He tucked into the pecan pie, groaning in pleasure. "Ach, this is really delicious."

Sam groaned in return. "Can you focus a minute here, please?"

Ben gave a sheepish grin before finishing up the pie. "Sorry."

Sam sighed. "It's okay. I've just got so much to lose. I feel that this might be a good way to work my way around to telling Jane what I did."

Ben swallowed some extra-sharp cheddar before answering. "You make it sound as if you'd committed some terrible crime. Sam, you accidentally gave a girl a nickname. You didn't even mean to do it! It's not the end of the world."

"But what I'm afraid of is that if I can't make her understand, it could be the end of my chances with her. And that sounds a lot scarier than the end of the world, to tell the truth."

Ben slapped Sam on the back. "I think everything will work out. She cares about you. I have inside information on this." He smiled knowingly at Sam while scarfing down a dill spear.

Sam's eyes sharpened on Ben. "What? Who?" Then he stopped, as realization dawned. "Eliza? Did she tell you Jane likes me?"

Ben's face became guarded, as if he realized he'd perhaps betrayed a trust. He finished another pickle spear before answering. "Maybe. But whoever my source was, I'm telling you that I think that the sooner you talk to Jane and get it all out into the open the better. So, you'll do it?"

"Yes. I'll leave her a gift tomorrow morning, with a note. I'll set up a meeting with her. And when she sees that I'm her secret admirer, I'll be able to get a feel for whether that makes her happy or not. And if she seems glad, I'll tell her the rest."

"Sam, you need to tell her everything, no matter what you think she feels. You can't always tell how people feel under pressure."

"I hear you. But I wish people came with instruction manuals. It would be so much easier!" Sam looked toward the house, where a few of the men who had finished eating were standing around, huddled into their black coats talking. "Denki for listening, Ben. We'd better get back or there won't be anything left for me to eat."

"I tried to tell you that."

Sam reached over and filched a brownie off his friend's plate. "At least I won't starve."

The two walked back to join the group.

Behind the barn, a tall figure stepped out from the shadow of a large water tank. He watched the two men walking back to the house, and a smile played across his lips. After a few moments he stuck his hands into his pockets and casually strolled around the barn, entering the house from the opposite direction taken by Ben and Sam.

"I ate too much," Eliza moaned, putting a hand on her tummy as she, Jane, Susan Bontrager, and Miriam Zook stood from the table.

Miriam grinned at her. "Ja, me too. But it's hard to resist, considering how gut everything is!"

Jane nodded, gathering up her paper plate and cup and the plastic utensils and strolling with her friends toward the trash can set up beside the steps leading into the kitchen. "I had two slices of Ruth's chicken pot pie, and big helpings of baked beans, potato salad, and Chow Chow. And now I plan to stuff at least one piece of pie into whatever space is left."

The other women laughed, but Susan said, "You're not the only one!"

Tossing out their trash, they headed to the dessert table, where there was still a good selection of cakes, pies, cookies, brownies, and gelatin.

"Oh! Look, someone made ice cream!" Miriam headed for the container heaped with homemade vanilla ice cream and accepted a generous serving from Sarah Bontrager, Jane and Susan's maem.

"Maem made it," Susan said, smiling at her mother and holding out her bowl for a serving. "Denki, Maem!" she said, grinning as she surveyed the selection of toppings to put on top of the frozen treat. "I can't decide between hot fudge, caramel, and strawberry, so I think I'll have all three." She heaped them onto the ice cream, followed by whipped cream, chocolate sprinkles, and a couple of cherries on the very top.

"Now that's what I call dessert!"

All four young women turned to see who had spoken, and Jane cringed a bit when she saw that it was Daniel Beechy from Wisconsin. "I already ate," he said, eyeing the ice cream with interest, "but that looks homemade. I think I have room for a little more dessert. Mind if I join you ladies?"

They looked at one another and shrugged. "Sure," Eliza said, building her own sundae. "We'll be sitting down wherever we find an empty table. You're welcome to join us."

"Great! See you in a few minutes."

The four young women took their desserts and coffee over to a table in the corner of the room and plopped down. "Ach," Jane whispered, sneaking a glance at Daniel, who was busy talking to her mudder while she served his ice cream. "I wish he hadn't asked to join us."

Susan and Miriam looked surprised. "But why not? He's new around here, right? Can't hurt to spend a little time with a handsome newcomer."

"I don't particularly like him," Jane confessed, leaning in so only her friends could hear. "He's said a few things I found objectionable."

At this, her sister and Miriam looked concerned. "Really? Like what?" Susan asked, peering over Eliza's shoulder to get a better look at him.

"Susan!" Jane hissed. "Don't look! He'll know we're talking about him!"

"But what did he say?" Miriam persisted before taking a large bite of her ice cream and moaning in delight. "Ach, this is so gut! Your mudder sure can make ice cream!"

"Ja, it's her specialty. Homemade is so much better than store bought, at least Maem's homemade!" Jane said.

"Hey," a deep voice complained. "I didn't see the ice cream when we went through the dessert line!"

Jane knew that voice, and she felt goose bumps creep over her skin as she looked up and saw Sam and Ben grinning at them.

"Hi, Sam. Hi, Ben!" Eliza cried. "Join us, there's plenty of room."

"First I have to go get ice cream. Sit and hold our places, Sam. I'll bring you a bowl with all the toppings." Ben sauntered off to the dessert table, and Sam sat down next to Jane and gave her a tentative smile.

"Hello, Jane."

"Hello, Sam," she answered after gulping down her mouthful of ice cream. "Oh, ow! Brain freeze!"

"Make your mouth into a small O and suck in air," Sam advised, peering closely at Jane, who was fanning herself in an attempt to relieve the sudden headache from swallowing the ice cream too fast.

She tried what he suggested, and after about ten seconds, a look of surprise came over her face. "That really worked! Denki, Sam. That's so awful."

"I hate brain freeze," Susan said, greedily finishing her own ice cream and looking over at the dessert table. "I wonder if there's enough for seconds?"

"How can you possibly have any more room?" Miriam asked. Then, with a giggle, she jumped up. "What am I talking about? I'll go with you. I can always eat more ice cream. Come on, Susan."

They hurried over to get a second helping of ice cream as Ben arrived back at the table, carrying two bowls. He placed one down next to Sam and sat down on his friend's other side.

"Denki!" Sam picked up his spoon and took a bite. "Yum, your maem hasn't lost her touch, Jane."

"Hey, I thought you girls were going to save me a seat."

Jane looked up and saw Daniel frowning down at Sam and Ben.

"Hi, Daniel," Ben said without much enthusiasm. "There's plenty of room. Have a seat."

Daniel eyed the space next to Jane, occupied by Sam, and shrugged. "Fine, I'll sit over there." He rounded the table and took the space across from Jane, temporarily vacated by Susan and Miriam.

"Actually, that seat is taken," Jane said.

"Oh yeah? I don't see anyone here," Daniel quipped.

"It's Miriam's seat. You know, Miriam Zook, the artist who painted the scenes of Amish life you were admiring the other morning at the gallery in town."

He gave her a tight smile, but she could see annoyance in his dark eyes. "Oh, right. Well, I'll budge over one."

"That seat is Susan's," Eliza said. "You can sit here, on the other side of me, across from Ben."

His eyes narrowed a bit, but he pasted a friendly smile on his handsome face and sat next to Eliza, across from Ben, who gave him a puzzled look.

"Were you in church, Daniel?" Ben asked. "I didn't see you."

"I got here late," the newcomer muttered. "I had trouble finding the place this morning. But I was there for most of it. I was directly behind you, a few rows back. Not surprised you didn't notice me there."

Ben nodded. "It can be hard finding your way around a new community. But you're here now. Like ice cream, do you?"

Daniel cast a glance at Jane, who pretended not to notice. "Ja, love it. And Jane's maem makes the best, I hear. So I had to try it. I've noticed that if you sample the maem's cooking, you've gotten a hint at the maedel's!"

He made a show of taking a big bite, and his eyes widened. "Ach, it is very gut!" He shoveled the rest of the treat into his mouth in record time. When Jane stood to go inside and help clean up, he stood too.

"Where are you going, Jane?"

"To help wash up. Are you coming, girls?"

"When I'm done," Miriam, who had just returned with her second helping of ice cream, said from her place at the end of the table across from Jane.

Beside her, Susan nodded. "Nearly ready."

"Well, I'm ready now," Eliza volunteered, standing and gathering her dish.

"Are you staying for the singing after?" Daniel asked Jane. "I'm looking forward to it. I hope you're staying."

Jane, who had never been pursued before in such an obvious manner, wasn't sure what to say.

"We're all staying," her sister helpfully volunteered. "What about you guys?" She looked at Sam and Ben, who exchanged a look.

"We're staying," Ben said with a firm nod. "Sam's a terrific singer, aren't you, Sam?"

Sam raised an eyebrow at his friend. "If you say so."

"Oh, I do!" Ben smiled at Jane.

"Let's get the cleanup done, girls," Jane said. "See you later, guys."

"Bye, Jane!" Daniel said with a saucy grin. "I'll look forward to trying your ice cream sometime!"

"I don't make ice cream, I'm afraid," Jane said.

Daniel smiled and said, "Well, I'm sure whatever treats you make are delicious!"

Jane couldn't help the groan that escaped her as she turned and walked toward the house, followed by Eliza. Susan and Miriam, who had finished their desserts while Daniel attempted to flirt with Jane, hopped up and hurried after them.

When they were far enough away not to be overheard, Eliza nudged Jane with her shoulder. "What was all that about?"

"Yeah," Susan said. "That new guy sure likes you, Jane!" She batted her eyelashes at her older sister, a silly grin on her face.

"Well, the feeling is not mutual," Jane muttered.

"What do you have against him? He's kind of a show-off, but he's new. Maybe he's just nervous," Miriam suggested.

"Maybe," Jane said, glancing back at the table, where the men had been joined by a few other young, unmarried guys. They were all chatting and drinking coffee. But Daniel was looking at her. She met his eyes for a moment before snapping her head around so fast she feared she'd end up with a stiff neck. "The other day in the art studio, he said some mean stuff about Miriam's paintings."

"What?" Miriam asked. "And here I was, disposed to like him!"

"What did he say?" Susan asked. Jane had already told Eliza about it, so she quickly explained to the others, who frowned.

"I think he was merely showing off," Miriam offered. "But I admit I don't think much of his technique." She exchanged looks with the others, and then they all laughed.

"Of course not!" Eliza said. "Not if he has to insult someone else to make himself look smart. Too bad, though. He is very handsome!"

They all laughed again, and the mood was lightened. "Well, I wish he wouldn't follow me around," Jane said. "But I suppose we'll have to be nice to him, since he's new."

"Ja, and give him a real chance," Miriam said. "Even if he has no taste in art."

Chuckling, they went into the kitchen to help with the cleanup.

"You need to hurry and ask Jane if she'll let you drive her home, Sam," Ben advised, giving his friend a small shove toward where Jane and her friends were talking following the singing.

Sam frowned at Ben. "She and Eliza and Susan all came together. I'm sure they plan to ride home together too."

Ben looked astonished at this. "Sam! Don't be dense, man! Susan and Eliza can ride home together, but if you give Jane a ride home, then they won't have to drop her off first."

"I'm surprised you're not asking Eliza if you can drive her home," Sam said pointedly to his friend, who squirmed a bit but gave Sam a small grin.

"Well, it did occur to me," Ben admitted. "But then I thought, if I give Eliza a ride, that would leave Susan all alone, and I doubt Eliza would like that."

"She wouldn't be alone. She would be with Jane," Sam pointed out.

Ben grinned and pointed at Sam. "Not if you're giving Jane a lift!"

Then his eyes widened as he looked at the four women over Sam's shoulder. "Uh-oh, you may be too late anyway. Looks like Daniel has beat you to it."

"What?" Sam spun around in time to see Daniel speaking to the women.

"Come on!" He grabbed Ben's sleeve and hauled him over to the group. They were in time to hear Jane giving her regrets to Daniel, who was obviously not happy to be rejected by the pretty maedel.

"But why not?" he practically whined. "I've got a nice rented rig and horse. And you'd be safe with me." Catching sight of Ben and Sam, he smiled at Ben. "You'll vouch for me, won't you, Ben? We work together, and you've seen what a gut worker I am."

Ben gave a small shrug. "Sorry, Daniel, I hardly know you." He looked at the women. "But I will say he's a very gut worker at the sawmill."

"There, you see? Ben recommends me!"

"That's not what I heard," Sam muttered.

"I'm sorry, Daniel," Jane said. "I'm riding with my sister and my friend. Maybe another time."

Sam listened to this with dismay.

Sis yuscht! Now that she's told Daniel no, she won't be able to say yes to me. What bad luck.

Sam frowned at the group, wishing he'd listened to Ben and asked sooner. He met his friend's eyes, and Ben gave a small grimace, acknowledging the hopelessness of the situation.

"I'm sure they wouldn't mind if you rode with me instead," Daniel persisted. "Would you, ladies?"

Susan and Eliza gave him a look of chagrin. "Um, well," Susan began, but Eliza cut in.

"Sorry, Daniel, but we're all going over to our place to work on a project that can't wait until tomorrow."

"You're working on a Sunday?" Daniel asked, an unpleasant gleam in his eyes. "I'm surprised to hear that."

"Nee, nee," Eliza said, obviously a fast thinker. "Not working. It's our new cats." She cast Susan a look. "They're acting up. Jane is coming over to help figure out why. Right, Susan?"

"Oh, ja." Susan nodded. "My big sister is amazing with cats. We're sure she'll be able to figure out why our new kitties haven't settled in yet."

"That's perfect! I'm gut with cats too! Why, just recently—" Daniel started.

Susan interrupted. "Denki, we'll keep that in mind if we can't figure it out on our own."

Daniel looked momentarily frustrated, but then his eyes lit up, and Sam was sure he'd come up with yet another suggestion to try to wiggle his way into spending more time with the girls—specifically with Jane—that afternoon. But before Daniel could say anything, Ben spoke up.

"Daniel, I've actually been meaning to ask your opinion on the new saw the boss is thinking of getting. I think you said something about using a similar one back in Wisconsin?"

Distracted, Daniel threw an annoyed look Ben's way. "New saw? What new saw?"

"You remember—we were talking about it at lunch one day last week. The bigger saw that can handle larger logs. Let's get some more coffee and talk about it. And I think I see more pie!" Ben took a few steps toward the dessert and coffee table that had been resupplied following the singing, and Sam could see that Daniel was torn between persisting with Jane and following Ben to get the scoop on this new saw—and eat more pie.

"You coming? I think I see pecan. My favorite!" Ben looked at Daniel, who gave the girls a regretful look before turning to follow Ben.

"I'll see you ladies later," he called, following Ben, who exchanged a quick look with Sam. Sam smiled his thanks at his friend's save. But when he turned to the women, it was to find them all looking at him with arms folded across their chests and frowns on their faces.

"What on earth is that man thinking, being so pushy?" Eliza asked.

"I see why you don't like him, Jane." Susan gave a sharp nod. "He's arrogant too."

"And obviously proud, and not in a gut way!" Miriam added with a sniff.

Jane looked at Sam, one eyebrow raised as if she expected him to have answers that would explain Daniel's behavior.

"Hey, don't look at me. I just met the guy a few nights ago, the same time you did," he said to Eliza and Jane. "Ben just did you all a favor. You'd best hit the road before Daniel breaks away from him."

They all looked over to where Ben was leading Daniel to a table half filled with other men. "It's a pity to miss pie," Susan said with a sigh. "But I agree, it's time to leave. And Jane, we really do need your help with the cats!"

"I think Lydia might be the better one to ask," Jane pointed out. "But I'm happy to try. Speaking of cats, the ad about Little Mouse comes out in the paper tomorrow. I hope it will be seen by whoever has her! I can't believe Lizzie hasn't called to check on us yet. And when she does, how will I talk to her without letting on that we've lost her cat?"

Miriam gave her a hug. "Don't lose faith, Jane! Gott knows where that cat is, and He'll keep her safe until we can get her back to the bakery, you'll see!"

"Ja, Jane, we have to believe Little Mouse is somewhere safe," Eliza said, squeezing Jane's hand.

"Let's pray," Susan suggested. "It always makes me feel better to give my problems to Gott."

So the four women, along with Sam, bowed their heads. Susan, who had suggested the prayer, said, "Vader, please keep Little Mouse warm, safe, and fed until we can find her and bring her home, where she belongs.

We pray to You for help in locating her. Please help us to figure this out. Your will be done, Vader."

Jane cast a grateful look at her little sister, who gave her a big hug. Sam heard her whisper, "Don't despair, Jane. He'll bring Little Mouse home safe and sound, just wait and see."

"But where can she be?" Jane cried, obviously overcome with worry.

"Probably somewhere we'd never even suspect—when we find out, we won't be able to believe it! You know how funny life can be sometimes."

Jane gave her sister a look of love and gratitude, and Sam smiled at the sisters' obvious love for one another and rubbed a hand over his heart as he wished Jane would one day bestow such a look on him.

"Good night, Eliza, Susan. Good night, Miriam," he said. Then, turning to look at Jane, he gave her a soft smile. "Good night, Jane. Listen to your sister. Don't lose hope. I have a good feeling that we'll soon find your cat."

She gave him a tremulous smile and thanked him softly, and once again he berated himself for not asking her to ride home with him sooner. He waved as the four women gathered their warm bonnets and capes and left the house together. Stepping outside, he watched them drive out of the Hershbergers' driveway toward town. Then he returned inside to get a piece of pie and some coffee, figuring just because he'd lost out on the chance to drive Jane home didn't mean he had to miss out on a piece of pecan pie.

Jane yawned widely as she entered the bakery kitchen the following morning and turned on the lights to start her day. Dawn was still a ways off, and the window outside the kitchen door revealed nothing but darkness.

Blinking sleepily, she stifled another yawn and decided to start with the coffee machine. She'd been out later than usual the previous night, trying to figure out what might be bothering Eliza and Susan's cats. The pair were having trouble settling into their new home. Something was obviously keeping them on edge, but the three friends had not been able to put a finger on it, whatever it was. Jane planned to consult Lydia as soon as she had the chance.

Large mug of black coffee in hand, she felt better prepared to face the day. She pulled a work apron over her deep blue dress, put a hairnet on under her prayer kapp, and got to work.

An hour later she heard the front door open and Eliza's greeting. Her friend tramped into the kitchen, a pale reflection of her usually cheerful morning self. She pulled off her black bonnet and hung it, along with her black wool cape, on hooks by the back door.

"Guder mariye, Jane." She yawned, walking over to help herself to some coffee, which she doctored up with cream and sugar before plopping onto one of the straight-backed kitchen chairs. "Ach! Susan and I barely got any sleep Saturday or Sunday nights. Those *deerich* cats kept us up both nights, yowling and running all around the apartment. I'm afraid we've made a bad mistake."

Looking at her friend, Jane noticed the faint blue smudges beneath her eyes that hinted at lost sleep. She decided the day's baking was well enough in hand that she could take a break, so she refilled her own mug and took a seat next to Eliza. "You do look tired."

"Great." Eliza propped her chin on her hand and yawned again, provoking an answering yawn from Jane. "I don't know if I can take another night like that, Jane. Secret and Little Mouse don't behave that way. Why do Friar Tuck and Little John?"

Jane shrugged. "Maybe they just need to settle in?"

"I hope so." Eliza yawned again. "Susan was like a zombie when she left for the quilt shop. I don't know how much use either of us will be today."

Jane's younger sister worked not far away at the Stitch-in-Time Amish Quilt Shop. She was a gifted quilter and divided her time there between counter help, stocking supplies and working on her latest quilting project. Jane admired her ability to create the tiny, hand stitches—twelve per inch due to her skill level—that comprised the complicated quilting patterns she favored. Recently she'd been excited to tell Jane that her boss had asked her if she'd like to start teaching beginner quilting classes for extra pay.

Jane considered herself a mediocre quilter, especially compared to Susan. She could do six stitches per inch, and they would be neat and even. But she had no aspirations to attain the skill level that would bring really good money from making stitches you practically needed a magnifying glass to achieve.

An exhausted Susan would be a Susan who couldn't quilt at her best. Not good.

"I do think it's more than just needing to settle in," Jane said. "But I can't think what. We searched the entire apartment last night. I didn't see anything that should bother a cat."

Eliza smiled at her friend. "We appreciate you coming over and trying."

"I really think we need to invite Lydia over to have a look. She has much more experience with cats than any of us."

Eliza shrugged tiredly. "I'm willing to try anything." She finished her coffee and stood up. "I'd better get to work. If I sit here any longer, I'll fall asleep."

Jane watched Eliza pick up a tray of pastries and push through the door into the front to set up for the day. "Ach, I hope this situation improves fast."

She walked over to pick up Eliza's mug and took it to the sink to wash. She glanced at the door and gasped when she caught sight of a white paper fluttering in the breeze. "Another note!"

Hurrying over to the door, she yanked it open and looked at the white paper, folded in half and taped to the door, with her name written on it.

"That's different from the first two." She carefully pulled the paper away from the door and glanced reflexively down at the stoop, but no gift awaited her there. "And so is that."

Thoughtfully she closed the door, first looking up and down the alley in both directions for a sign of who might have left it there. A scuffle over by the dumpster caught her attention, and hope blossomed in her chest. She shoved the note into her apron pocket and stepped outside, peering at the dumpster in the early morning light. A small meow made her gasp, and she hurried toward the dumpster. A large gray tomcat bolted out from behind it, startling her. "Oh!" she cried, pressing a hand to her chest. The tom hissed and spat before streaking away down the alley. Jane had to chuckle at how much he had scared her. "That was not Little Mouse." She turned to return to the bakery but had only taken a couple of steps away from the dumpster when a small, plaintive meow issued from inside, again filling her with hope. "Little Mouse? Is that you?"

The lid to the dumpster was closed, and the meow came again, from inside. "Little Mouse?"

She carefully lifted the lid, filled with hope that she'd found her friend's cat. But instead of Lizzie's sweet gray kitty, Jane was surprised by another angry tom that leaped from inside to the rim, glaring at Jane with baleful yellow eyes. His dirty white fur and ragged, battle-scarred ears were testimony to his hard life as a stray. He hissed a warning at Jane before jumping to the ground and, with a flick of his ragged tail, racing away down the alley.

"Hey, I'm not the one who closed you in there!" she called after him. A disgusted yowl answered her, and she giggled at the realization that she'd just defended herself to an old stray cat. "Still, I'm glad I came out and found him. Poor thing. I'm going to have to mention to the people from the shelter that we've got a couple of toms that need to be caught and neutered before they start families."

She peered hopefully behind the dumpster, calling for Little Mouse, but no meow answered her. Dejected, she returned inside, closing the door behind her.

"Where are you, Little Mouse?" she whispered, forehead pressed to the window in the door overlooking the alley. With a sigh, she turned and surveyed the kitchen. Most of the opening chores were completed. "I'll need to change my apron, and I'll be ready for the day."

Reaching into the pocket of her baking apron for whatever she might have shoved inside, she encountered the note. "Ach! I forgot about this!"

Drawing it out, she opened it and read it over once, then again, more slowly. "That's odd. It seems different somehow."

"What have you got there?" Eliza asked, peering over Jane's shoulder. "Hey, is that another note from your secret admirer?"

"Seems to be," Jane murmured, reading it yet again. "It's odd, though. It seems different somehow."

Eliza looked around. "Where's the present?"

Jane looked up at her friend. "Oh, there isn't one today."

"No present? What kind of secret admirer is he, not leaving you a present, especially after the first two times?"

"It says he wants to meet me," Jane said. "Tomorrow."

"Ja, I saw that. Are you going to go?"

"I don't know." She nibbled her thumbnail, and Eliza reached over and pulled her hand away. "Don't bite your nails, Jane. You told me to remind you."

Jane laughed. "So I did." She looked at the note again. "Do you think I should go?"

"What is it that bothers you about the note? Is it that it didn't come with a nice gift this time?" Eliza's eyes twinkled mischievously. "That might put me off too."

Jane laughed again. "Gifts are nice, and my secret admirer seems to know what I like." She pondered the question a few moments before giving a decisive shake of her head. "I'm happy to be able to honestly say I'm not that shallow, though. It's not the lack of a gift. It's something I'm having a hard time defining."

"Okay, let's look at this logically," Eliza suggested, picking up another tray of French pastries and heading toward the front to place them in the display case. Jane followed.

"Logically?"

"Ja, of course. The note is different. The other ones came in envelopes, right?" Eliza pulled on a pair of disposable plastic gloves and carefully began placing the fresh baked treats on trays inside the display case.

Jane's eyes widened. "Ja, they did." She looked at the outside of the note again. "Huh! My name is written in block letters this time. Before, it was done in a nice cursive, like we learned in school."

"Interesting," Eliza said, closing the door on the display case and straightening up. She peeled off the gloves and tossed them into a trash can. "That's the last of the baked goods. I'll put the coffee on. It's almost time to open."

Jane followed Eliza as she got the coffee ready. "It's different enough that it almost seems as if. . .but no, that's deerich."

Turning on the coffeepot to brew, Eliza placed her hands on her hips. "I don't think it's silly, Jane. It almost seems as if it came from someone else, is that what you were going to say?"

"Well, ja. But how could that be? I haven't talked about this to anyone. Only you and I, Susan, Sam, and Ben know about it."

Eliza shrugged. "Who can say? When did it say the secret admirer wants to meet?"

Jane looked at the note again. "After we close tomorrow afternoon, at the gazebo in the park."

"Romantic," Eliza pointed out, wiggling her eyebrows. "So, let's say it's the same guy, and he changed his MO because he's done fooling around and wants to cut to the chase."

Jane blinked. "MO? Cut to the chase? Have you been watching more television?"

"Nee, we don't have a television. That's all left over from when I first got here, and Reuben was still Mennonite. MO means a method of doing something. It's short for some Latin phrase. What was it?" She closed her eyes a moment then snapped her fingers and exclaimed, "Modus operandi! That's it!"

Jane shook her head. "You are a font of weird knowledge."

"I know. Isn't it fun? Anyway, he could have changed because he wants to let you know who he is. It seems odd that he'd leave out the gift, though." She tapped her finger against her lips then shrugged. "Who knows? So, are you going to meet him?"

"I'll think about it and let you know."

"Okay." She reached out and placed her hand on Jane's arm. "But Jane, you shouldn't meet him alone. You have no idea who he is. It could be dangerous."

Jane narrowed her eyes at her friend. "I thought you might have a pretty good idea of his identity."

Eliza blinked. "Okay, I thought I did, but now, with this new note, I'm not so sure. The guy I suspected wouldn't do this. At least, I don't think so. He would give you another, even better, gift. The first two were big hits, nee?"

Jane nodded. "Gut point. I won't meet him alone if I decide to meet him."

"I think we should tell Ben and Sam about this."

Jane frowned. "Why? What do they have to do with this?"

"Come on, Jane, don't be obtuse. You know Sam is obviously sweet on you."

"What? Why would you think that? He had his chance. I'm not sure I even want it to be him!" Jane stalked up front and turned the lock on the door with a snick, opening for the day.

"At least keep an open mind. I want to hear what they think about this new note," Eliza wheedled.

Jane blew a puff of air from her cheeks. "Fine."

"Great! Good decision. Something tells me they need to know about this. Here, have a beignet!"

Eliza tossed a beignet, still warm, to her friend, who caught it reflexively with a poof of powdered sugar. "Ach! Now I've got powdered sugar all over me."

Eliza giggled. "You look tasty!"

Jane rolled her eyes. "Very funny. I thought you were too tired for shenanigans today." She dusted herself off.

"The caffeine and sugar have revived me!"

Jane rolled her eyes, but the jingling of the bells on the front door cut off her response to that. "Here come the first customers. Here we go!" Three Englisch tourists entered the bakery, oohing and aahing at the delicious scents and tantalizing array of treats displayed in the cases. "Guder mariye!" Jane sang. "Welcome to The Plain Beignet!"

CHAPTER NINE

"Tomorrow evening?" Sam muttered, eyes glued to the piece of notepaper Eliza had handed him moments after he and Ben had entered the bakery that afternoon shortly before closing time.

"Is that significant?" Eliza asked, watching Sam closely through narrowed eyes.

He glanced up. "Significant? What do you mean?"

She scrunched up her face. "I don't know. You're the one who seems to find it odd that Jane's secret admirer wants to meet tomorrow evening."

"Oh no, not odd," he said, going for casual. "But it seems strange. I'm just surprised. If this secret admirer is ready to meet Jane in person, why doesn't he just come see her and tell her who he is?"

Ben, seated with Sam and Eliza at the table in the bakery kitchen, blew across a cup of hot coffee to cool it. "Ja, you'd think that would make sense, wouldn't you?" After taking a careful sip of his coffee, he pointedly met Sam's gaze and added, "And I think it's odd that there wasn't a gift this time, since there was the first two times."

Sam nodded emphatically and pointed at Ben. "Ja! You'd think there would be another gift, especially if the fellow wants to meet her—you know, to increase the anticipation."

"Or the motivation," Ben muttered into his coffee cup.

"What was that?" Eliza asked Ben. "Motivation? Surely you aren't implying that Jane can be bought with pretty gifts?"

Her eyes flashed, but Sam thought he noticed a twinkle hidden behind the fierce facade.

"Of course not," Ben allowed. "But maybe someone else does think she can be bought. Hence my surprise that this secret admirer didn't sweeten the deal with a final gift. He missed his chance at a big gesture." He spread his arms wide, sloshing a bit of coffee onto the floor. "Oops. Sorry about that. I'll clean it up."

"Nee, nee, I've got it. Stay put so you don't spill anything else." Eliza walked to the sink and grabbed a sponge from a plastic container marked FLOOR, which she used to quickly wipe up the mess. She rinsed the sponge and dropped it back into the container, which Sam had noticed before was filled about halfway with some sort of disinfectant.

Sam squirmed a bit in his seat, worrying about whether they would go back to the matter of the missing gift. In fact, he had included a gift, and a very nice one at that. Where was it? And this note wasn't his; it was from some impostor who had stolen his note and his gift and replaced them with his own bogus note—and kept the gift! The nerve of it!

Frowning, Sam examined his conscience. Had he been trying to buy Jane's favor with the little gifts? He hadn't thought of the gifts as bribes, or anything of the sort. He just wanted to make Jane happy. The missing gift had been another thing geared toward cats, since Jane had been so tickled by the kitty water fountain. He smiled to remember how much that had pleased her. The missing gift was actually another cat toy of sorts—a special bird feeder that could be mounted on a window, allowing the birds to feed in plain sight of anyone in the room. He thought the cats would get a kick out of that, though the birds might not be as pleased.

And now some impostor had taken his gifts and his note and requested a meeting with Jane the following evening.

Ben had been right. Sam had also asked for a meeting with Jane—also the following evening. And that didn't feel like a coincidence. He felt very frustrated at having some unknown person steal his thunder. But he had no idea what to do about it. *Ach!* How had the simple gesture gone so wrong?

"What did Jane think about this note?" Ben asked before biting into a cream cheese pastry. "Mmm, this is so gut!"

Eliza grabbed a pineapple pastry for herself. "It struck her as odd, especially after I asked her about the differences between this note and the previous two."

She put her untasted pastry down and walked across the kitchen to a drawer, opening it and pulling out the two other notes Jane had received from her original secret admirer.

Sam's heart skipped a beat as he saw his handiwork in Eliza's hands. Ben's eyes lit up. "Oh, please let me see those." Turning to Sam, he held out his hand. "And the new one, if you don't mind, Sam. I'd like to compare them."

"Gut idea!" Eliza exclaimed, handing the first two notes to Ben, who accepted the newest from Sam. "When my bruder was living above his office, before he decided to be baptized into the Amish faith, we watched a lot of detective programs on television. I especially loved old reruns of *Murder, She Wrote*, starring a smart Englisch woman named Jessica who was a novelist and amateur sleuth! They were so fun to watch! One thing they would do when the villain left a note was to compare the handwriting to samples from all the suspects. That helped them narrow it down." Resuming her seat, she took a bite of the pastry and then reached for the coffeepot to refill her mug.

Ben spread the three notes out on the table and looked at them intently. "I'm no handwriting expert, but the first two look like they came from the same person. Same handwriting to my eye, even the same color ink. And the same notepaper. Plus, the same envelope, with Jane's name written in cursive. Very nice penmanship."

"That's what I said!" Eliza grinned at Ben.

"But this last note is quite different." Ben picked it up and turned it over. "No envelope. The name is in block letters. And the handwriting is not the same. It's quite easy to see that."

They all examined the notes, and they all nodded their agreement.

"So, we appear to have two different secret admirers," Ben concluded.

Jane, who had just entered the kitchen without being noticed, dropped the empty tray she'd been carrying with a clatter and cried, "What? Two secret admirers? One was bad enough!"

Sam jumped up from the table and hurried over to Jane, bending to pick up the fallen tray, unfortunately at the same moment she did. Just like characters in a scripted comedy routine, they crashed their heads together, both stumbling back and holding their heads. Jane would have ended up on her *hinnerdale*, except she came up against the counter. Sam wasn't as lucky—he plopped right down onto the floor on his bum.

"Oh, that smarts!" Jane moaned, holding on to the counter with one hand and rubbing her head through her kapp with the other. Sam was rubbing his own head, biting his lips to keep from saying any words a proper Amish man shouldn't know.

Ben and Eliza had jumped up, and while Eliza checked Jane's head for any visible injury, Ben offered Sam a helping hand up from the floor. "That looked painful."

Sam grimaced, checking his head for blood. "You could say that." Finding none, he smiled wryly at Jane, who was also uninjured. "It's a gut thing we both have such hard heads!"

She snorted out a laugh and covered her mouth with her hand. "Oh! Sorry. I've never been praised for my hardheadedness before."

Sam smiled tenderly at her. "Are you sure you're okay? That was very clumsy of me."

"I'd say it was clumsy of both of us. Your head didn't bash into mine alone. I was right there with you."

Eliza picked up the fallen tray and put it in the sink to wash. "We were just figuring out that there have to be two secret admirers, not only one, Jane. That's what you heard when you walked in."

Sam, who was thinking about what she'd said right before they'd collided, asked quietly, "Jane, before, you said one secret admirer was bad enough. Was it really that bad, having someone who liked you but was afraid to come out and say so leave you gifts and notes?" He bit his lip, afraid he'd given himself away but having to know the answer. Had he wasted all his time and efforts to please her? He hated to think he'd frightened her instead!

Jane sat heavily down on one of the kitchen chairs. Sam thought she looked a little spooked—not her usual condition, as she was tough as nails as far as he'd seen. "You know, this started out kind of fun," she said. "I mean, who wouldn't enjoy receiving gifts and poetry from a secret admirer? It's very romantic. But now it feels a bit. . .sinister. Why would someone else claim to be the person who's been leaving me notes and gifts? What could they have to gain? What do they want from me?"

She looked at her friends with wide eyes, and Sam reached out and caught hold of her hand where it rested on the table. Her eyes widened even more, and he hoped he wasn't overstepping. He hadn't even thought about the gesture. It had felt totally natural to him, as if holding her hand were a right he could claim.

She didn't pull away, which emboldened him to reveal a little bit of his feelings for her. "Jane, I'm not surprised that men are competing for your attention. You're a lovely maedel, with a lot to offer."

Her mouth fell open, and she looked at him, as if searching his eyes for the truth. "Do you really think so?"

He swallowed nervously. Should he tell her everything, right here and now? He glanced at Ben, who gave a tiny nod of encouragement. Then he looked at Eliza, who had a strange, pensive expression on her face. What was she thinking?

Looking back at Jane, who seemed uncharacteristically vulnerable at the moment, Sam lost his nerve. He couldn't hold this conversation in front of witnesses—even if they were good friends. Instead of telling Jane that he was the original secret admirer and, further, that he was the scoundrel who'd unwittingly bestowed the unfortunate nickname on her a decade before, he chickened out and merely nodded. "Sure, Jane. Everyone thinks so."

Disappointment filled Jane's expressive brown eyes. She dropped her gaze to the floor and pushed the ties of her kapp behind her shoulders, not meeting his eyes. Sam felt like a heel. Had she been hoping for more? Did she feel something for him? Well, he'd missed the chance to fess up for the moment. Perhaps he'd feel more comfortable talking to her one-on-one later.

He glanced at Ben, who shook his head sadly at him, and dropped his eyes. Great. All he needed was yet another person letting him know he'd messed up and missed his opportunity.

He prayed there would be another opportunity, and soon.

"So, what are you going to do, Jane?" Eliza asked. "You can't go meet this guy, whoever he is, alone."

Jane frowned. "I don't know. I think I have to meet him. I need to find out who he is and why he's interested in me. I mean, sure, he's off to a bad start, but maybe that's a glitch and he's really a gut person. Who knows?"

Sam's jaw dropped. "A gut person? Someone who stole your gift and note and left you some imitation? How could he be a gut person?"

Everyone stared at Sam, and he realized he'd yet again given away too much. Only the fact that Jane was so *ferhoodled* by everything that had happened that week had kept her from putting all the pieces together so far. But it wouldn't be long before her confusion cleared up and she did put the pieces together; especially with Eliza to help her figure things out. He licked his lips and cast for something to say.

"I mean, if there *was* a gift this time, which there probably was, since there was before."

Eliza cocked her head thoughtfully, studying him. "Sam, what makes you think there was a gift, or another note? It's as if you're implying he exchanged his own note for one that was already there. And took away a gift that was there too. But how would you know that?"

Sam glanced at Ben, who was shaking his head again, and panic filled his heart. His mouth opened and closed as he desperately tried to think of something to say that would sound logical and explain his gaffe, but nothing came immediately to mind. He was about to give up and confess all, which might actually be better and would at least get the secret off his chest, when the kitchen phone rang.

"I have to get that," Jane said, standing and walking over to the wall. She picked up the receiver and said, "Gut afternoon, The Plain Beignet. Jane speaking."

The sudden panic on Jane's face—something Sam could absolutely relate to—tipped her friends off that the caller was probably Lizzie, checking in after her first week away.

This was confirmed when Jane, speaking in a slightly breathless tone of voice, said, "Lizzie! So gut to hear from you! We expected you to call, and here you are, calling! Everything here is fine! Just fine! Nothing we haven't been able to handle!"

She squeezed her eyes shut and pounded her forehead gently with her fist, no doubt realizing that she sounded slightly unhinged and absolutely not as if everything were actually fine.

But Lizzie must have been floating on a cloud of newlywed bliss, because she apparently didn't notice anything odd about her best friend's voice. After a few moments, Jane nodded, and said, "Ja, ja. Gut!" A short pause. . . "Oh, really? How fun!" Then she listened for a while and shook her head. "Of course we didn't forget Mary's bruder's birthday cake. He loved it. Mary plans to order another one next month for her next bruder's birthday." She listened some more, then pulled the phone away from her ear, and Sam could hear Lizzie loudly calling to someone that she'd be right there. After another thirty seconds or so, Jane said, "Okay, got it. No worries, we can accommodate them. No, it's fine. You don't have to come home early! Aren't you enjoying yourselves?" A pause, then, "Okay, then, keep on having fun. When do you leave for Wisconsin?" Another pause, and Jane nodded. "Gut, gut. Give my love to Ruth's parents, and let me know when you get safely to Wisconsin. I'll talk to you next week." A final pause, and Jane's face paled a bit before she said, "Of course I'll kiss Little Mouse for you, the minute I see her. Uh-huh. Uh-huh. Okay, bye."

She hung up and stood there, hand on the phone, staring at the wall.

"Jane, are you *oll recht*?" Eliza walked over and rubbed Jane's shoulder. When Jane let out a small sob, Eliza turned her around and pulled her into her arms and started rubbing her back comfortingly.

"Shh, shh, it's going to be oll recht. You'll see. We'll find Little Mouse, and next time you'll be able to tell Lizzie that the cat got out for a couple days but is just fine now."

Jane gave a great sniffle, and Eliza reached into her apron pocket and handed a napkin to her friend, who stepped back and blew her nose. Then she gave a watery laugh. "Ha! If I told her that, she'd be on the next bus home. I'll wait until she's back to tell her what happened, find the cat or not." She sniffed again and heaved a sigh that seemed to come from the soles of her feet. "I just hope the story has a happy ending."

Sitting by helplessly, unable to offer comfort as Eliza had that covered, Sam hoped so too. He wanted to say something wise and inspirational, but he typically couldn't think of a thing.

The bells on the front door jingled, and they all looked at each other. "Oops, I must have forgotten to lock it at closing time," Eliza said. "I'll see who it is."

She jumped up and hurried up front. They heard her talking to someone, and in a moment they heard the bells ring again and Eliza returned to the kitchen, a copy of the *Willow Creek Examiner* in her hand.

"That was Philomena Jones, editor at the *Examiner*. She said she knew we'd be anxious to see our ad, and asked if we'd found Little Mouse yet. Turns out she's a cat lover."

"How nice of her to bring us a copy!" Jane exclaimed, jumping to her feet and hurrying over to peer at the paper over Eliza's shoulder.

Eliza grinned and handed Jane an envelope. "She also said she'd noticed we didn't subscribe to the *Examiner* and gave us a form to do so if we like. She said they're running a special."

Jane chuckled. "You've got to respect her for trying. Maybe we will subscribe. I'll give this to Lizzie when she comes home."

Eliza had opened the paper and was turning the pages, examining each carefully. "Here it is!" she exclaimed. Look how gut Susan's drawing looks! And they put the whole thing in a nice box to set it apart."

"Read it out loud, Eliza," Jane instructed.

"Lost: gray female cat, spayed, downtown Willow Creek. No collar. If seen or found, please call The Plain Beignet." She looked up. "And it gives our number. Oh, whoever has her just has to see this and call! By now everyone in town must know we're looking for her!"

"Ja, that's what worries me," Jane said. "I can't believe word hasn't reached Lizzie in Texas!"

"If we'd run an ad in the *Budget* it would have," Ben said.

"That's partly why I didn't," Eliza said. "And also because they've stopped their local publication in Sugarcreek."

"That's a shame," Jane said. "We need local news."

"Well, we've got the *Examiner*. I guess we Amish will just have to rely on it more than we have in the past. I am going to subscribe."

They all nodded their agreement. If the bakery had a subscription, they could share the paper with each other.

Sam, meanwhile, was pondering something else. He wondered if there was any chance he might convince Jane to have supper with him again that evening. He looked casually at Ben, who had driven separately, and found his friend trying to send him some kind of signal with his eyes. He had no idea what the message might be, so he just shrugged. Ben looked disgusted. But he turned to Eliza and smiled charmingly at her. "Eliza, could I give you a lift home? I'd like to take a look at your apartment and see if I can help figure out what might be upsetting your new cats."

Eliza's face lit up, and she nodded eagerly. "Oh, denki, Ben. Ja! We had no luck last night." She bit her lip then added casually, "And maybe you'd like to stay for supper? We're having meat loaf and mashed potatoes. There's plenty."

She batted her eyelashes at him. Sam was sure she did. He'd heard that was a thing, but this was the first time he'd seen it in practice. It was nothing like he'd expected. In fact, it was charming, and it seemed to do the trick, as Ben's smile grew a bit dopey and he nodded. "I'd love to stay for supper, denki." He stood up. "Maybe we should get going. It's getting late, and tomorrow is another workday!"

Eliza stood and smiled shyly up at Ben through her lashes, causing him to blush. "Can I get your cape and bonnet? Which ones are they?" He hurried over to the garments hanging on pegs by the back door and waited for Eliza to point them out before eagerly carrying them back to her, and even helping her with the cape.

Glancing at Jane, Sam saw her roll her eyes at her young friend. Then she caught his eye and twinkled at him in amusement, and he forgot all about Eliza's outrageous flirting with Ben and his friend's amusing reaction. All he could do was give Jane a silly grin in return.

"See you tomorrow, Jane!" Eliza chirped.

She and Ben waved and left through the dining room, the bell on the front door signaling their departure.

Jane and Sam were alone. After a moment, he realized he shouldn't waste his friend's efforts to set up this very situation, so he cleared his throat and said, "How about we lock up and go out and look for Little Mouse for an hour or so?"

Her eyes misted up. "You'd do that? You worked all day. You must be tired."

He shrugged. "Well, ja. I just said so."

She smiled sweetly. "You did. Okay, let me get my bonnet, and we can go." She looked at him shyly for a moment then added, "And if you like, we could have supper back here after?"

Although he loved the idea of having her all to himself, he didn't think it was smart for the two of them to spend too much time alone in her residence. Not only was there her reputation to consider—and his—but he wasn't sure he could resist the temptation to kiss her if he spent too much time alone with her. So he offered an alternative. "Or, we could get dinner at Rebekkah's Country Kitchen? It's baked steak night again tonight."

"Oh, I love her baked steak."

"Perfect! First we'll look for Little Mouse. Maybe this is the night we'll find her."

Jane's countenance sobered. "Oh, I pray we do, Sam. That would relieve my mind so much! It's a terrible burden I've been carrying."

"And it's partly my fault. I feel terrible too."

"Nonsense. You were trying to help. It was a crazy day, and really it was nobody's fault."

He gave her a small smile. "Well, then, that means it wasn't your fault either, ain't so?"

She stared at him a moment, and then she laughed. "You got me there, Sam. I like how you can make me laugh, even when I'm feeling down. It's nice. Ach! I need to remember to call the cat shelter tomorrow and tell them about a couple of unaltered stray toms I saw this morning." She paused as if a thought struck her. "I wonder whether Eliza thought to give them a call and tell them about Little Mouse so they can keep an eye out for her?"

"I happen to know the answer to that," Sam said. "Ben told me the cat shelter was one of the places he and Eliza stopped when they were handing out flyers. He told me they looked over all the cats, and Little Mouse wasn't there. They promised to call if anyone brings her in."

"Oh well, it was a thought."

She headed toward the front door, and he followed, thinking about what she'd said about him being able to make her laugh and wishing he could always make her feel gut. But if he were honest with her—and he had to find the courage to be!—it was bound to make her feel bad. And how he dreaded that!

As Sam pulled his horse up in front of the bakery a couple hours later, Jane felt a bit let down. They'd had no luck finding Little Mouse; it was as if the cat had disappeared from the face of the planet. Though they called for her at every intersection, no small gray cat answered as they walked the streets of Willow Creek, mostly deserted as the businesses were closed and the residents were mostly tucked away in their houses and apartments for supper. They saw several of their flyers fluttering in the evening breeze, the little tearaway tabs at the bottom of each still intact.

After an hour they'd returned to the bakery and climbed into Sam's buggy for the short drive to Rebekkah's Country Kitchen where they'd enjoyed a delicious baked steak supper with all the trimmings, including mashed potatoes, pickled beets, corn, Chow Chow, and apple pie a la mode for dessert. But they hadn't really been able to talk about anything significant, as their meal was interrupted several times by friends and acquaintances who'd stopped to chat for a few minutes, not bothering to hide their speculative glances as they commented on how nice it was to see Jane and Sam out enjoying dinner—together. Jane was sure she blushed several times, and she hoped Sam wasn't put off by the blatant curiosity and well-intended nibbiness of their acquaintances.

Jane had thought that Sam had something important he wanted to say to her. She'd sensed it for a few days, and she'd thought he'd been on the verge of it that afternoon before Lizzie's phone call had interrupted their conversation. It had occurred to her that maybe he hadn't wanted to say anything too personal in front of Ben and Eliza.

But when Ben had quite obviously engineered things so that he got to spend the evening with Eliza—with Eliza's obvious and eager compliance, something that gave Jane food for thought—and she and Sam were left to spend the evening together, she'd really thought he'd finally get around to whatever it was he wanted to discuss.

She had secret hopes on that topic!

As they approached the bakery after dinner, she thought furiously about how she could extend their evening long enough for him to come to the point, whatever that point might be.

"Sam, I've enjoyed this evening. But we didn't have any coffee with our pie. I could use a cup. Would you like one?"

She held her breath, praying he would say yes despite his reluctance, she suspected, to be alone in the bakery with her in case gossips got wind of it and caused them trouble. He turned and smiled at her and said, "Ja, you know, I could use a cup. Maybe decaf, though, at this time of the evening."

She was certain her face glowed with happiness, and she didn't care that he would be able to see her feelings written on it. But when they turned onto Main Street, she frowned and leaned forward.

"There's a buggy in front of the bakery," she said.

He nodded. "Ja, I see. Who could it be?"

He pulled in next to it and jumped out to tie his horse to the hitching post, and as he did the occupants of the other buggy climbed down. Jane exclaimed with surprise as she rounded the back of the buggy. "Maem! Lydia! What are you doing here?"

Jane's mother, Sarah Bontrager, gave her daughter a hug. "Is that how you greet your maem?"

Sam helped Lydia descend from the buggy, and they all walked to the bakery, which Jane unlocked by the bright light of the vintage-look sconces on either side of the door. She looked at her mother and Lydia and tilted her head. "I assume you both plan to come in and stay a bit?"

Lydia grinned at her. "Ja, we do! We want to talk about Little Mouse, and about what you're doing to find my baby, Miss!"

Jane's heart plummeted. So word was out in the community. Well, that shouldn't have surprised her.

"You heard."

Lydia tilted her head, looking like a tiny but fierce sparrow. "Of course I heard! What happened?"

"Please, come in. I was just about to make coffee for Sam and me. I'll just make a bigger pot."

"Decaf, I hope," Lydia said, walking inside the bakery followed by Sarah, Sam, and Jane.

"For me too," Sarah said, looking around at the darkening space. "You say you were going to make a pot for you and Sam? But nobody else is here. Surely you weren't planning on spending time alone here together, where Jane lives?" She gave Sam a serious look. "Are you trying to damage my daughter's reputation, young man?"

"Nee! Of course not. We just had dinner at Rebekkah's for that very reason."

"Maem, it wouldn't have hurt anything for him to come in for a few minutes. Look at the windows! They're huge. Anyone can see inside, and we weren't going upstairs." She blushed.

"Well, now we're here to have coffee with you!" Lydia chimed in cheerfully. "So no harm done, Sarah. Your chick is fine. Come, let's sit. My old knees are aching."

They sat down at a table, and Jane went to make coffee. She could hear their conversation and was relieved when neither older woman asked anything outrageously personal or embarrassing. She hurried back with the coffee and a few cookies as soon as possible and set it all on the table before taking a seat.

"So, when were you going to tell me that Lizzie's cat had gotten out?" Lydia doctored her coffee the way she liked it, light and sweet, while waiting for Jane's answer.

Jane bit her lips. "I was really hoping she'd be back before I had to say anything," she confessed miserably.

"What have you done to find her?" Sarah asked, patting her daughter's hand. "We saw the ad in today's *Examiner*. That's how we found out."

"Which didn't please me," Lydia said, sipping her coffee. "Is Secret safe?"

"Ja! She's upstairs. Want to see her?" She jumped up and hurried into the kitchen to open the door to the upstairs and called for Secret, who trotted right down. When Jane carried her into the dining room, the brown tabby purred at the sight of Lydia, who was one of her favorite people.

"There's my baby!" Lydia accepted the cat and held her on her lap, stroking her while she looked at Jane and Sam.

"Now, tell me what happened to Little Mouse. And don't leave anything out."

Jane and Sam explained what had happened with the water leak and the open door, and how they'd found Secret quickly but not Little Mouse. They told how they'd been searching the neighborhood daily, and about the flyers and the newspaper ad.

"What about Facebook?" Lydia asked, making Jane blink in surprise.

"I hadn't thought of that. We don't have a page, although we've discussed creating one. We'd have to get permission from Abram first, of course."

"Other Amish businesspeople have Facebook," Sarah said. "You should get one of them, or one of your Englisch friends, to put a post on Facebook tomorrow. It might help."

Shaking her head at being schooled on social media by the older generation of Amish women, Jane promised she would talk to Lizzie about it when Lizzie got home.

"Does Elizabeth know?" Lydia asked, finishing her coffee. She declined a refill by placing her hand flat over the cup. "Nee, denki. That's enough."

"Nee. I didn't tell her when she called earlier to check in. I'm hoping to have Little Mouse back before she gets home in a couple weeks. If I told her now, she would insist on cutting their wedding trip short, and I don't want them to do that."

Sarah and Lydia looked at each other, and Lydia nodded. "Gut decision. I agree, that was the right thing to do."

"You do?" Jane was relieved. She'd dreaded this conversation and was afraid that either her mother or Lydia would insist she call Lizzie and tell her Little Mouse was missing.

"Ja. Keep looking. And pray."

"Oh, I pray all the time, Lydia. Gott is surely getting tired of my pleas to return Little Mouse home."

Sarah shook her head. "Lieb, Gott never gets tired of hearing our needs. He loves us. Keep praying. It will all work out."

Lydia nodded. "Ja, keep praying. Now, it's time for an old woman to get home to bed. Come, Sarah, let's go."

They stood and Jane and Sam walked them out to their buggy. He helped Lydia climb up into the vehicle and then stood back.

"I imagine you'll be leaving now too, young man," Sarah said, leaning across Lydia to look at Sam. "It's growing late."

"Um, ja, I'm leaving now too." He cast a helpless glance at Jane, who shrugged. There was nothing for it. They would have to have their talk—whatever it was about—another time.

"I'll see you tomorrow afternoon, Jane," Sam said pointedly. "Remember, you, Ben, Eliza, and I are all going out together after the bakery closes."

"Ach, ja, Sam. Denki. I remember."

"How nice! I like that Ben," Lydia said. "Good night. Better get on the road, Sam. It's dark, and I imagine you have animals to tend at home."

He smiled at the old woman and nodded. "Yes, ma'am."

"Don't you 'ma'am' me! Let's go, Sarah."

"Good night, dear," Sarah said to Jane before giving her horse the signal and trotting down the street.

Sam and Jane watched them go, and then Sam turned to Jane and smiled. "Well, I guess I'd better go. I wouldn't put it past them to go around the block and make sure I left."

She giggled at that. "You're not wrong."

"I'll see you tomorrow. I want to talk to you about something important, but it can wait. Good night, Jane."

She hoped he would do something to show his feelings—take her hand, maybe dare a good night kiss. But he didn't. He smiled and climbed into his buggy. "Go inside and lock up before I leave, please," he said. "I'll feel better about you being here alone if you do."

She turned to the door and saw Secret sitting in the window, watching them. Jane waved at Sam and went inside, locking the door securely behind her. She peered through the window and saw Sam wave and drive off, and she picked up her cat and snuggled her, comforted by Secret's steady purring. "Ach, Secret," she whispered. "That man has had me tied around his little finger since we were kinner. But how does he feel? Will he ever tell me? I don't know. But I'm going to pray extra tonight, for Little Mouse, and for Samuel Mast to find the courage to speak up if he has feelings for me." She put the cat down and gathered up the coffee and cookie things, taking them into the kitchen. She washed up then turned off most of the lights before calling Secret and following the cat upstairs to their apartment.

She went into her living room and sat in her reading chair. She turned on a battery lantern and looked around the pleasant space. "Denki for this lovely place for me to live with my little Secret, Vader," she prayed. "But You know my heart, and You know my loneliness for the kind of relationship I see between Lizzie and my bruder, John, and between my parents. And even, lately, between Lydia and Abram. Please let Sam feel the same for me as I do for him. And please, please bring Little Mouse home soon, Vader. Your will be done."

Picking up a book, she welcomed Secret into her lap and stroked her while she read a chapter before bed, taking comfort from her little friend's purring and warm presence.

CHAPTER TEN

The following day seemed to creep by like a chameleon Jane had once seen at the zoo—step by shaky, painstaking step, moving so slowly one could barely discern the progress.

Finally it was closing time, and she could barely remember a thing that had occurred all day. She and Eliza quickly finished the closing chores and then readied themselves to go out to meet Jane's mysterious second secret admirer.

Jane had an inkling who the first secret admirer might be, though she barely dared to hope. But this second person was a worrisome development, and for some reason, she dreaded the encounter and was very glad her friends would all be with her.

The men arrived at five sharp and came inside but didn't sit down. "The meeting is at five thirty, right?" Sam asked, standing by the door with his hands in his pockets while Jane and Eliza put on their bonnets over their prayer kapps.

"Ja, so we'd better get going," Eliza confirmed.

"Bring all three notes," Ben suggested.

"Why?" Jane asked.

"I'm not sure," Ben admitted. "It feels important, though."

"Okay, I'll run and get them." Jane hurried back into the kitchen and returned quickly with the three notes, which she placed into her purse. "Got 'em. Let's go."

Out at the street they stopped before climbing into Sam's buggy. "I think the women should ride up front, and us out of sight in the back,"

Ben suggested. "We don't want to scare him off, whoever he is."

They all agreed, and Ben and Sam climbed into the back of the two-seat buggy. "Won't he recognize your horse, Sam?" Jane asked worriedly.

"Nothing we can do about that. It's already growing dark, so maybe he won't, and if he does, maybe he'll think you needed to borrow a buggy. You don't have one, right?"

"I have a pony cart, but it's at my parents' farm, along with my Haflinger, Goldie. We don't have a stable at the bakery."

"There you go," Sam said as they set off for the meeting at the village park, a mile away. As they drove, they chatted, comparing ideas about who might turn out to be Jane's second secret admirer. Jane had accepted the opinion of her friends that there had to be two different men behind the gifts and notes, and she was eager, if a bit nervous, to find out who at least one of them was, for sure and certain.

She suspected she would very soon discover the identities of both.

Jane turned Sam's mare, Millie, into the park and drove her to the pavilion specified in the note left yesterday. It was dark enough by then that she had trouble seeing much, though there were streetlights spaced regularly down the road, and one by the pavilion.

There was another buggy parked nearby, and as they drew near Ben whispered from the back of the buggy, "I don't believe it!"

Jane turned to look at him, just as the last person she'd expected stood up from a picnic bench inside the shadowy pavilion into the light of the streetlight.

"Daniel Beechy!" she exclaimed. He stood, hands in pockets, frowning at the approaching buggy. Eliza was visible in the passenger seat, and he clearly wasn't happy that Jane had brought a friend. There was no way he could see into the back seat in the gloomy twilight. Little did he know that there were three friends there to support and protect her that evening.

"I'm getting out," Sam said in a ferocious tone that had Jane turning in surprise.

"What? Nee! I need to talk to him alone for a minute to see what he has to say. You all have to stay here. I mean it!"

"Sam, she's right," Eliza said soothingly. "We're right here, and it's not like he's going to hurt her."

"Can you be certain of that?" Sam demanded fiercely.

"He is Amish," Eliza said.

"We only have his word for that!" Sam shot back.

Eliza bit her lip at that, and Jane glared at all of them. "Nonsense. Of course he's Amish. He speaks *Deitsch*, and not with an Englischer accent. Now hush. We're almost there."

Jane parked the buggy and climbed down, and Daniel secured the horse to the hitching rail. She walked around him to the picnic tables, which were in the shadows. She didn't like that, but there was nowhere to sit in the light of the streetlamp. With a final glare at Eliza, he followed her.

Daniel jerked a thumb toward the buggy. "Why did she come with you? Don't you trust me?"

"First, I didn't know it was you, and besides, I just met you, so nee, I don't trust you. Second, it would be foolish for me to come alone to meet someone who hadn't identified himself, don't you think?"

She faced him, not sitting down, still in full view of the buggy containing her friends though she stood in the darkening pavilion.

"Well, at least come over here where we can be private," he insisted, pointing to a secluded corner of the pavilion, which was blanketed in shadow.

She glanced over to where he wanted to go and then back at him, brows raised in disdain. "Nee, Daniel. I'm staying here where Eliza can see me. She can't hear us. I want to know what you were thinking, leaving me that note." She shivered as a cold breeze wandered through the space and pulled her wool cloak more tightly about her. "And please hurry. It's cold out here!"

Frowning, he kicked at the floor of the pavilion with his work boot. "I think I've made it plain that I'm interested in you, Jane. I thought the note might be a gut way to get you alone so we could talk. After all, you seemed to like the first two well enough." He folded his arms and stared at her boldly, daring her to deny it.

"How do you know about those first two notes, Daniel Beechy? I didn't tell anyone except my close friends!"

He looked flummoxed; then he shrugged. "I overheard Sam and Ben talking after services Sunday. They were saying something about it. So I thought I'd give it a try, since you seem to like gifts from secret admirers."

"Gifts? What gifts? You only left a note."

Again, Daniel looked taken aback, but in his bold certainty that he was doing nothing wrong, he shrugged again. "I heard them say you'd gotten gifts from whoever your first secret admirer was. But I didn't have time for that. I just wanted to set up a meeting so I could explain to you why you should let me court you, not some other lame guy."

Jane was astonished at the newcomer's audacity. "Why on earth would I let you court me, Daniel? You've insulted my friends, pushed and shoved your way into conversations where you weren't wanted, and now you've lied to me, trying to convince me you were the person who had left me notes and gifts. You haven't done a thing to make me want to spend time with you. Just the opposite, in fact."

He frowned at her. "You don't know me. You'd like me if you gave me a chance."

"I might have, if you'd been patient and kind, and approached me honestly, but that's not what you've done. I don't want to see you again, Daniel. I think we're done." She turned to walk back to the buggy, but Daniel grabbed her arm and spun her around to face him.

"I'm not finished talking to you!"

Whatever else he might have said was lost in the shouts of her friends as they all jumped out of the buggy and rushed toward them. Seeing them coming, Daniel's eyes widened, and he released Jane's arm and stepped back, hands raised in defense.

Jane's heart was thudding in her chest. She couldn't believe an Amish man had grabbed her and treated her roughly. Sam reached her first and stood beside her with a protective arm around her shoulders. She knew he would feel her trembling, but she couldn't help it.

"That was foolish, Daniel," Ben said, stepping between Sam and Daniel, as if afraid of what Sam might do. "We don't condone rough treatment of women around here. Of anyone, for that matter."

"Aw, I didn't hurt her," Daniel muttered, eyes shooting daggers at Sam and Ben. "What are you doing here, anyway?" He sneered at Jane. "Afraid to meet and talk without all these friends to protect you?"

Eliza stepped forward, eyes flashing. "And with gut reason, as it turns out! I've never seen anyone treat a woman like that! What were you thinking?"

Daniel dropped his eyes before Eliza's fury, but he continued to scowl.

"I just wanted to talk."

Jane found her voice. "We're through talking, Daniel. I made that clear."

He glared at her and then sneered some more. "Oh yeah? Well, what makes you think he's any better than I am?" He jerked his chin in Sam's direction. "He's a liar too. He's been lying to you all your life! Just ask him!"

"Ach, nee," Ben muttered. "This is why I've told you and told you to tell her the truth, Sam. Now you have no choice, and no time."

Jane's head was spinning. "What is he talking about?" She looked up at Sam, who was looking back at her miserably. "Sam? Have you told me a lie? When?"

Sam licked his lips and opened his mouth as if to reply, but Daniel again beat him to it. "Ask him about a nickname he gave you when you were kinner. I don't know what it was, but from his conversation with Ben I know it was something mean." He sneered again. "Explain that, if you can, Mast."

Eliza's jaw dropped in shock, and Jane's eyes widened in dismay as Daniel's meaning struck home. Nee. It couldn't be true! The boy she'd loved since she was a little girl couldn't be the one who'd given her the nickname Plain Jane. Gott wouldn't let something like that happen, would He? She raised tear-soaked eyes to Sam and saw him wince. And she knew it was true.

She stepped away from him. "Sam," she whispered brokenly. "How could you?"

"It wasn't like that. I didn't mean to!" Sam tried desperately to explain, too late.

Jane put up a hand. "Nee! Stay away from me. Are all the men in our community liars?" She looked at Eliza. "I need to get away from here."

Eliza nodded. "We'll take Sam's buggy." Looking at Ben and Sam, she said, "You two can walk back to the bakery."

When Sam tried to speak, Ben put a restraining hand on his arm. "Nee, Sam, not now. Give it some time. We'll walk, and you can both cool off." He turned to look at Daniel. "I'll expect you to apologize to everyone involved in this tomorrow, Beechy. You've caused a lot of trouble."

"Me? How can you blame me? He started all this with his lies, notes, and gifts! I just jumped on his bandwagon."

Jane looked sadly at Sam. "So, you were the first secret admirer?" At his nod, she sighed. "I thought you might be. I even hoped." Her eyes filled again. "I'm such a fool."

His eyes flared with hope. "You hoped?"

"That was before I knew you were a liar and a coward."

Eyes glistening with unshed moisture, Sam held out a beseeching hand. "I'm so sorry, Jane. I didn't mean for any of this to happen."

Daniel jumped into his buggy. "You're all a bunch of losers." He reached down and picked something up from the floor, and he tossed it out the open window of his buggy at Sam, who caught it reflexively. "Here, have your lame gift back!"

"You stole my gift to Jane? So you admit it? And that you replaced my note?"

Daniel laughed. "Ja. I didn't know about the gifts until I saw that one sitting on the stoop outside the back door of the bakery after I followed you there yesterday morning. When I saw it was for cats, I took it. I got a cat recently, and I thought she might like it. But I don't want anything that came from you." He started to back his horse away from the hitching post, but Ben stepped forward and grabbed the horse's bridle.

"Wait!" he said. "You said you recently got a cat? What kind of cat? Where did you get it?"

Daniel shrugged. "Just a stray. I found her in Willow Creek, not far from the bakery, actually. I was driving home one day last week from an errand, and she was sitting on the sidewalk. I thought she was cute, and I—I live alone. So I got out of my buggy and approached her. I thought she'd run, but she's really friendly. She must have belonged to someone once. She let me pick her up and take her home. Now let go of my horse so I can leave."

While he was talking, everyone's eyes grew large. Jane almost didn't dare hope. She stepped forward and spoke quietly to Daniel. "Daniel, please, what color is this cat?"

He frowned at her. "Why do you care?"

Striving for patience, she answered calmly. "Because I lost a cat last week. A little gray female. Is the cat you found gray?"

His eyes narrowed and he scowled. "What if she is? She's not yours. She can't be. There must be lots of cats who look like her."

Sam gave Daniel a steely look that promised he had better answer honestly. "What color is the cat, Beechy?"

Daniel frowned at all of them, as if taken aback by their intensity. "She's gray. So what? She's my cat. I named her Betty."

"Haven't you seen all the flyers around town, man?" Sam asked incredulously. "Haven't you noticed someone lost a cat just like that? Didn't you care?"

Daniel blinked in astonishment. "I. . .no! I haven't seen any flyers. And I didn't know anyone was looking for a cat." He looked at Jane and frowned. "Do you really think she's your cat?"

"I think she's my friend Lizzie's cat. Lizzie is on her wedding trip, and last week I left the door open at the bakery by mistake, and both she and my cat got out. I found my cat quickly, but Little Mouse—that's her name—vanished. We've been looking everywhere ever since. We even placed an ad in the *Examiner*."

"I don't read that," Daniel grumbled. But Jane could tell from his expression that he was starting to think maybe he had her cat. He raised his eyes to her, and she could tell it was a struggle for him to ask, "What day did you say you lost your cat?"

"Last Monday. She's been gone just over a week."

Daniel sighed then reluctantly said, "Follow me home. You can look at the cat. If she's your friend's cat, you can take her. I didn't mean to take someone else's cat. I'm not a total jerk, you know."

Jane's expression softened. "Denki, Daniel." She looked at her friends. "Let's follow him now."

They all nodded, and she threw a look at Sam. "You drive. It's your buggy."

He nodded, and Ben and Eliza quickly climbed into the rear of the buggy, and Jane climbed into the passenger seat while Sam jumped into the driver's seat after untying the horse. He looked at her and started to speak, but she held up her hand. "Nee, Sam, not now, please. I have a lot to think about. But right now, all I care about is finding out if Daniel has been the one with Little Mouse all along."

He nodded reluctantly and pulled out, following Daniel's buggy toward his apartment.

Ten minutes later they pulled up in front of a business, and Daniel drove around back to unhitch his horse and put him in his stall. He reappeared a couple of minutes later, and they all climbed out of Sam's buggy. "I'll rub him down and take care of him after you look at the cat," Daniel muttered. They followed him up the outside steps to the second-floor apartment. He unlocked it and went inside, lighting a couple of lanterns in the kitchen.

The first thing Jane saw was the lovely gray cat comfortably curled up in a cozy cat bed on the counter by a window overlooking the street. She gasped. "It's her! Oh, thank Gott! Little Mouse!"

The cat blinked sleepily and looked at them all, and she gave a little chirp of acknowledgment before sitting up and commencing to take a bath.

"Oh, you darling thing!" Jane cried, hurrying over and scooping the small cat up in her arms. Little Mouse purred and rubbed her head against Jane's chin. She looked all around. "It is her! It's Little Mouse! Oh, I was so afraid we'd never find her, and how would I have told Lizzie?" Her eyes filled with tears, and Eliza went and put an arm around her.

"Well, here she is, safe and sound, so you don't ever have to find out." Eliza looked around Daniel's tidy kitchen, seeing the bowls of kibble and clean water against one wall, and the cat tower visible in the adjoining living room. "And I can see that she hasn't suffered during her stay here either. Daniel has taken gut care of her."

"I told you," he muttered. "Well, I guess you'll be taking her now." He gestured at all the items he'd clearly purchased for the cat. "You might as well take her things too. I won't be needing them."

Jane looked at Eliza and found herself feeling a bit sorry for the man. He had no idea how to behave with a human woman, but he obviously knew how to take care of a cat. That meant he couldn't be all bad. Didn't it?

Eliza rolled her eyes. "Look, Daniel, there are plenty of cats in need of a home. My roommate, Susan, and I got two last week from the local cat shelter. Go over there and pick out a cat of your own. You'll have to fill out an application and pay for spaying or neutering, but it's not much. And then you'll have a cat that actually belongs to you."

He looked at her uncertainly. "Really? You can just go in and choose a cat you like?"

"Ja, although sometimes it turns out that the cat does the choosing. It's just outside Willow Creek, on the road to Berlin. You can't miss it."

Daniel looked regretfully at Little Mouse. "Well, I really liked Betty— er, Little Mouse. But I know how I'd feel if someone stole my cat. So take her, and maybe I'll check out this shelter tomorrow."

Jane nodded and started across the kitchen toward the door. She stopped and met Daniel's eyes. "Denki for taking such gut care of her, Daniel."

He shot a look at the two men then returned her small smile. "You're welcome." He cleared his throat. "I don't suppose this means you've changed your mind about dating me?"

Jane rolled her eyes. "Nee! I'm not dating anyone! Thanks for the cat, but that's all. Goodbye, Daniel."

As she headed for the door, she heard Ben say, "Try not to be such a jerk, Daniel, and you'll meet a woman who will like you for yourself. Give it a try."

The men and Eliza followed Jane outside and down the steps. They walked out front to Sam's buggy, and Jane glanced back and saw Daniel standing alone in the dark driveway, hands thrust into his pockets, looking like the poster child for loneliness. He was a jerk, but maybe he'd change his ways. She hoped so.

Looking at Sam, she felt a welling-up of sorrow. Here was a man she'd trusted and loved for years. And he'd turned out to be a liar too. "I'm only letting you drive me home because I don't want to risk losing Little Mouse again, Sam. I do not want to talk to you right now."

He nodded, and they all climbed into the buggy and drove to the bakery, where Jane, Little Mouse held tightly in her arms, quickly climbed down and hurried to unlock the front door and disappear inside where she could make certain the cat was fine and be alone to lick her wounds.

Sam watched Jane close and lock the door. Her eyes met his for an instant, but then she drew down the shade on the front door, hiding herself from his view.

He leaned his head back against the seat and closed his eyes. If only he'd listened to Ben's advice. Now it was too late.

"I know what you're thinking, Sam," Ben spoke up from the back seat. "And you're wrong. Ja, you were narrish not to tell her years ago about the stupid nickname. And you should have told her this week, about that and the secret admirer thing. But she cares for you, man. Give her time to cool off, and go see her with an honest, open heart. She'll give you another chance."

Sam rolled his head, which was starting to ache from holding back tears in front of his friends. "I'm so tired. I need to go home." He sat up. "I'll drop you both off. Where's your buggy, Ben?"

"It's at your house, remember? I stopped by after work and we drove over together."

"Oh, right. I forgot." He steered Millie toward Eliza's apartment above the doctor's office, and when they arrived, he pulled up. He waited while Ben and Eliza climbed out.

"I'm walking Eliza up to make sure everything is fine here. I'll be right out. Wait for me, please."

Sam nodded. He watched his friend walking up the front steps of the big house. Eliza unlocked the front door, and they disappeared inside. There were lights on upstairs, indicating that Susan Bontrager was home. Sam stared out the front window of the buggy, not seeing his horse, who was cropping grass from the berm to the right of the buggy. He was seeing all his mistakes, in a long line leading back to that day behind the school where he'd stupidly, unwittingly coined the nickname Plain Jane.

"Ach, why did I do it?" he moaned. "Why was I ashamed of my feelings for her? Even then, she was the best girl I knew. And I hurt her. Now I'll never have a chance to make a life with her. I'll live alone on my farm, with only animals for company, building buggies for other people's families until I'm old. And it's only what I deserve."

"Okay, whatever you're thinking, just stop it," Ben's voice said as he opened the driver door of the buggy. "Shove over. You're in no shape to drive, and I don't want to die, not when things with Eliza are looking so promising."

Sam scooted over into the passenger seat, and Ben climbed up and took the reins, steering Millie onto the road home.

"You must think I'm the biggest fool you know," Sam muttered, staring out at the passing scenery without really taking it in.

"Ja, I do."

Sam laughed humorlessly. "Well, at least you're honest, which is more than I can say for that Daniel Beechy."

Ben glanced at Sam. "Wouldn't that be the pot calling the kettle black?"

Sam shot him a surprised look but then nodded miserably. "Ja, you're right. I've been dishonest too."

Ben drove in silence for a few minutes. "Sam, you're my best friend. I love you like a bruder, so I'm going to be straight with you. You messed up big. But it's not hopeless."

When Sam tossed him a disbelieving look, Ben shook his head. "I'm telling you. Eliza agrees."

"Really?"

"Ja. But it's going to take time. And probably groveling. You can't expect her to let this go quickly. Apparently, according to Eliza, she hated that nickname, and it hurt her badly. And she hasn't forgotten it. I was wrong thinking she had. I'm sorry for that."

Sam shrugged. "I knew she wouldn't. She's sensitive. And it was really mean. A girl that age—or a boy, for that matter—doesn't forget a hurtful nickname."

"Okay, so just give it time. And when Eliza says you can, go over there, start by apologizing and explaining everything that happened, and why you felt you couldn't tell her before. And also why you started the narrish secret admirer stuff in the first place."

"I'm afraid it's hopeless."

"Sam, nothing is hopeless, not with Gott on your side."

Sam gave another empty laugh. "I rather think Gott is on her side, not mine."

"Don't be narrish. Gott is on both of your sides. You're both His kinner, and He loves you both and wants you to be happy. For some reason, you usually make Jane happy, so Gott will help you unravel this mess. Just probably not real fast, fashtay?"

Sam sighed. "Ja, I understand. I only hope you're right."

Ben gave him a level look. "You know I'm always right."

"What about that pie thing?" Sam asked, giving Ben a small smile.

"You can't win 'em all," Ben tossed back, pulling into Sam's driveway. "Work on buggies. Take care of those ugly sheep of yours."

"Hey! My Tunis sheep aren't ugly! And I'm helping to preserve an endangered, historically significant breed of sheep."

"Bah." Ben grinned at Sam, who couldn't help smiling a bit in return.

"Sam, just do your thing here. Give Jane a few days. I'll let you know when you can go over there."

"Okay, Ben. And. . .denki for being such a gut friend. I should have listened to you all along. About everything."

Ben nodded. "Yep. You should have." He reached over and patted Sam on the arm before climbing down. "I'm out of here. Eliza and Susan invited me for dinner. See you later."

Sam watched him lead his horse, Cupid, from the barn and hitch her to his buggy. He climbed down from his own buggy as Ben drove away and then unhitched Millie. From inside the barn, he heard Ralph greeting his friend with a loud whinny. He led Millie inside to her large box stall and gave her a good rubdown and a measure of oats along with her evening feed; then he turned his attention to caring for Ralph and his other stock.

When he was finished he went outside and turned his eyes to the clear November sky and prayed, tears rolling down his face.

"Gott, I'm sorry for being so foolish. I hope You aren't disappointed in me. I've made so many mistakes." He swiped at the moisture on his cheeks. "I pray You'll help me gain a second chance with Jane. I love her and want to make a life with her. Please help me say the right thing so she'll forgive me." He walked up the steps to his dark, empty house. "Your will be done, Vader. Amen."

Pausing a moment to take in the wonder of Gott's creation, he saw a meteor streak across the sky, and he smiled.

There was beauty here, even when his heart felt as if it were broken. He drew in a deep breath of clean, cold air and let it out again before going inside to heat up leftovers for his lonely supper. He needed to be alone to think. He needed to reflect on his mistakes, so maybe he wouldn't repeat them. He would read his Bible and look for comfort in the scriptures. And he would wait to hear from Ben. Then he would go, when it was permitted, and try to fix his broken life.

CHAPTER ELEVEN

Jane found herself making excuses several times the following day to run up to the third floor to check on Little Mouse, just to make sure she was still there and fine.

She figured the cats must think she was a little cracked, but she couldn't help it!

Eliza and Ben had spent a couple of hours early that morning driving around taking posters down, and Jane had called the newspaper to let the editor, Philomena Jones, know they wouldn't need to run the ad a second week and that the cat was home safe.

Philomena, an animal lover herself, had promised to tell anyone who called that Little Mouse was safely home.

I wish Lizzie would call. I could tell her honestly now that Little Mouse is just fine!

"What are you thinking about?" Eliza asked when she dashed back to the kitchen where Jane was washing up dishes during the lunch rush.

"Oh, just that I'm so happy I don't have to lie to Lizzie anymore! What a relief!"

"I hear that!" Eliza grabbed another tray of sandwiches from the fridge. "Got to run. Customers waiting."

"Do you need help?"

"Nee, I've got it. The rush is dwindling to a trickle. Hey, did you remember to call the shelter to tell them we found Little Mouse, and about the stray toms in the neighborhood?"

"Ja, I called them this morning."

"Great!" She pushed through into the dining room with her tray, letting the door swing shut behind her.

"Of course, I still can't tell Lizzie that her cat was missing for a week! She would probably insist on coming home to be certain Little Mouse was okay." She nibbled a soapy thumbnail. "I hope nobody else tells her."

The door blew open again, and Eliza hurried in with a stack of dirty dishes, which she set into soapy water in the sink. "Talking to yourself? That's a bad sign!"

Jane chuckled as Eliza grabbed a pot of fresh coffee to carry out front. "I answer myself too."

"Another bad sign. And stop biting your nails."

Eliza's laughter trailed her into the dining room. Jane finished up the dishes and looked around the kitchen. It was easier running the place without Lizzie than she'd thought it would be. But she'd be glad to have her friend back home in a couple of weeks. With only two of them there, they couldn't take any days off. Not that she really had any need of a day off. It wasn't as if she had a life beyond working at the bakery anyhow.

"Still, maybe I should call in some extra help," she mused. "I could do my laundry instead of just rinsing things out in the sink upstairs." They'd used extra help from time to time, but it wouldn't really make a difference. She couldn't imagine taking a full day off right now anyway. And Lizzie would be back soon enough. "Nee," she decided. "We'll push through."

The bell on the front door jingled as Jane walked into the dining area to see if Eliza needed any help.

A glance at the counter reassured her that Eliza was down to her last customers, Officers Ron Jakes and Maryann Anderson, whom she knew from the year before when they had helped solve the mystery of who was trying to put Lizzie's bakery, newly opened at the time, out of business.

She grinned at the pair and welcomed them like the friends they'd become during that investigation, and in the time since.

"Jane! How are you?" Officer Anderson, an athletic, middle-aged woman with her long graying hair pulled back into a ponytail that fed out through the back of her uniform cap, grinned when she saw Jane. "Where are those smart kitties of yours?"

"Are they still keeping the bad guys away?" Officer Jakes asked. He was younger than his partner, with a well-trimmed beard that matched his vivid red hair and eyebrows, and the freckles to match. Jane considered him to be a handsome man, and she figured all the young Englisch women in town must be chasing after him.

"Oh ja, and the mice too!" Jane winked at Officer Anderson, who had a bit of a mouse phobia.

"Well, that's good to hear. We're grabbing a quick lunch, then it's back to work for us," Officer Anderson said.

"Actually, we heard Little Mouse got out for a few days. We were glad to learn from Eliza that she's home safe and sound," Officer Jakes said. "We saw your flyers and the ad in the *Examiner*."

"We kept an eye out for her, but we didn't see any lost gray kitties," Officer Anderson added. "But now she's home safe, so all's well!"

"Ja, and before Lizzie got back from her wedding trip and found out I'd managed to lose her cat the very day she left!" Jane said. She glanced over to see who had come in the door, and was surprised to see Lydia Coblentz standing there, an uncharacteristic look of uncertainty on her dear face as she took in the fact that there were other customers there.

Concerned that something was bothering the old woman who was universally loved in their community, she excused herself and hurried over to her elderly friend.

"Lydia! How nice to see you again so soon." She gave Lydia a hug and stood back, studying her face. "But something is bothering you." She glanced at the counter where Eliza was still visiting with the officers and decided to take Lydia into the kitchen, where they could talk privately.

"Come back to the kitchen with me. I'll make tea."

"What I have to talk about requires something stronger." When Jane blinked at Lydia, her friend pinned her with a pained look. "I'm talking about chocolate, child! I need some gut, strong hot cocoa. Possibly with marshmallows if you have any of the tiny ones."

She marched back to the kitchen, and Jane followed, shrugging at Eliza's questioning look. "Gut to see you both!" she told the officers. "Come back soon, and I'll try to sit down and visit for a bit. I want to catch up. But Lydia needs to talk about something."

They waved and she pushed through to the kitchen, where she found Lydia getting out the ingredients for hot chocolate.

"I figured you wouldn't mind."

"No, of course not. The marshmallows are in the cookie cabinet in a plastic container." Jane helped prepare the treat, and soon the two women were seated at the kitchen table, large mugs of fragrant cocoa heaped with tiny marshmallows in front of them.

"Got any cookies?" Lydia asked.

"Of course. Gingersnaps?"

"My favorite."

Jane brought over the cookie jar and pushed it toward Lydia. "Let's not stand on ceremony. Help yourself."

Lydia smiled and reached inside, pulling out two cookies. She nibbled on one, staring pensively into her cocoa.

"Lydia, what's wrong?"

The old woman sighed. "Jane, I've lived a good, long life. I've been very blessed. My late husband was wunderbar, and my children and grandchildren love me and include me in their lives. Ruth and Jonas have welcomed me into their lives as well, treating me like family, putting me up in the *dawdi haus* and sharing their sweet bopplin with me. I can't complain about anything."

Seriously worried, Jane asked, "Lydia, are you sick?"

Lydia pulled her eyes from the mug and blinked at Jane. "What? Sick? Nee!" But her eyes filled with tears, and Jane caught her breath. She grabbed her friend's hand, holding on tightly. "I hate to see you so upset! Tell me what's wrong, please. I want to help."

Lydia sniffed and rooted in her apron pocket for a handkerchief, which she used to dab at her eyes and nose. "Oh, it's nothing terrible. I'm being a silly old woman."

Jane shook her head. "You could never be silly, Lydia. Do you know how much the people around here value your opinion? You're wise. You always help your friends, including me. So give me a chance to return the favor and tell me what's wrong."

Lydia raised drenched eyes to Jane's. "It's Abram! That old fool wants to get married!"

Jane sat blinking at her friend, unsure what she meant. Carefully, she asked, "Married? To whom?"

"To me!" She lifted both hands and gave Jane an expressive look that she must have thought would explain everything to her young friend, but Jane was still at sea.

"Okay. . .and that's a bad thing?"

Lydia tossed her hands into the air. "Of course it's bad! Why does he want to go messing everything up? We have a perfect arrangement right now." She gestured widely with her arms, illustrating her points. "He has his place, I have mine. I like it that way. Do you know how annoying an old codger like Abram can be? Sometimes I need my own space!"

She stared at Jane, who could only nod and wait for Lydia to continue while pondering how she felt about hearing the bishop referred to as an old codger. Coming from anyone else, she would have taken exception, but from Lydia? Jane figured her friend had probably earned the right.

Finally, Jane asked, "So. . .where do you think this sudden proposal has come from? What triggered it?"

Lydia rolled her eyes and chose another cookie, gesturing with it as she spoke. "He says his son is ready to take over the farm, and they don't have a dawdi haus. He says if we get married, we can both live in my little dawdi haus on Ruth and Jonas' farm. Can you imagine? The two of us in that little place? We would be at each other's throats!"

Jane wasn't sure what to say. She knew both Abram and Lydia had strong personalities and stronger opinions, so she imagined the two of them might need plenty of space to spread out, so to speak. To be fair, as fond as she was of Lizzie and John, she valued her own space up on the third floor of the big historic building that housed The Plain Beignet. So she understood where Lydia was coming from. On the other hand. . .if a man she loved wanted to get married and set up house together, she could probably make room for him. If Sam wanted to get married and move in with her, she thought wistfully, she would definitely be able to make room for him! But to be fair, the third floor of the bakery building was considerably larger than the dawdi haus at Ruth and Jonas' place. Still, she'd happily share a smaller space with Sam, if necessary.

So why didn't Lydia feel the same? Was it simply a factor of age? Of the different places they were in their lives?

Trying to understand what had her friend so upset, Jane asked, "So, Abram's son wants to move into the big house on his farm? Where has he been living?"

"With his wife and their kinner in the dawdi haus on his wife's parents' farm, not far away. I asked why Abram didn't build himself a nice, tidy little dawdi haus on his place, and then he could stay on his farm and be near his *grosskinner*. But no! He wants to move into my little house. He wants me to bake him cinnamon rolls every day, like his late wife used to do. His wife was a lovely, patient woman, Jane. A gut friend of mine. I'm not at all certain I can fill her shoes. Besides, he's not twenty-five anymore. Cinnamon rolls every day? Ha! Does he think I want to give him diabetes or a heart attack? Does he think I want to look at his face twenty-four hours a day?"

Lydia scrubbed her hands over her face then looked at her young friend. "Ach, Jane," she said plaintively. "I'm happy with things the way they are. Why isn't he?"

"You and Abram have been friends a long time, right?"

"All our lives. When our spouses were alive, we were all good friends. We did a lot together. Now it's just the two of us, and we've grown close, first because we were lonely and it was nice seeing a familiar face, but later, I actually came to care for the old man for his own sake. But enjoying having a regular partner for Scrabble doesn't mean I want to get married!"

"But, Lydia, don't you love him?"

Lydia pulled in a deep breath and let it out slowly before answering. "Yes, child, I love him. But what's the point in getting married at our age?"

"Lydia, I can think of a lot of good reasons for you and Abram to marry, and really no insurmountable roadblocks. If you had more room, would you want to marry him? Or is it something else?"

Lydia propped her chin on her hand, sipping coffee. "Child, I don't know. Maybe I'm too set in my ways. Maybe he just took me by surprise. We were going along just fine, and suddenly, bam! He's talking marriage!"

Curious, and since Lydia had brought it up, Jane probed a bit. "How did he propose? Was it romantic?"

Lydia threw back her head and chortled gleefully. "Ach, Jane, have you been reading romance novels? Nee, he wasn't romantic. As you'd expect from Abram, he just blurted it out." Imitating a deep voice, Lydia said, "'Woman, you should marry me and we can live in your little house. It'll be more convenient.' Then he ate a cinnamon roll." Lydia stared at Jane expectantly.

"Ah. I see. Not romantic at all, then."

"Nope." Lydia stirred some more mini marshmallows into her cocoa and popped a couple into her mouth for good measure.

"Maybe he feels as if he needs to set a gut example, since he's the bishop and all," Jane suggested.

Lydia nodded. "That's part of it. There's apparently been some gossip about all the time we spend at each other's homes." She looked outraged. "Can you imagine? It's not as if either of us is young and hot blooded. Goodness!" She took an angry gulp of her cocoa and gasped. "Ack! Too hot."

Jane poured a bit of cream into Lydia's cup, and the old woman nodded her thanks before taking a cautious sip. "Better, denki."

"I'm sure nobody is listening to malicious gossip about you and the bishop, Lydia. It's nonsense."

Lydia waved a hand in the air. "Of course it is, but people love to talk. And it could lead to trouble for us. Especially Abram, who is supposed to set an irreproachable example." She heaved a sigh. "How can he chastise others for doing what he is giving the impression of doing? Ugh. It's not what I want, but maybe I need to stop spending so much time with him, let the gossip die down some."

"Oh, that would be a shame, though!" Jane said, wondering if she could diplomatically point out that Lydia and Abram, both in their late seventies, didn't have all that much time to waste. She decided she couldn't, so she ate another cookie instead.

But Lydia gave her a playful smile. "I know what you're thinking, young woman. You think Abram and I don't have time to wait for gossip to die down, that we both have one foot in the grave already! Ha!"

At Jane's surprised look, Lydia nodded with satisfaction. "I can't read minds, but I can read faces, dear."

Jane chuckled. "I'm sorry. But honestly, why do you care about what people say?"

"I don't for my part. But I wouldn't want Abram's position in the gmay being compromised."

"Lydia, why don't you take a few days and think about Abram's proposal. Ask yourself, and maybe ask him, why he proposed now, after all this time. Tell him what you told me. And maybe the two of you can come up with a solution, a compromise. Maybe a bigger house and cinnamon rolls two or three days a week." She shrugged. "You like him a lot, and enjoy spending time with him, which is not the same as loving him. But since you do love him, why not find a way to be together under one roof? A way that doesn't take away from your independence and freedom. You're smart. I bet you can come up with something."

Lydia seemed to be contemplating Jane's words for a bit, then she nodded. "You're pretty smart yourself. I'll do that. Now, let's talk about your problem."

At Jane's look of alarm, she cackled. "Oh, you didn't think I was going to ask about that, did you? Ha! How long have you known me? I don't bother with gossip. I go right to the source and get the facts. So. You and Samuel Mast. What's going on with the two of you?"

Sam found himself at loose ends. So he did what he always did when he was chewing on a particularly difficult personal problem—he immersed himself in work.

On a farm there was never a dearth of chores. His Tunis sheep, an American breed valued for its delicious meat, were also pretty and easygoing. Their creamy coats and red faces and legs were interesting, and they were good breeders and easy to keep. That, along with the fact that the breed was considered endangered, had intrigued Sam when he was considering getting into keeping sheep.

He'd gone to the Ohio State Fair to check out all the different breeds, and the Tunis had caught his eye. He'd learned more about the breed from the people showing them at the fair, and once he met them, he was sold.

He'd even joined the Ohio Tunis Sheep Association and, through them and the contacts he'd made at the fair, had started a couple of years ago with a few ewes and one buck, and he'd been blessed. His herd was growing.

While he raised the sheep primarily for their meat, he also had a contract with a local woman who purchased their fleeces each spring. She told Sam she liked the fact that the wool was resistant to felting, which meant it worked well for the textured knitting, crocheting, and weaving she did, remaining well defined even when the item made with it was used for a long time.

The arrangement worked for both of them, and Sam enjoyed watching his little herd grow. He spent enough time with the sheep that they knew him, and they didn't run when he entered their stalls or paddock. He loved the feel of their fleece, often running his fingers through it when he was mucking their stalls or feeding them.

His favorites were the three original ewes and the buck. He'd named them after King David and his three wives, Michal, Abigail, and Bathsheba. He called them King, Mikey, Abby, and Sheba. The names had caused Bishop Abram to raise an eyebrow and to remind Sam of the trouble the biblical king had found as a result of his polygamy. But he'd let the names stand, and Sam was very fond of his founding stock. None of them would ever be sold for meat.

"Guder mariye!" he called to the sheep as he entered the barn the morning after Jane had basically sent him packing. "How is everyone this morning?"

He carefully looked everyone over. The ewes were all expecting lambs and looked fat and happy, with their warm winter coats coming in thick and tight. Their lambs were due between March and May, and that would be a very busy time. But now was the quiet time, when last spring's lambs had been weaned, and all the sheep were concentrating on eating as much as they could to prepare for the coming winter.

Of course Sam's sheep would not be staying outdoors during the cold months, except on nice days when they'd go out for a bit of foraging. They all had nice, big, clean, warm stalls in Sam's large, modern barn.

They greeted him gladly, since he was the source of food and good scratches on the places they couldn't reach themselves. He smiled at the antics of the young ones, born that spring. And laughed at the expression on a few of the more mature faces as they regarded the antics of the lambs recently weaned from their patient mothers.

"Okay, everyone, it's a nice day. Let's head outside. There's grass yet, and the water's not frozen in the trough. Feed in here later." He opened up the barn doors leading to the protected, enclosed farmyard where his sheep went before being let out into the adjoining field. He scanned the field for any potential dangers and thought, not for the first time, that now that he had a growing herd he really needed to get himself a pair of herd dogs to protect them from predators such as coyotes, bobcats, and the occasional cougar passing through the area.

"I need to talk to Ruth Hershberger," he said to himself. She kept goats and had a pair of Great Pyrenees dogs that guarded her herd. "She could tell me where to find such dogs. Maybe she even has puppies! And maybe she'd be willing to give me some tips on training them." He decided to talk to Ruth at church services on the next church Sunday in two weeks.

"Or maybe I should get a donkey. I like the idea of a donkey." He thought about it for a few minutes as he cleaned out the sheep pens. "Or maybe both! Why not?"

He knew a man who bred donkeys. He'd go see him and talk to Ruth the following Sunday.

Satisfied with that plan, he finished up in the barn and decided to do his laundry. It was a fair day, and the breeze would dry it quickly. Unlike most Amish women with a houseful of people to care for, he didn't have a routine laundry day. He just did it whenever he was running short of clothes. He took a last look at the sheep out in the field before heading inside to check that tedious chore off his to-do list.

Half an hour later he carried a basket of damp clothes outside to hang on the line. He was holding a clothespin in his mouth and securing the second leg of a pair of his work pants when he heard a buggy pull into his driveway.

Turning to see who was coming, he was surprised to recognize Abram Troyer's buggy, pulled by his mare, Spot.

Had it been a week? He didn't think so.

Securing the pants on the clothesline, Sam left the rest of the laundry in the basket and walked out to his driveway to greet Abram.

"Guder mariye, Abram! What brings you back so soon?"

Abram climbed down from his buggy, taking a bit more time than usual, and Sam thought maybe the older man's arthritis in his knees was acting up. It was common knowledge in the gmay that the bishop needed a knee replacement, but he was stubborn and had no intention of doing it before he absolutely had to.

Since that was exactly what Lydia Coblentz had done about her hip when it needed to be replaced—in fact, she'd waited too long and her hip had broken spontaneously, leaving her no choice in the matter—Sam smiled to himself, thinking the elderly couple were well suited.

"Does a fellow need an excuse to visit a member of his community? I just thought I'd come by and see how you're doing." The old man cast Sam a speculative, sideways glance, and that was what tipped Sam off—someone had told the bishop that he and Jane were bickering. Or to be more honest, since Sam really needed to work on being more honest, he and Jane weren't currently speaking.

Sam sighed. "Why don't you come on up and have a seat on the porch while I finish hanging my laundry? I'll get you some *kaffi*."

Looking pleased, Abram headed to the porch. "Don't mind if I do!" Sam noticed that the old man's limp was more pronounced than usual. *Maybe he's not going to be able to put off that knee replacement for all that much longer,* he mused.

He winced as he watched Abram's pinched expression as he climbed the porch steps, hobbled over to one of a pair of red Adirondack chairs on Sam's porch, and settled down with a sigh. "Ach! These old knees aren't getting any younger!"

"Wouldn't you rather go inside where it's warm? It's a chilly day."

"Nee, nee. The sun is warm here on your porch. I like it here."

Sam excused himself to go inside and make coffee, wondering what the bishop had to say and when he'd get around to saying it. He was back in a few minutes with two steaming mugs, and he placed one on the wide arm of the bishop's chair, taking a sip of his own before going over to the laundry still waiting in the basket to be hung on the line. He began clipping the items of clothing on the line that stretched between house and barn, playing it out across the farmyard as he added new pieces.

The bishop sipped his coffee and watched the sheep grazing peacefully in the field. After Sam finished hanging his laundry, he walked over and took the chair next to the bishop's, stretching his legs out before him on the porch. A red wooden table sat between the two chairs, and Sam set his mug on it and folded his hands across his stomach, waiting to see what was on Abram's mind.

"I've come to ask your advice, Sam."

Startled, Sam turned to look at Abram. This was not what he'd expected. "My advice? I'm not sure what I know that you don't, but if I can be of any help, I'll be happy to."

Abram pursed his lips, staring out at the field. He sighed. "It's about women. One in particular."

Sam laughed softly. "I can't imagine why you'd think I'd be able to advise you on women, Abram. Surely you know a lot more about that subject than I do. You've been married. I can't even seem to get a girlfriend."

Abram smiled gently at Sam. "Ja, I heard about you and Jane's fight."

"Fight? I wouldn't call it a fight," Sam said defensively. "What did you hear? And who from?"

Abram shrugged. "This and that, here and there."

"Ah."

"I guess you didn't get around to telling Jane about what happened with the nickname before she learned about it from someone else?"

"Ja, that sums it up. Now she thinks she can't trust me. She's pretty mad."

"Give her a few days," Abram advised. "I think she cares enough about you to come around once she cools down."

"That's what Ben said."

"Smart boy, that Ben." Abram took a sip of coffee then looked at Sam. "But I really do want your opinion. It's about Lydia. I asked her to marry me."

"Really? Well, congratulations! I guess you have gut news to share after all!"

Abram cast a sour look at Sam. "She said no."

Sam blinked. "No?"

Abram nodded. "In no uncertain terms either."

"Ah." The two men sipped coffee and watched the sheep grazing. After a few minutes Sam mused, "Well, if she said no, that seems like an end to it. What can I possibly say that you don't already know?"

Abram chuckled. "It's not an end to it, Sam. It's the beginning of negotiations."

Sam's eyebrows shot upward. What an interesting concept. Negotiations. "Huh. Maybe I should look at my situation with Jane like that. Negotiations. I kind of like the idea of that. It leaves room for. . ."

"Hope?"

Sam smiled wryly. "Ja. Hope."

"Well, I certainly hope so. In my case, I probably could have gone about the asking a bit differently."

"How did you ask? Did you get her flowers? Take her to dinner? Write her a poem?"

Abram chuckled. "Who do you think you're talking to? Nee, unfortunately, none of those. We were enjoying a perfectly nice breakfast at my house. She comes over a few mornings a week and cooks me breakfast. Truthfully, the other mornings I usually head over to her place. She often bakes me cinnamon rolls." He sighed happily. "It reminds me of my late wife, Amelia. She made the most appenditlich cinnamon rolls!"

"Er, did you tell her that when you proposed? That she reminded you of Amelia?"

The bishop cast a sour look at Sam. "Of course not. I'm not that dumm."

"Sorry."

Abram nodded. "I was enjoying my second roll, and I must have been overcome by the sugar. I just came right out and asked her—blurted it out, really—let's get married, I said. It would be so convenient, and I mentioned she could make me rolls every morning."

Sam gave him a blank look. "How did that go over?"

Abram winced. "Not too good."

Sam nodded. "I'm not surprised."

"That's not all. I went on to explain how my son and his family need a bigger place than the dawdi haus on his *frad*'s parents' farm, and that it would make sense for me to give up the big farmhouse to them. I'm seventy-five now, and even though I still like to get my hands in the dirt, I'm not as young as I was."

Sam nodded, and Abram continued. "I pointed out that we could live in her little dawdi haus at Ruth and Jonas' place."

Distracted by Abram's comment, Sam interrupted. "Funny, I was just thinking about them. I want to ask Ruth about those big dogs of hers. I'm thinking I need some for my herd."

"They're gut dogs." The bishop chuckled. "Ask Jonas about them sometime. He was pretty leery of them at first." The smile slowly slid off his face behind the snowy white beard, and his laughing blue eyes dimmed. "Anyway, Lydia didn't like the idea."

Abram just stared at Sam, a look of disbelief on his weathered face, as if waiting for Sam to agree with him that women were a puzzle, and Lydia in particular. But Sam shrugged. "Okay. What part didn't she like?"

"All of it! She said she wasn't going to bake me cinnamon rolls every day and give me a heart attack, and besides, she needed her space and didn't want to see my mug every morning." Abram looked hurt.

"Ah."

"Narrish, right? The woman is crazy. People are talking! I told her we spend all our time together, we might as well make our vows before the gmay and Gott."

"Again, not very romantic, Abram."

The older man scowled in disgust. "What do I need with romance at my age?"

Sam drummed his fingers on his leg for a moment before commenting, "Maybe you don't, but it seems she might."

Abram blinked at Sam. He was silent for a couple of minutes while Sam finished his coffee.

"Huh. I hadn't thought of that. Romance, huh? What should I do?"

"You're asking me?" Sam tapped his fingers against his chest, eyebrows raised. "The guy who messed up his chances with the only woman he's ever cared about?"

Abram shrugged. "You took her those little gifts. She liked that, nee?"

"She did. But the things I didn't do, namely, tell her the truth for the last ten or so years, meant more to her."

Abram nodded sagely. "Well, I've been honest with Lydia, and it didn't get me far either." He stared into the distance, frowning. "Maybe I should buy her some little frippery. Something silly and unnecessary. Women like that, right?"

"How would I know? I got lucky with my gift choices because I bought things for Jane's cat. That was just a gut guess. And honestly, Lydia doesn't seem like the type to want a bunch of unnecessary clutter in her home."

Abram thought about that. "True. She's pretty minimalist in her decorating. Back to the cat thing, though. Lydia has two cats, and she sure sets store by them. Maybe I should get her something for them. What did you get?"

Sam told Abram about the kitty water fountain and the bird feeder, and Abram's expression brightened. "I like those ideas! I can do that!"

"But at the end of the day, Abram, you need to talk to Lydia and find out what she wants. And see if what you want can work with what she wants out of life. If not, you might need to accept what she's offering now."

The bishop frowned again but nodded slowly. "See, that's why I came here. You have a good head on your shoulders, Sam." He pushed to his feet. "I need to get to the hardware store and see if they have one of those cat water fountains. I'll talk to you later. And Sam?"

Sam stood and waited to hear what the bishop had to say.

"Don't give up. You messed up, but you still have a chance. You need to let Jane know how much she means to you. Do a better job of it than I did. That shouldn't be hard."

Sam laughed. "I'll try."

Abram smiled and made his way to his buggy and waiting mare. "I'll let you know how Lydia likes the romantic gifts you suggested." He grinned. "And if she hates them, I'll blame them on you."

Sam laughed as he watched Abram turn his buggy around and head down the road toward town. He wondered whether Lydia would consider cat gifts romantic. He shrugged. Lydia loved her cats, so who could tell? To his mind, a gift was romantic if it demonstrated one person's caring about another's needs.

"Time to get some work done on the buggy waiting in the shop. It won't build itself."

He headed for the buggy shop, thoughts of how he might win back Jane's good opinion tumbling around in his mind. Knowing he couldn't do it on his own, he prayed.

Tomorrow, Vader, I have to see her. I know Ben said to give her a few days, and that will only be one day, really, or maybe two if I count tomorrow as the second day, but I just can't wait any longer. Please, help me find the right words to let her know how sorry I am about that narrish nickname! And to apologize for lying about it all these years. And please help me to convince her how much she means to me, and how much I want to get to know her better, so we can start working toward a future together. I'm so clumsy, Vader! I'm hopeless, but with Your help, I have hope. Your will be done.

CHAPTER TWELVE

"It's got to be something they can hear that we can't," Jane said, carefully going through Eliza and Susan's apartment the following evening in another attempt to discover what was preventing their cats from settling into their new home.

It obviously wasn't because the cats were lacking for anything material or nutritional. When she'd arrived an hour earlier, having walked over with Eliza after closing the bakery for the day, the two young women had eagerly showed Jane everything they'd done for the cats.

The fact that little had changed from her last visit on Sunday made no difference, and since Jane's younger sister and Eliza were so excited to show off their kitty supplies, Jane didn't have the heart to remind them she'd seen it all before.

Susan and Eliza followed her anxiously around the apartment as she peered into cabinets and closets.

"What are you looking for, Jane?" Susan whispered as Jane got down on her hands and knees to look underneath the living room furniture.

"No idea. I'm hoping I'll know when I see it." Finding nothing new, and no closer to figuring out what was wrong with the cats, who even now were running around the space, unable to rest and relax, Jane thought they looked a bit wild-eyed as they darted from place to place in the small apartment, yowling occasionally and shaking their heads from time to time. They'd better figure out the problem soon, or all the residents of the apartment, human and feline, were going to have mental breakdowns from sheer exhaustion.

"The way they shake their heads," she said thoughtfully. "Have you checked for ear mites?"

"Oh ja," Susan assured her older sister. "We took them to the vet last week. They're perfectly healthy."

"Hmmm. So if not ear mites, then why are they shaking their heads as if their ears are bothering them?" Jane murmured. "Could it be something they can hear? Maybe something we can't?" She watched the cats for a while and was about to turn away to have another look around when she noticed that both cats avoided an air vent in the floor. They ran all around the room but steered well clear of the vent. It could be that they just didn't want their little paws going through the metal holes. . .or it could be something else.

She walked over and looked into it and saw that it was closed. There was a small lever on one side. Crouching down, she shifted the lever, and the metal slats slid open, revealing not a heating or cooling duct as she'd expected but rather enabling her to look directly into the room below.

"What's down there, below us?"

Eliza shrugged and Susan walked over and peered into the vent. "I'm not sure. The waiting room, maybe? I know the vent was from back when the house was built, and there was no central heat or cooling. Radiant heat from below would rise up through the vent, heating the second floor. There are similar vents in both bedrooms."

"They're closed too?" Jane asked.

"Ja," Eliza confirmed. "We have radiators in all the rooms now, and there are vents for the air-conditioning."

Susan gave a sheepish look. "The benefit of living above a business."

Jane nodded. "Ja. It's a balancing act living by our standards, for sure and certain. But you don't use electric lighting up here, and your appliances are all gas." She shrugged. "It's a compromise. The heat and cooling are here. You pretty much have to use them."

She peered into the vent again. "Have you got a flashlight?"

Susan hurried into the kitchen and returned quickly with a powerful flashlight, which she handed to her older sister.

"Denki," Jane said, turning on the light and pointing it down through the vent. The doctor's office was closed for the evening, so she wasn't worried about violating anyone's privacy. Curious, she asked, "Do you ever hear voices through these vents?"

"Occasionally, but muted," Eliza said. "We can't make out any words. When Reuben lived up here he made sure none of the vents were above examining rooms or his office. Just public areas, like the waiting room, the nurse's station, the hallways. Like that."

"Okay. This one is above the waiting room, I think. What could be down there that might bother the cats?" She stood up. "May I see the ones in your bedrooms?"

"Sure," Eliza said, leading the way down a short hallway. "The bedrooms are on either side. Bathroom is at the end of the hallway."

Before they could proceed, the doorbell rang.

"Oh! That'll be Ben. He said he'd stop by this evening after work," Eliza said happily. "I'll go let him in while you have a look."

She scurried away, and Jane and Susan exchanged an understanding smile. "She really cares for him, doesn't she?" Jane whispered.

Her sister nodded. "Oh, ja. And I can see why. He's terrific." She stopped at the first room on the right. "This is my room, you remember. You can look in here first."

The cats zoomed down the hallway and into the bedroom, racing underneath the bed and back out again, and Jane noticed that they both avoided the vent in there, as they had in the living room.

She'd been in Susan's room before—had helped her move in, in fact. She admired the beautiful quilt on the double bed that had come with the house. It was an Irish Chain pattern in shades of light green and violet. "Oh, Susan, that quilt is just lovely. You made it?"

"Ja, denki! I just finished it. I liked it so much I decided to keep it instead of selling it as I'd originally planned. My old one is in my hope chest."

Susan's hope chest, made for her by their father, was a thing of beauty as well. Jane reflected that her family was blessed with many artists. In addition to the bed, there was a carved walnut bedside table, the hope chest, a small dresser with a few personal items on top, a bookcase filled with Susan's childhood favorites such as the Little House on the Prairie series and some works by Jane Austen, along with some sweet romances and cozy mysteries and, Jane was amused to see, a new cat tower in front of one of the windows.

"That's new," she said, pointing at the five-foot-tall cat tower, which had several enclosed spaces for a kitty to hide inside, all covered in plush carpet in a lovely violet shade that went very well with the new quilt. Susan gave a sheepish smile. "I couldn't resist. I think Friar Tuck likes it. Or he would if he could ever settle down!"

Jane nodded, reminded of her purpose in being in the room. She got down on her hands and knees, opened the vent, and then pointed the flashlight down through the hole between the first and second floors.

"See anything interesting?" a deep voice inquired, and Jane turned to see Ben in the doorway—and standing behind him, a nervous expression on his mobile face, was Sam.

Jane quickly turned her attention back to the vent. "I'm just about to look. It occurred to me that the cats avoid all these vents between floors, and I wonder if whatever is bothering them might not be up here. . ."

"It might be down in the doctor's office! Smart thought!" Sam, never able to resist a challenge, stepped into the room. And Jane wondered if the challenge calling to him was the mystery of what was bothering the cats—or her.

Shaking her head, she concentrated on trying to see what was in the room below Susan's. "Hmm. Looks like a storage closet of some kind." She moved the beam of the flashlight around. "Oh, ja, I see boxes of toilet paper and paper towels. And there are cleaning supplies, mops, brooms, and a vacuum cleaner. It's the janitor's closet."

She went to stand and caught her foot in the hem of her calf-length pink dress. But she didn't stumble, for a strong hand caught her arm and assisted her in regaining her balance. Unsure how she felt about Sam's presence, let alone his touch on her arm, she shrugged him off as soon as she was on her feet.

He stepped back, a look of uncertainty on his face.

Confused by her feelings, Jane averted her eyes. "Let's check the vent in Eliza's room next." She marched out of Susan's room and across the hall to Eliza's. It was set up much like Susan's, with a double bed covered with a blue chenille bedspread; a dresser; an old steamer trunk in one corner; a bedside table with a battery lantern and battery clock on it, both sitting on a lovely antique doily; and a pretty navy-blue braided rug on the floor.

"Where's the vent?" She looked around the room. "Is it under the bed?"

"Nee, under the rug." Eliza, who had just entered the room, pulled the rug up and revealed the vent, which, unlike the other two, was open to the room below. "Huh, I didn't realize that was open."

Sam stepped into the room, but Ben remained outside in the hall, as if uncomfortable entering. Jane was okay with that. She knelt down on the floor and shined the beam into the hole.

"Mind if I look?" Sam stood respectfully by, as if waiting to see what she would say.

She thought about telling him to leave, then realized she really didn't want to stay angry at him. Maybe they had lost their chance at a deeper relationship and maybe not. That remained to be seen, but in the meantime, it didn't mean they couldn't tolerate one another's company. After all, they would see each other often at church services and other places. It was inevitable. She might as well get used to it.

"Sure." She handed him the flashlight, and he knelt down next to her, his arm briefly brushing against hers, and shined the beam into the vent. "Nice flashlight," he commented absently while he leaned closer to have a look. After a few moments he said, "Seems to be some kind of medical equipment in there. There are a few lights on. Diagnostic machines, I bet." He sat back on his heels. "It wonders me that this vent wasn't sealed, since it's above a room where patients go for tests."

Eliza nodded. "I'll tell my bruder about it. We can put a piece of plywood or insulation or something into the vent and seal it off."

Jane was considering what Sam had seen. "Machines? And they're turned on?"

Sam nodded. "Ja, they seem to be."

She nibbled her thumbnail. "I wonder if they make some kind of noise that we can't hear?"

The others looked surprised at the notion. "Huh," Eliza said. "Interesting thought. You mean some sort of noise that's maybe too high pitched for human ears but not for feline ones?"

Jane nodded, and Eliza looked excited. "I wonder whether those machines have to be left on when not in use?"

They all looked at each other, and Ben said, "It might be worth it to ask your brother about that, Eliza."

"I will! Tomorrow morning I'll run back over here from the bakery when the doctor's office opens at nine, if you don't mind, Jane?"

"Sure. You can take my bicycle. I hope you find an answer to your problem."

"Ja, that would be amazing!" Eliza and Susan exchanged exhausted looks. "We could finally get some sleep! Maybe as soon as tomorrow!" Susan said wistfully.

"Anybody hungry in the meantime?" Eliza asked. "I have dinner ready, and then there's pie." Jane, Ben, and Sam readily accepted the invitation, and all of them walked to the kitchen, the cats still zooming around the apartment yowling.

"I don't know how you stand this," Sam commented.

"Neither do we," Susan told him. "It's getting really old, really fast. If we can't figure it out soon, we're going to have to rehome them."

"No one would blame you," Jane said as they took seats at the table and Susan and Eliza bustled about getting everyone's meal. "This is more than anyone could bear!"

Sam sat down across from Jane and met her eyes cautiously. He gave her a small smile, and she nodded in return, a serious look on her face. Sam winced inwardly. He clearly had a lot of ground to make up with her. He glanced at Ben, who gave him a look that said, *Well, what did you expect?*

Eliza and Susan finished setting out the food and drinks and joined them. After a silent prayer they all enjoyed the meal and companionship, and the conversation ranged from Sam's desire to find a couple of dogs to guard his sheep to Abram and Lydia's romance to whether Daniel Beechy would get himself a cat to when Lizzie and John would return.

Finally they all stood and carried their dishes to the sink. Sam puttered a bit, offering to wipe down the table as he tried to decide whether he dared offer Jane a ride home. It was dark out and she had no buggy of her own, so he knew she must have walked over with Eliza after work.

"Well!" Eliza said brightly, "Denki so much for coming over tonight and helping us figure out what's going on with the cats."

"We still don't know if we have," Ben cautioned.

"I know, but I'm praying this is it," she answered.

Sam sucked in a breath and caught Jane's eye. "Can I give you a ride home?"

Jane looked at Ben, who smiled back and said, "I'm going to hang around for a bit and play some cards with Eliza and Susan. You should let Sam drive you. It's dark out and kind of chilly."

Jane's face fell. "Oh, okay." She chewed on her thumbnail and looked at Sam, who gazed quietly back, waiting to see what she would decide. It wasn't as if he'd left her a whole lot of choices, but he thought it would be best to pretend she had some.

She sighed and nodded. "Then denki, Sam. It's pretty cold out for a walk. I accept."

"As if we'd allow you to walk home alone in the dark anyway," Susan scoffed.

Sam got her cape from the peg by the front door and helped her with it, then handed her the black winter bonnet, which she tied over her prayer kapp.

Not quite meeting his eyes, she said, "I'm ready. Good night, Eliza. Good night, Susan, Ben."

They all chorused their good nights, and Sam and Jane trooped down the steps followed by Susan, who gave Jane a hug and whispered in her ear, "I feel like such a third wheel! I need a boyfriend of my own."

Jane laughed. "Don't be in a big hurry. You've got time." She kissed her sister on the cheek and then went out into the cold night. "Brrr! It smells like snow," she said, walking over to Sam's buggy. His horse gave a loud whicker, making it clear that he was tired of waiting in the cold. Next to him, Ben's mare snorted and whinnied.

"Sorry, Cupid, you've still got some waiting ahead of you," Sam said as he opened the passenger door for Jane and gave her a hand up.

"Denki." She settled into the buggy, pulling a warm lap robe over her legs as Sam climbed into the driver's seat and turned his gelding, Ralph, toward the bakery.

"Where's Millie?"

He shot her a glance, and she turned her gaze back to the road in front of them. "It was Ralph's turn."

"Ah."

Nobody spoke again as they traversed the empty streets of Willow

Creek, and Sam wondered what Jane might be thinking.

After a short ride, they pulled up in front of the bakery, and Sam sat quietly, wondering what to say.

After a minute, he said, "Jane, I want to apologize again for—"

Just as Jane said, "Sam, I want you to know that—"

They both broke off, laughing self-consciously, and then they both said, "You go first" at exactly the same moment.

Sam snuck a glance at Jane, whose eyes were twinkling with amusement in the light of the streetlamp outside the bakery. Relief filled him. If she was amused, then she'd already started to forgive him.

He sent up a silent prayer of gratitude to Gott, even as he was aware that he still had a long way to go. "You first, Jane."

She nodded. "Okay." She turned to face him in the buggy, a determined expression on her face. "Sam, I've thought about this a lot. I realize I can't blame you for something you did when you were just a youngie."

He started to reply, and she held up her hand. "Please, let me finish."

He pressed his lips together and nodded.

"Denki. I can't stay mad at you for that, even though I won't lie—it really hurt me at the time, and for years afterward. What I am having trouble getting past is the fact that as we've gotten to know each other these past couple of weeks, you still never told me it was you who coined the nickname Plain Jane. Instead you hid behind your secret admirer persona, still afraid to come talk to me man to woman, and let me know you had feelings for me. It's as if you're still a youngie, afraid of an adult relationship. I need a man who can face his feelings, even when they're hard. I need a man who can admit his mistakes, not try to hide them. I need a man who will be a mature, honest partner to me." She looked at him seriously, and his breath caught in dismay at what he saw in her face.

"I need someone who won't lie to me, Sam, even by omission. And as of right now, I don't see that being you."

She might as well have hit him over the head with a brick and pushed his body out of the buggy, Sam thought. Her rejection hurt that much. And he couldn't even defend himself, because she was exactly right. He had somehow become emotionally stuck at the point he'd been when he'd made up that name at fourteen years old. If he'd actually matured, he would have found the courage to tell the woman he loved about his mistake, begged her forgiveness, and let her know how much she meant to him.

Instead, he'd hidden behind a mask of false innocence, avoiding Jane for over a decade because he was afraid of facing her with the truth.

How ironic, he thought, rubbing his belly, which hurt as if he'd been physically punched there. He'd lost her anyway, through cowardice and inaction.

He swallowed several times before finding his voice. "I understand, Jane," he croaked. "I don't blame you. I've been a coward. If I could take it back, I hope I would, but I can't be certain because obviously I'm still that same guy—the one who was afraid to admit he'd done something stupid and covered it up for years rather than telling the truth to the most important person in his life."

Her mouth fell open a bit at his admission that she was the most important person in his life. She looked as if she were going to say something, but then she closed her mouth and nodded. "Denki, Sam. I appreciate your candor, late as it is. I'll. . .see you when I see you."

She opened her door and climbed down. Turning, her eyes searched his face for a few moments before she closed the buggy door and walked to the bakery, which she unlocked. She went inside and was about to close the door when he called out to her. "Jane! Wait."

She hesitated then waited while he jumped down from the buggy and hurried over to stand facing her in the doorway.

"Will you give me some hope?"

Shaking her head, she opened her mouth, as if to tell him there wasn't any hope when he raised his hand to forestall her.

"Jane, please, I'm not asking you to let me court you, not now. What I'm asking—begging—is that you'll keep an open mind about me. Give me a chance to show you I actually am a grown man, all evidence to the contrary. To show you how much you mean to me. Bishop Troyer recently told me that with Gott, there's always hope." He studied her face closely, eyes searching hers. "Please at least say you'll give me a chance."

She pressed her lips together before raising a hand to her mouth to nibble on a thumbnail, but she caught herself and lowered her hand. "I'll think about it, Sam. It's true, with Gott there is always hope. But I can't see the hope right now for us."

"Denki, Jane. I'm hoping Gott will help us both see it, together. For now, know this—I care about you. I always have." He shrugged. "For whatever good that does us now."

He stepped back, his eyes still locked on hers, and she nodded slowly. "I. . .care about you too, Sam. But without trust, what is there? I'll see you. . .when I see you. *Gut nacht.*"

She closed the door and drew the blinds.

Sam stood there for a few minutes until he saw the lights come on up on the third floor, and he knew she was safely home for the night. With a heartfelt sigh, he returned to the buggy and turned Ralph for home.

"I should have faced this heartbreak ten years ago. At least it would be over now. Or maybe if I had, I wouldn't have had to face heartbreak, because she would have forgiven me back then."

He headed home to his empty house, feeling it was unlikely that would ever change.

As he pulled into his driveway a little later, Ralph snorted and pranced a bit as if spooked by something Sam couldn't see. He rolled down his window and listened to the darkness, but he heard nothing. He shook the reins and called, "Okay, Ralph, there's nothing to be afraid of, boy. Let's go to the barn and you'll get some oats."

But Ralph wouldn't move forward. "What on earth?"

Sam peered into the dark night, unbroken here in the country by the lights of streetlamps. Only the stars and a sliver of moon offered any illumination. It was cold but not frigid, thankfully, since Ralph still didn't seem interested in heading to the warm barn. Sam clucked and shook the reins and again Ralph danced in the traces, snorting nervously. He was answered from inside the barn by Sam's team of Belgians and Millie, all of whom sounded uncharacteristically nervous. They were all generally very laid back.

Starting to feel a bit nervous himself, Sam opened the buggy door and climbed out, looking around. He saw nothing out of the ordinary and heard nothing other than the wind in the stand of white pines that stood as a windbreak between the farmhouse and the north fields. Not even a coyote sang in the distance. It was very quiet. Maybe. . .too quiet?

Sam walked up to Ralph's head and took hold of his bridle, petting his sweaty neck and murmuring soothing words. The horse's eyes were rolling, showing white all around, indicating that he was seriously spooked by something. Maybe he smelled a bobcat nearby, not that the medium-sized predator could hurt a grown horse. "Come on, boy. Let's get you into the barn."

Sam tried to lead Ralph toward the barn, but the horse wouldn't budge. He dug his front feet into the ground and tossed his head up and down, whickering and snorting. "Ralph! Cut it out! What are you doing?"

Suddenly the horse screamed and reared, almost pulling Sam's shoulder from its socket as he struggled to control the twelve-hundred-pound animal made unreasonable by whatever was spooking him.

"Ralph! Ralph, calm down!"

But the horse screamed and lashed out with his front feet, nearly hitting Sam, who swung aside at the last moment. As he struggled to hold the crazed beast, another scream rent the air, but this one didn't come from the horse. Sam froze, the hairs on the back of his neck and arms standing up as Ralph bugled a challenge, echoed by the horses inside the barn. And that was when Sam saw the cause of the furor—a huge cougar slid from the shadows of the barn where it had been crouched, watching Sam and Ralph approach. It moved with terrible grace into a patch of faint moonlight and looked directly at Sam, its eyes glowing gold in an otherwise shadowy face.

Sam felt a terror he'd never experienced. He had no weapon and knew he wouldn't make it to the house if the cat decided to chase him down. He stood staring back at the big cat, fear sweat soaking his shirt, skin prickling with adrenaline, as time seemed to slow down until Sam was aware of each thundering heartbeat. Then, with a final scream, the cat made its move—away from Sam and Ralph, disappearing under a fence into the dark. Sam caught a glimpse of the cat moving at a ground-eating lope as it crossed his field and disappeared into the trees down by the creek.

The cat was gone, at least for now. Immeasurably relieved, Sam turned to lead Ralph into the barn, but the horse was still panicking. It reared up, catching Sam off guard, pulling him off his feet and causing him to stumble. He pitched forward, reaching out blindly to catch hold of the horse's reins, but Ralph was descending from his rear and his near front hoof caught the side of Sam's forehead in a glancing blow that was nevertheless enough to send him to the ground, where his last thought before darkness claimed him was a prayer that the cat wouldn't return while he was helpless.

CHAPTER THIRTEEN

Jane had just handed over Rebekkah's standing order the following morning, Friday, when Eliza returned from biking over to her brother's medical practice to talk to Reuben about the cats and her thoughts about it maybe being the machines making some kind of high-pitched noise inaudible to humans that was making her cats bonkers.

"He said it was a definite possibility, and they'll make sure to turn off all the machines when they're not using them! They don't have to be left on, it's just a bad habit they've developed," Eliza told Jane breathlessly as she hurried to don her apron and put a hairnet on under her prayer kapp.

"Ach, I hope and pray it's the answer! How long do you think it'll take to see results?"

"If that's what was causing the trouble, and the machines are turned off, right away," Eliza said.

"Here's hoping!" Jane said. "I'm glad you're back, though. We're crazy busy this morning for some reason."

Philomena Jones rushed in, a look of concern on her expressive face. She glanced around quickly, and when she spotted Jane she made a beeline for her.

"Jane! I hurried over here because I just heard something I think you need to know." She paused a moment to catch her breath. The newspaper editor, a curvy brunette with luxurious waves of dark hair and wide-set brown eyes that transmitted her feelings as readily as words, was not a spring chicken.

A woman of about fifty, she held up a hand, catching her breath before continuing. "Sorry, I practically ran over here. I should have taken time to grab the van keys and driven over. Give me a moment."

Eliza hurried over with a glass of water and handed it to the editor, who accepted it gratefully and gulped half of it down before lowering the glass and wiping her mouth with the back of her hand. "Sorry." She looked around and seemed relieved to find that there were no customers at the moment.

"I'm glad you're not busy yet," she said, dropping into a chair.

"We were! If you'd been fifteen minutes earlier you'd have found us packed!" Jane said. "Why don't you sit down, and I'll bring you a coffee and pastry on the house."

Philomena stepped closer to Jane and put a hand on her arm. "I just heard something from the sheriff I need to tell you about before the gossips start pouring in here."

Starting to feel alarmed, Jane led Philomena over to a table and sat down with her. Eliza hovered nearby, listening. "What is it? Did something happen?"

Philomena blew out a breath and nodded. "Yes, I'm afraid so. Now, nobody is dead, but—"

The rest of her sentence was cut off by the front door slamming open and Lydia and Abram hurrying inside. "Jane!" she hollered. "Oh, there you are, and Eliza too. Gut, gut," Lydia said, hand on her heart. She paused to catch her breath before continuing. "We can tell you both at once. Lock the door, Abram."

Philomena looked at Lydia askance. "Actually, I can't stay . . ."

Lydia hurried over to where the three women were, and Philomena murmured, "I guess I'll stay a bit." She sat back, as if she knew that whatever she had come to tell them was about to be revealed by their friend, Lydia, and the bishop.

Lydia glanced at Philomena, and her eyes widened. "Oh, hello, I'm sorry, I didn't see you there." She stopped, as if unsure whether to go on.

"Lydia, this is Philomena Jones, the editor of the *Examiner*," Jane said. Lydia nodded.

"Of course, I know who she is, child. Has she. . .told you any news?"

"I was about to," Philomena said, and Lydia nodded again.

Abram walked up to stand behind Lydia, setting a hand on her shoulder. Their eyes met, and he nodded at her to go on.

She took a fortifying breath then blurted it out. "Sam Mast has been hurt. He was kicked in the head last night by that big gelding of his."

Jane gasped and surged to her feet. "Nee! Is he all right?"

"Well, that's what I'm not sure of, child. He's alive, I know that." She looked helplessly at Abram, and Philomena cleared her throat.

"Maybe I can shed a bit of light on this?"

Everyone looked at her. "Ja, please do," Abram said before plopping into a seat at a nearby table. Lydia sat down beside him, and everyone waited for Philomena to explain whatever more she knew.

"The sheriff called me a while ago. It seems that your friend, Sam Mast, was found unconscious in his driveway this morning by a customer who stopped by to talk about a buggy they want him to build."

Jane's hands covered her mouth, and tears filled her eyes. "Unconscious? This morning? How long did he lie there?"

"They aren't sure. The theory is that he returned home sometime last night, and for some reason he got out of his buggy and tried to lead the horse the rest of the way to the barn. Something must have spooked it, and it must have accidentally clipped Sam in the head with a hoof."

"Oh no," Jane breathed. "Where is he? Can I go to him?"

"He's at Pomerene Hospital in Millersburg," Abram said. "We'll all go in a while. We can call a driver. But there's more, ain't so?"

Philomena nodded. "The sheriff also told me he has a pretty good idea what spooked the horse." When everyone looked at her, she continued slowly. "It seems that there were animal prints in the mud just outside the barn doors, where something tried to get inside to reach the sheep." She paused before adding, "The sheriff said they looked like mountain lion prints." At Eliza's and Jane's gasps, she paused a moment. "Sam must have come home and surprised a cougar—and from its prints and the scratches it left starting about eight feet up on the barn doors, it's a big one!—sniffing around the barn hoping for a lamb dinner. It looks like the horse freaked out and reared, clipping Sam in the head with a hoof. The horse was found still hitched to the buggy, grazing in the yard. Sam was lying in the driveway. The lion was long gone, its prints leading off across the field down toward the creek."

"A mountain lion?" Eliza looked amazed. "I've never heard of one around here before!"

"We get them passing through from time to time," Philomena said. "But they aren't common. Fortunately, this one must have decided the angry horse was more trouble than the sheep it couldn't get to anyway, and it took off."

Lydia shuddered. "I hate to think of poor Sam lying unconscious all night. It was cold out, and the lion could have come back."

"But it didn't, and he survived," Abram said. "Now, I assume you will want to put a sign on the door saying you're closed due to an emergency, and come with us to Millersburg?"

Jane nodded. "Oh, ja, denki." She stood up and took a few steps toward the kitchen before stopping and staring at her feet.

"What is it, Jane?" Eliza asked.

"He dropped me off after we left your place last evening, Eliza," Jane whispered. "It was around seven, right?"

Eliza nodded. "Ja, about that."

"He must have gone straight home, and if the accident happened before he even made it all the way up the driveway, then he must have been lying there all night! He could have frozen to death!"

"It wasn't that cold last night," Philomena said reassuringly. "Only got down to around forty-five."

"And I wasn't very nice to him," Jane said brokenly. "I told him I couldn't trust him, since he didn't tell me the truth about the nickname."

Philomena looked confused. "Nickname?"

"He accidentally gave Jane the nickname Plain Jane when they were both kids."

Philomena's eyebrows rose. "Huh. Not nice but clever, the way it plays off your culture. . . Never mind. How old was he at the time?"

"About fourteen," Jane said. "I was twelve."

The editor winced. "Ouch. Hard time for a young girl to get saddled with an unfortunate and catchy nickname."

"And exactly the kind of stupid thing a fourteen-year-old boy would do to prove he didn't have a crush on a girl he absolutely did have a crush on!" Abram added.

Lydia nodded. "The fact that it was clever made it stick. It tormented Jane for years."

Everyone sat quietly for a moment, and then Philomena said, "Look, why don't I close the newspaper for a couple hours? I can drive you all to Millersburg. You'll have to catch a ride home later, but it'll save you calling a ride now."

"Oh, denki!" Jane said, hurrying toward the kitchen. "I'll make a sign for the door and get my cape and bonnet. Are you coming, Eliza?"

"Ja, I'm coming." She stopped. "I wonder if anyone has told Ben."

Abram and Lydia looked at each other. "I don't know," Abram said. "Why don't you call the mill, and if he can get off we can swing by and get him on our way."

"I will." Eliza hurried to the kitchen to place the call. A few minutes later, she and Jane both emerged carrying their capes and bonnets. Jane taped her note to the front door then turned and looked at everyone impatiently. "Coming?"

They went outside, and Jane locked up. "We need to pick up Ben on our way. Where's Philomena?"

"She went to get her van," Lydia said, putting her arm around Jane's shoulders. "It'll be all right, lieb. We'll all pray on the way. Oh! Here she comes now."

The roomy minivan pulled up to the curb, and everyone piled inside, Abram taking the front passenger seat and the three women piling into the back. As they pulled away from the curb Philomena called, "Everyone fasten your seat belts."

Eliza leaned forward from the back row. "Would you please swing by the sawmill? We need to pick up Sam's best friend, Ben Fisher, on our way."

Jane found her thoughts scattering down one avenue after another. Central to all was her fear that when they arrived at the hospital they would find that Sam had succumbed to his unknown injuries. She sobbed, and Lydia put her arm around the young woman, murmuring soothing words.

Abram cleared his throat from the front seat and said, "I'm going to offer a prayer for Sam's recovery. Gott, please hold Your son, Samuel, in the palm of Your hand and help him recover from his injuries. We don't know how extensive they are, but You know what he needs. So we entrust Your child to You. Now, let us all say the Lord's Prayer together."

Together they prayed the comforting, ancient words, and Jane felt a calm steal over her. By the time they stopped at the sawmill and Ben, who must have been watching for them, hurried outside and climbed into the back with Eliza, Jane was able to calm her racing thoughts and offer up a silent prayer of her own for Sam's health—and for the opportunity to tell him that even though he'd hurt her she still cared for him.

The knowledge that he could have died alone in the cold night with no closure between them had brought home very strongly to Jane that whatever had transpired in the past didn't matter. What mattered was that she still loved him. And she hoped and prayed he still felt the same about her, after her coldness toward him.

Please, Gott, don't let it be too late.

As if through a barely penetrable fog, Sam became aware of an insistent voice calling his name. "Sam, please try to open your eyes. Sam? Can you hear me? Come on, now. Open your eyes."

Sam was pulled to the surface of his mind by the voice that wouldn't go away and let him sink back into the comfortable dark nothingness. He didn't want to wake up, because as he surfaced from sleep, he realized he had the worst headache he'd ever experienced.

"Oh, my head is coming off," he groaned.

"There you are," the voice said, sounding pleased. "Come on, now, open your eyes. I want to check your pupils. Come on, Sam, open your eyes."

"Nee, let me sleep," he begged.

"I don't understand much Deitsch, honey. I should really learn. But for now, just open your eyes."

Sam hadn't realized he'd spoken in his first language. He couldn't straighten out his thoughts. And he was so thirsty. "Water, please."

"Here, have some ice chips. I know your mouth is dry." A spoon touched his lips, and Sam allowed cool ice chips to slip in and moisten his parched tongue. They felt wonderful, and he croaked, "More, please."

"I'll give you more, and then you open your eyes for me. I've got the lights low in here. I know your head hurts, but I need to look at your eyes," the voice said quietly. The spoon delivered more ice chips, and Sam let them rest in his mouth, soothing his tongue and the parched tissues of his mouth.

"Okay, let's see those baby blues," the voice coaxed, and Sam pried his eyes open, groaning as the dim light caused his headache to double. He groaned again and then rolled to his side and retched, losing the contents of his stomach. Tears burned his eyes as he retched again helplessly, and the voice soothed him as his back was gently rubbed and a cool compress was pressed to his forehead. "Poor baby, okay, it's over. Here, roll back, and I'll give you a little water to rinse your mouth."

"Sorry, sorry," Sam whispered, and the cool compress swept over his face, wiping away his tears and evidence of his sickness.

"It's okay, Sam. You got kicked in the head by a horse. No wonder your head hurts and you're sick. We're just happy you're awake. Now, I'm going to raise the head of the bed a little, and give you water to rinse your mouth. Are you ready?"

His eyes still tightly closed, Sam gave the slightest nod. Even that movement caused pain to slash through his head, and he groaned. As he felt the head of the bed raise up a few inches, he worried that he might be sick again, but he managed to push it back.

"Okay, here's a little water. Swish it around then spit it into the bowl. I'm holding a bowl right under your chin. I'm giving you a straw; here you go."

He felt a straw tap his lips, and he cautiously drew in some water, which he swished around, washing away the taste of vomit; then he spit it weakly into the bowl he felt touching his chin. "More," he croaked, and the straw tapped his lips again. He repeated the process twice more until his mouth tasted and felt better. Then he relaxed against the pillows, exhausted. He heard the owner of the voice speaking quietly with someone else for a moment.

"We've put some anti-nausea meds into your IV, Sam," the voice said as the soothing hand wiped another cool compress across his sweaty forehead, taking away some of the ache. "In a few minutes you'll feel better. Then you need to show me those baby blues."

"My eyes are hazel," Sam whispered, a tiny smile playing across his lips.

"Oh, my bad! Well, you let me know when you're ready to prove it to me. I'll let you rest for a few minutes, and then we'll try again." The pleasant voice went away, and Sam let himself sink back into a comfortable half sleep, where his head didn't feel as if someone were hitting it with baseball bats.

What seemed like seconds later, the voice was back. "Okay, Sam. You open those eyes now, and we'll make sure you're doing okay. Then we'll be able to give you some meds for that headache. Come on, honey, open 'em up for Nancy."

Sam cautiously slit his eyes open the tiniest bit, and when that didn't cause him to throw up again, he dared to open them a bit wider. A woman with intricately woven burgundy braids piled high atop her head swam into view. He blinked a few times to bring her into focus. She was smiling reassuringly at Sam and held up a little flashlight. "There you are. And your eyes are hazel. What do you know? Now, honey, I'm Nancy, your nurse. I've got to take a good look in those pretty eyes, and I need to use this little light to do it. It's gonna hurt, not gonna lie. But then we'll be able to give you better pain meds, okay?"

He gave a tiny nod and kept his eyes open as she used the light to look first in one eye, and then the other. Her touch was cool and gentle on his face, and she clucked to herself a bit, and then she turned off the light with a little snick. "Well, we knew you had a concussion, Sam. I'll bet your head is just pounding. But the good news is your pupils are the same size, and reactive to light. So that means we can order you some meds to dull that headache. It won't be going away totally for a couple days, I'm afraid. But it'll help."

She patted his shoulder and gave him another spoonful of ice chips. "Oh, I nearly forgot. You've got some very worried people out in the waiting room who want to make sure that you're not going home to be with Jesus today. I told them you would live, but they want to see for themselves." She waggled her high, arched brows at him. "Maybe one of them is your sweetheart, hmm? There are a couple of very pretty young ladies out there! I'll let them in after you get your pain meds." She gave him a considering look. "And I think you could stand it if we cleaned you up just a little bit, gave you a new gown. Not to put too fine a point on it Sam, but you stink."

Her frank comment startled a laugh from Sam, who winced as his head pounded in response.

"Oh, don't make me laugh, please. It hurts."

"I know. Well, now, here's Dr. Seifer. Oh, and Dr. King too. Well, you've got all the important people coming to check you out."

She turned to the doctors and had a quiet discussion with them before returning to Sam's bedside. "The docs are going to have a look at you. I'll be back in a few minutes." She squeezed his shoulder reassuringly and gave him another spoon of ice before leaving him to the physicians, one of whom he knew well. Dr. Reuben King was the family practitioner in Willow Creek. He was Beachy Amish, and therefore able to practice medicine and drive his truck. Originally from Pennsylvania, he'd moved to Willow Creek a couple of years before and married a friend of Sam's, Mary Yoder. If Reuben was here, that meant everyone in the community had heard he'd been in an accident. He grimaced at the thought of all the worry he'd caused people.

"Reuben? What happened to me?"

Reuben, along with the other doctor, a man Sam didn't recognize, stepped up to the bed. The second doctor picked up his chart and began reading while Reuben gave him some more ice. "Seems you were kicked in that hard head of yours by your horse. You had us pretty worried when you arrived here this morning by ambulance. You'd spent the night on the ground, and it was down in the forties last night. You were hypothermic and dehydrated. And you have a heck of a concussion. But we warmed you up and hydrated you with IV fluids, and it looks as if you'll make it, I'm happy to say. This is your actual doctor, Dr. Seifer. I'm just here because there are a bunch of people who want to know how you are, so I'm abusing my position on staff by horning in on Dr. Seifer's territory."

He smiled at Sam, and it made him feel much better knowing that Reuben cared about him enough to come out to check on him. He could tell that Reuben had been genuinely worried, despite his humorous tone.

"Don't let this guy take care of me," Sam croaked to Dr. Seifer. "I'm not sure he's a real doctor."

The strange doctor, a young, bald man with striking green eyes, smiled at Sam before pulling out a little flashlight like the one the nurse practitioner had used. "He's a real doctor. I checked his diploma to be sure. Now, I need to look into your eyes. If they're as good as Nancy said, I'll give you some pain meds that will seriously reduce the thumping in your head."

He checked Sam's eyes and, apparently satisfied, promised him pain meds. "You're going to be here a couple days until we're sure you're safe on your own. I hear you live alone."

"Who is taking care of my animals? Reuben?"

"Not to worry, Sam, we've got it covered," Reuben assured Sam. "So, the waiting room is full of people who want to see you. We're not going to let them all in. But there are a couple you'll probably want to see? Abram and Lydia? Ben? And I believe Jane Bontrager is here, wringing her hands and looking mighty worried, along with my little *schwester*, Eliza." He smiled knowingly at Sam. "I hear they're going to get you cleaned up first, once the pain meds take the edge off. I'll send everyone down to the cafeteria for lunch, and by the time they get back you'll probably be feeling more human again, nee?"

Sam smiled. "Ja, denki, Reuben. Denki, Dr. Seifer."

"No problem, Sam. I'll be back to see you in a few hours. Don't be stoic. Tell the nurses when you hurt, okay? And tell them if your vision gets any blurrier than it probably is right now, or if you get nauseated again, or anything else. Okay?"

Sam promised he would, and Dr. Seifer bid him and Reuben goodbye and left the room.

"Reuben, I have no idea what I'm doing here," Sam croaked. Reuben gave him more ice and frowned in concern. "You don't? Well, that's not unusual, considering. What's the last thing you remember last night?"

Sam frowned, trying to recall. "Um, I had dinner at your sister's place, with her, Susan, Jane, and Ben. Then I drove Jane home. We. . .didn't part on the best terms. In fact I'm surprised she's here. I thought she'd washed her hands of me."

"Hearing you almost went home to heaven may have softened up whatever hard feelings she was harboring toward you, my friend."

"Was it really that bad?"

Reuben shrugged. "Well, it's a gut thing your customer stopped by. It seems something caused your horse to attempt to kick your head off. You don't remember what that could have been?"

Sam thought hard but couldn't remember anything after dropping Jane off at the bakery. "Nee, I've got nothing."

"Well, it might jar your memory loose to hear that mountain lion tracks were discovered all around your barn, and down by your creek. And it put some scratches mighty high up on your barn doors. Seems you had a big cat there last night."

Suddenly, it all came back to Sam. He half sat up in bed but then groaned when the sudden movement made his head burst with pain and nausea rushed into his stomach. Reuben put a hand on his shoulder and pushed him gently back onto his back. He felt weak as a baby, but he grabbed Reuben's wrist. "I remember! When I turned into the driveway, Ralph got jittery. Halfway up he wouldn't go any farther. I got out to lead him up, and the horses in the barn started screaming, and Ralph screamed and reared up. That's when I saw the cat! It had been in the shadows of the barnyard, and it ran out into the moonlight and looked right at me, maybe ten, fifteen feet away. I was never so scared!"

"I'll bet. That would frighten anyone."

"Ralph reared up, and—that's all I remember until I woke up here."

"Ralph must have caught you a glancing blow when he reared. Knocked you out. Good thing the cat decided you were all too loud and scary, and ran away."

Sam grabbed Reuben's sleeve. "Reuben! Are you sure it's gone? My animals!"

"It's long gone, don't worry. A trail camera caught it miles from there this morning. It's just passing through its territory and hoped for some mutton last night, would be my guess."

Sam couldn't help worrying about his horses and sheep. "Who's taking care of my place?"

"Some folks from the gmay. I promise you, everything is under control. All you need to do is recover your strength. Ah! Here are your pain meds. This may make you take a little nap, Sam. Don't fight it. Sleep is healing. I'll report to our friends and see you later, okay?"

Sam smiled weakly at Reuben and watched the nurse add something to his IV. Soon he began to notice his headache easing, and along with that came a comfortable, irresistible sleepiness. Heeding Reuben's advice, he let himself drift off, trusting Gott and his friends to take care of him and his farm.

As he fell asleep, he thought of Jane, out in the waiting room, and his final thoughts before sleep took him were hopeful ones.

CHAPTER FOURTEEN

"Ach, look at the bruises! And the bandage on his head! He has stitches. They had to shave some of his hair. Thank Gott he's going to be oll recht," Eliza whispered to her friends as they stood near Sam's bedside, gazing down at Sam, who was sound asleep.

Ben stood across from them on the other side of the bed, and it seemed to Jane that he was having trouble controlling his emotions.

And no wonder. None of us are accustomed to seeing our friend, who is so strong and able most of the time, helpless in a hospital bed.

One side of Sam's dear face was covered with a rainbow of bruises. And there was a bandage covering part of his forehead, where she'd been told he had a line of stitches where Ralph's sharp hoof had caught him. Jane reached over and caught Eliza's hand, holding it tightly for reassurance. "It's so hard to see him hurt like this!"

"But the doctors said he'll be okay," Ben said, raising his eyes to Jane and Eliza. "We have to cling to that. He looks bad, but he's going to be oll recht."

Since Sam's parents had passed away years ago and he was an only child, the nurses had allowed Abram and Lydia in to see him first. They'd only spent a couple of minutes in the room before returning to the waiting area and reporting what Reuben had already told them—that Sam was asleep but making progress and he'd be able to go home in a couple of days. In addition to their elders, only Jane, Eliza, and Ben would be permitted to see him that evening. He needed his rest, after all.

Hearing this, many of the concerned members of their community who had come to offer their support and prayers had gathered their things, praising Gott for delivering Sam from possible death, and after giving hugs and reassuring words to the young friends, they'd headed home to see to the evening chores.

"I'm going to Sam's place tonight to care for his animals," Ben said. "I'll stay there until he comes home. And maybe for a few days after, if he needs help."

Jane teared up. Ben was a much better friend to Sam than she was. Her breath hitched a bit, and Eliza squeezed her hand. "Now Jane, don't cry. He's going to be fine. You'll see—my big brother said so, and he's never wrong."

From where he was propped up in bed, eyes still closed, Sam croaked, "I sure hope so, because right now my head still feels as if someone's using it for horseshoe practice."

"Sam! You're awake!" Jane cried, dropping Eliza's hand. She moved closer to the bed and reached a trembling hand out to touch Sam's shoulder. He cracked his eyes open and looked up at her, swallowing painfully. "You're here. You came."

She nodded, tears trickling down her cheeks. Ben and Eliza looked at each other, and Ben took a step closer to the bed. "Sam, I'm so glad you're okay. I'm going to stay at your farm until you can come home to be sure everything is okay. Any instructions?"

Sam pulled his gaze from Jane's and looked at his best friend gratefully. "Nee, it's all common sense. Denki, Ben. I owe you."

"Nonsense. You'd do it for me." He squeezed Sam's shoulder and said, "I'll be back tomorrow after work. Tell the doctor your head hurts again." He looked at Eliza, who nodded.

"Good night, Sam. See you soon," she said, following Ben to the door. "We'll be in the waiting room when you're ready, Jane."

Jane nodded and turned back to Sam.

"Would you please give me some water?"

She looked around and spotted the tall plastic cup of water on a table near the bed. Condensation was beaded on its sides, and she grabbed a paper towel to dry it off so water wouldn't drip on Sam when he sipped the water.

After he had his fill, he handed the cup back to Jane. "Denki."

"You're welcome. Wait a minute." She pulled a chair close to the bedside and sat down, leaning forward and resting her arms on the side of the bed.

They stared at each other awkwardly for a bit, then both started to speak at once. Sam smiled. "We always do that. You first."

She nodded, unsmiling. "Sam, I'm so glad you didn't. . .didn't. . ." Helplessly she shook her head, a trembling hand pressed to her lips.

"Die?" He supplied helpfully, a wry smile tugging at his lips.

She let out her breath. "Ja, that! I realized when I heard what had happened that I'd been a fool. A huge fool!" She cast about for another paper towel to blot at the tears that were again escaping her reddened eyes.

"You?" He croaked. "I was the fool, Jane. I'm the one who coined that awful name. And I'm the one who didn't have the courage to tell you about it all these years."

"You were fourteen. I believe I can see how it happened. But I have a question, Sam."

"Anything."

"I just wondered if that nickname was the reason you would never talk to me all these years? If you had never made up that name, would things have turned out differently?"

He picked up the water and drank again. His eyes wandered the room a bit before coming back to hers. "Yes. I hate to think of all the time I've wasted! All these years, I couldn't bring myself to tell you what I'd done, because I didn't think I could stand it if you looked at me with hatred and unforgiveness when you found out."

He looked miserable and ashamed. She reached out tentatively and slipped her small hand into his large one. His eyes widened, and he looked at their joined hands then up at Jane's face. "Sam, I could never hate you. I've cared for you since we were kinner."

"I never knew," he admitted, his own eyes tearing up. "I've wasted so much time! If only I'd spoken to you back then, when I saw how that stupid nickname was hurting you. Would you have forgiven me?"

She tipped her head to the side, considering. "I think so, but I can't be certain I would have right away. It was really painful. The other kids called me Plain Jane for years. It's why I never dated. Who wanted to ask Plain Jane out on a buggy ride?"

Sam closed his eyes in dismay. "Ach, Jane, if I could take it back, go back to that day and make the boy I was look those other boys in the eyes and admit that, ja, I had a crush on Jane Bontrager—oh, I would do it. I promise you I would."

She grinned through her own tears. "Well, you can't go back and kick your younger self in the hinnerdale, but you can make up for lost time now."

"Really? It's not too late?"

"Nee Sam, it's not too late."

Before he could say anything else, a middle-aged nurse with neon orange hair bustled into the room. "How's the patient?" She hurried over, and Sam and Jane let go of one another's hands. Jane stood up and stepped quickly back from the bed, and the nurse took Sam's vitals. She gave him a good looking over and asked, "Does your head hurt?"

He nodded. "Ja, like men with jackhammers are trying to build a road through it."

She laughed. "That bad? Time for more meds. I'll ring for them." She looked at Jane. "I'm afraid it's time for your pretty friend to go home, though. Sorry, Miss, but this young man needs his beauty sleep."

Sam opened his mouth to argue, and the nurse raised her eyebrows. "Don't bother arguing, young man. Your friends can come back tomorrow. I'll give you one minute to say goodbye to your sweetheart."

With a saucy wink for Jane, she hurried out of the room, and Sam's eyes flew to Jane's. "I need to talk to you. There's so much more to say."

She gave his arm a reassuring squeeze. "I'll be back. I promise. After work tomorrow."

His eyes searched hers. "Promise?"

She nodded. "Ja, I promise. We have plenty of time to talk."

She turned to go, and he reached out and caught her hand. "Jane, wait. I have to know. Do you forgive me?"

"Oh, Sam, of course I do. And really, it's not all your fault. I could have done more to let you know I was interested in you instead of acting like a hermit." She smiled. "I'll see you tomorrow. Sleep well tonight."

"Now that all this is out in the open, I am so relieved," Sam said.

"Ja, me too. It's as if an enormous weight has been lifted from my shoulders." Impulsively she darted back to the bed, leaned over, and planted a gentle kiss on his forehead. His eyes widened and his mouth formed an O of amazement. She laughed delightedly.

"No more shy girl! Feel better, Sam!"

He grinned. "I do now!"

Jane giggled at her own audacity and left the room as the nurse returned with meds for his IV.

As she walked down the hallway to the waiting room to collect Ben and Eliza, she offered up a silent prayer. *Vader, denki for Sam's survival. And for what he just said to me. I know we're going to be oll recht now. Denki! Oh, denki!*

When she entered the waiting room, she was smiling. Now that they had aired the old hurts, everything would work out, she just knew it.

The following morning, Sam awoke to find a strange woman with beautiful burgundy braids piled high on her head taking his blood pressure. He blinked a couple of times to clear his eyes and then pushed himself up to a sitting position.

"What? Who?" he muttered as he looked around in confusion.

"Now just be still a minute while I take your blood pressure, Sam," the woman said, raising one arched eyebrow at him as she readjusted the cuff on his arm and began pumping it up again. He sat still, trying to recall whether he should know her, since she'd called him by name as if she knew him.

"Looks good," she said, writing something on a clipboard. Then she hung her stethoscope around her neck and smiled at him. "So how are you feeling this morning? Better than yesterday, I hope?"

He frowned, trying to figure out who she was and where he was. He looked around and realized he was in a hospital room.

And he had a headache that felt as if his whole herd of sheep were trampling across his brain.

"I'm sorry, but do I know you?"

Her dark eyebrows arched high. But then she chuckled. "You're joking with me, right, Sam?"

He shook his sore head slowly, and the smile slipped from her lips. "You don't remember being here yesterday?"

"I got here yesterday?" He took in the fact that he was in a bed, wearing a hospital gown. "I was here all night? I can't be here all night! I have a farm to take care of. My animals will be hungry!"

He swung his feet around and tried to get out of bed, and she placed a hand on his shoulder to stop him. "Now you just stay in that bed, Sam. You're hooked up to an IV in case you forgot. You'll hurt yourself."

"But my sheep. . ."

"Are being well cared for by some of the members of your community," she said, keeping her hand on his arm and reaching for the call button on his bed. She pressed it and coaxed him to slide back into the hospital bed before tucking the covers back around him. "In fact, I believe your friend Ben is staying at your place until you can go home. Do you remember Ben?"

"Of course I remember Ben! I'm not narrish!"

"I assume narrish means crazy. No, you're not crazy, Sam. But I am concerned that you're experiencing some memory loss." She glanced at the door as Reuben King walked in.

"Good morning, Nancy! How's our patient this morning?"

"Dr. King, good timing. Sam doesn't recall waking up here yesterday. He doesn't recall any of it."

Reuben frowned. "Hi, Sam. Do you remember me?"

"Of course I remember you! You're both acting as if I'm nuts. She wants me to believe I've been here since yesterday, but I clearly remember being at home yesterday, and going over to your sister's place, and driving Jane home. . . But then I went home last night. How could I have been here?"

He looked at them both, feeling the need to prove that they were wrong. But fear started gnawing at the edges of his bravado as they stood looking back at him, saying nothing.

"Reuben? What's going on?" Sam heard his voice come out sounding small and unfamiliar to his ears.

"Nancy, please get Dr. Seifer on the phone. I think we need to order a CT scan on Sam here. And depending on what that shows, possibly an MRI."

"Yes, Doctor." She left the room, and Reuben pulled up a chair and sat next to Sam's bed.

"I'm getting a little concerned here, Reuben," Sam said. "Why am I in the hospital? And why can't I remember?"

"You were kicked in the head by your horse the night before last, Sam. You were found unconscious yesterday morning and didn't regain consciousness until yesterday afternoon, indicating a severe brain injury. Now it appears you may have developed post-traumatic amnesia. I want to have a look at your brain, hence the CT scan. I feel your doctor will agree."

"Ralph kicked me? I can't remember!" Sam felt his headache increasing as his fear and frustration mounted, and Reuben reached out and pressed a hand over one of Sam's. "Sam, look at me."

Sam brought his eyes to Reuben's and saw reassurance and caring there. He took a deep breath and then another to try to calm down. "This is bad, ja?"

"Well, it's not good, but it isn't necessarily bad either," Reuben said. "These things are often unpredictable. We want to make sure you don't have any bleeding going on in your head. Barring that, you've got swelling. It should resolve in a few days, and the amnesia will also get better, though you might not remember what happened. But we can fill you in. You told us yesterday after you woke up."

"I. . .did?" He pulled his hand away and pressed his hands to his face. "I don't remember. Please tell me what I said."

Reuben filled Sam in on the horse's reluctance to go up the driveway, on Sam getting out to lead Ralph the rest of the way, on the big cat jumping out of the shadows of the barn and the horse rearing, and Sam's subsequent injury, exacerbated by lying outside all night in the cold. When he finished, Sam was amazed by the tale.

"That sounds like something you made up, Reuben," he said, hoping his friend would laugh and admit he was just pulling Sam's leg. But Reuben smiled wryly and shook his head. "I wish I had. But it all happened. The mountain lion is long gone according to authorities, and Ben Fisher is taking care of your farm and animals until you can get home. Any more questions?"

Sam shook his head. "Nee." He slid back down in the bed and closed his eyes, hoping if he slept a bit, he'd awake and either remember everything or find out it was all a bad dream. "I could use something for this headache, though. It's just awful."

"I know, Sam. We'll get you something. First I need to see what tests you're going to have. I'll be back soon. Rest, friend."

"Wait," Sam said before Reuben left the room.

His friend turned and looked at him inquiringly.

Sam swallowed and hoped he wouldn't sound too desperate. "Does Jane Bontrager know I was hurt?"

"Why, yes, and she was here all day yesterday. You two spoke for a while last night, in fact."

Sam felt hope at that news. "We did? So, she came to see me?"

"Ja, she did. In fact, my sister, Eliza, told me that Jane said the two of you had a good talk last night."

But I can't remember any of it! Did she forgive me? Ach, this is terrible!

"I wish I could remember," he murmured.

Reuben came back into the room. "Sam, there are no guarantees, but in my experience, people in your situation generally do eventually recover much of their memory. But not always, and not necessarily all."

"What am I going to say to Jane if she comes back, expecting me to remember what we talked about last night?"

"Just be honest, Sam. Tell her you don't remember."

Sam nodded glumly. "Ja. Sounds like some kind of ploy to renege on something."

Reuben laughed. "It would be a good one. I'd better go check on those tests and talk to Dr. Seifer if I can get hold of him. I'll be back soon."

Sam heard Reuben walking out of the room, and he allowed a couple of tears to escape his eyes.

Vader, what did I do to deserve this? Please let me heal. I just want to go home. I want to take care of my sheep and horses. I want my memory back. I want to know what Jane and I talked about last night! I'm afraid, Vader. And I'm all alone. Please help me.

He lay blinking at the ceiling, fighting his growing fear, before silently adding, *Your will be done.*

CHAPTER FIFTEEN

"It's almost closing time, Eliza! What time is our ride getting here?" Jane hurried to finish the last few dishes then tossed her kitchen apron into a hamper and took off her prayer kapp to remove her hairnet, which she tossed into the trash.

Hurrying to a small mirror on the kitchen wall, she straightened up her hair then replaced the kapp.

"There. Good as it gets!" She grinned at herself in the mirror. "And everything is going to be fine now!" With a little twirl that sent the skirts of her eggplant-purple dress swishing around her legs, she tossed her arms up into the air, beaming with newfound happiness. "I'm so happy Sam and I finally talked!" She cocked her head thoughtfully. "I could wish it hadn't taken so long, but better late than never! Okay, time to close up and head for Millersburg!"

She turned toward the door to the dining room and let out a little shriek of surprise when she saw Eliza leaning against the doorjamb, a smile playing around her lips.

"Please, don't stop dancing around and talking to yourself just because you noticed me. You were on a roll there!"

Heat climbed up Jane's face, and she planted her hands on her hips. "Why didn't you say something? You just let me go on and on!"

Eliza smoothed the skirt of her robin's-egg-blue dress and white apron, then raised mischievous eyes to her friend. "Well, I didn't want to interrupt! You were enjoying yourself."

Jane rolled her eyes. "Fine. Are you ready?"

"Ja, the driver will be here soon." Eliza handed Jane her cape and bonnet and swirled her own cape over her dress.

A horn tooted out front, and the women turned off the kitchen lights and hurried out through the dining room, only leaving one light on for Jane for when she returned later that night.

"Lydia, Abram, and Ben should already be in the van," Eliza said as they locked the door to the bakery and walked over to the vehicle.

Eliza opened the door and climbed into the back row with Ben, while Jane joined Lydia in the middle. Abram was up front with the driver. Soon they were on their way, and Jane could hardly wait to see Sam again. She prayed he hadn't suffered any setbacks since last night.

But we'll deal with whatever comes together. Now that we've talked to each other openly and honestly, there's nothing to keep us from getting to know each other and hopefully get married one day!

Lydia interrupted Jane's pleasant thoughts. "I hear Lizzie called home last night. I ran into her mudder today in the grocery store, and she said that Lizzie and John will leave Beeville tomorrow for Wisconsin. They're going to Dalton, which is a little northeast of Madison."

"Have you been there?" Jane realized she didn't know a great deal about Lydia's life.

"Nee, but I have family there, as do you. That's where your second cousins live. Their grandparents left here as young marrieds, and they've made a gut life for themselves there."

"I've heard Maem and Dat talk about them, but we've never met them."

"Well, your bruder and Lizzie can tell you all about them when they return in a couple weeks."

Jane nodded absentmindedly, and Lydia peered at her more closely. "Something has changed with you. Care to share with an old woman?"

Jane chuckled. "If I see an old woman, she can ask me. But I'll share with you." She told Lydia about her conversation with Sam the night before. The driver had the radio on, and country music was playing loudly enough that she didn't think anyone else would overhear them. And besides, Ben and Eliza were too engrossed in their own quiet conversation, heads close together in the back seat, to bother trying to listen in on anything Jane and Lydia said.

Jane looked eagerly at Lydia. "So? What do you think?"

"I think that sounds like a promising beginning. Your biggest hurdles were the fact that neither of you would talk to the other long enough to do more than say hello and goodbye." She rolled her eyes. "And of course, the fact that Sam had kept that silly secret for so long—long enough that it took on a life of its own and came between the two of you." She gave a satisfied nod. "Ja, I'm very glad he finally told you about that."

"Well, he wouldn't have if that Daniel Beechy from Wisconsin hadn't spilled the beans first!"

Lydia's eyebrows rose. "He did? How did that happen?"

Lydia already knew about Jane's secret admirer, so Jane updated her. "So it turned out that Sam was my secret admirer!"

Lydia smiled knowingly. "I am not surprised by that. The young man has always been too shy and too clever for his own good! Trust him to concoct a scheme like that!"

"Well, I got a third note but not a third gift..." Jane explained about how the new secret admirer, posing as the first one, had set up a meeting and had turned out to be Daniel Beechy.

"You don't say!" Lydia exclaimed. "I know his grandparents. They would not be amused by such behavior."

Jane thought about how lonely Daniel had looked as they drove away with Little Mouse, leaving him standing in his dark driveway with no friends and no cat. She felt kind of bad for him. "Lydia, maybe don't tell them about this."

"Nee?"

Jane shook her head. "I think we should let him settle in a bit more and see if he's learned his lesson. Maybe he's not so bad. Maybe he's just lonely."

"So, are you thinking about letting him court you after all?" Lydia's eyes twinkled teasingly, and Jane laughed. "Nee, but I don't want word of his very awkward beginning here getting back to his home folks. I have a feeling he'll come around and behave better. People can be remarkably narrish when they're all alone in a strange place, can't they?"

"That they can." Lydia paused a moment and glanced up front. Then she leaned in closer to Jane and spoke in a quiet voice. "You'll never guess what Abram is up to."

Jane leaned in closer to her friend and whispered, "What?"

An odd look crossed Lydia's face—a mixture of exasperation and reluctant enjoyment. "He's decided since I won't marry him, he's going to court me. He asked me out to dinner and gave me a gift!"

Jane clapped her hands and laughed out loud, attracting the attention of the others. "Sorry, sorry, just something Lydia told me." She leaned in close again. "Sorry, I'll be quieter. What did he give you?"

"The most darling little cat water fountain!" Lydia whispered a bit breathlessly. "It's the perfect gift. I don't want any dust catchers sitting around my house, and at my age I don't need candy, goodness knows. But a gift for my cats?" She sat back and shook her head in wonder. "Well, that just about knocked me flat. It was so thoughtful. And Hepzibah and Zed can't leave it alone. They're acting like kittens again, playing in the water. Zed has a little woolen mouse he's taken to dropping into the water and then fishing it out, over and over. I'm afraid it'll mildew because it's never dry!" She chuckled, and Jane thought it was very interesting that Abram had purchased Lydia the exact same thing Sam had given her—truly the perfect gift for a cat lover. But she decided not to mention it to Lydia. She didn't want to take any of the shine off the gift by letting on that Abram probably hadn't come up with the idea all on his own. And what did it matter? He'd made Lydia very happy. And if Jane didn't miss her guess, the cagey old bishop was making real inroads into Lydia's reluctance to remarry.

"What a wonderful gift!" Jane gushed. "So thoughtful. He must really care for you, Lydia."

Lydia blushed a pretty shade of pink. "Well," she said. "Hmm. Ah! We're almost at the hospital!" She busied herself gathering up her things, and Jane felt butterflies take flight in her stomach at the thought of seeing Sam again now that they'd sort of, kind of, come to an understanding. They were dating, weren't they? Or would be when he was well again. She heaved a sigh. She wasn't exactly certain what they were. But whatever it was, it was better than what they'd been before!

They pulled up to the front doors of the hospital and slowed to a stop.

"What time would you like me to come back for you?" The driver, a middle-aged Englisch man named Ned who always seemed to have on a colorful, patterned sweater, looked at Abram, who glanced back at Lydia.

"Visiting hours end at eight, right?" Lydia asked. "So how's eight?"

"Fine with me," the bishop said, "as long as we plan to eat dinner here. The restaurant is pretty gut, and I'm hungry."

"I could go for some food," Ben chimed in from the back. So it was agreed that Ned would collect them at eight, and they all piled out of the van and into the lobby of the hospital.

"It's almost six," Ben said, looking at a clock on the wall. "I vote we eat first and go see Sam after."

The others agreed, except for Jane, who couldn't imagine eating a thing before assuring herself that Sam was no worse off than he'd been the previous evening.

"I'm not really hungry. You guys eat and I'll see you upstairs."

They teased her good-naturedly and walked off down the hallway leading to the cafeteria. Jane stood a moment watching them go before turning and studying the window displays outside the small gift shop.

Sam had given her several very thoughtful gifts, and she'd never given him anything. She thought she could find something he'd like in the little shop.

She pushed through the door and inhaled the heady scent that came from the multitude of flower arrangements on display. She wandered around the store, considering and rejecting a number of items. Finally, she decided on a single sunflower bloom and a bag of dark chocolate candies. Having hoarded little facts about Sam nearly all her life, she knew he loved dark chocolate. And the sunflower was just cheerful.

Jane took her purchases up the elevator to Sam's floor and stepped out near the nurses' station. She recognized the woman with the beautiful braids from the day before and smiled at her. The nurse's eyes widened a bit, but she was talking to someone else on the telephone and couldn't say anything to Jane.

"That's all right, I remember where Sam's room is," she reassured the nurse before turning to walk down the hall. She thought the woman's expressive brown eyes indicated that she wanted to say something, but Jane was too impatient to see Sam to wait and find out what that might be. She hurried down the hall, and when she came to Sam's door, it was partly closed.

Suddenly feeling unsure of herself, she chewed on a thumbnail a bit before deciding the thing to do was to knock softly in case Sam was sleeping. She didn't want to wake him, but she had to do something to let him know she was there.

Using the knuckles of two fingers, she rapped softly on the door. A faint call of, "Come in" reassured her that Sam was awake, and she pushed the door open a bit and called, "It's me, Jane. May I come in?"

Silence greeted her request, then Sam called, "Sure, come on in, Jane."

She thought he sounded odd, and an uneasy feeling gripped her as she pushed the door open and stepped into the room, leaving the door open behind her.

Sam was sitting up in bed, and her first thought was that the bruising was worse today, which was to be expected. Then she looked into Sam's lovely eyes and was taken aback by the caution she saw there.

Did he regret their conversation last night? Had she spent the day rejoicing at what she saw as their newfound understanding while Sam spent it regretting that they'd moved so fast?

"Nice flower," he said, noticing the sunflower sticking out of a blue glass vase clutched in her hand. She glanced down at it blankly for a moment then remembered she'd bought it for him.

"Oh, I just thought it looked so happy, and it might cheer you up since you're stuck in here when I know you'd rather be home on your farm." She walked forward and set it on his little table by the bed. He blinked at it then raised solemn eyes to Jane's.

"Denki, Jane, it's really pretty."

Recalling the chocolates, she reached into her purse and pulled out the bag, handing it to him. "I got you some candy too. Dark chocolate. Your favorite, I recall."

He accepted the bag and frowned at it. "You remember my favorite kind of candy?"

Feeling embarrassed, she nodded mutely. "Well, ja. I've sort of made it a point to remember things about you over the years, Sam," she admitted. "But not in a creepy way!"

A small smile raised one corner of his lips. "Of course not. You couldn't be creepy. Denki, Jane. I love the chocolate and the flower. That was really considerate of you."

She shrugged. "I wanted to give you something since you gave me all those nice gifts for the cats when you were being my secret admirer."

He raised his eyes to hers, and she thought again that he looked strange. "So, you're not still angry about that?"

She frowned. This wasn't right. Hadn't they settled all this the night before? "Nee, Sam, I get why you did all that. It was silly but also kind of endearing and adorable. I liked it."

"What about the other thing?" he whispered.

"Other thing?" She cast about for his meaning; then it dawned. "The nickname?"

He nodded silently, and it was as if he were holding his breath, waiting for her answer. "Sam, we talked all this out last night, don't you remember? I forgive you for the silly nickname. That was a long time ago, and we were both really still kinner."

He brushed a finger along a soft yellow flower petal before looking her in the eye. "The thing is, Jane, I don't remember. I'm sorry."

"What do you mean you don't remember? We sat right here and talked about everything! How the nickname Plain Jane followed me around for years, and how you were so sorry you'd made it up trying to convince your friends you didn't like me. Remember?"

He shook his head and then winced as the motion apparently caused him pain. "Nee. I'm so sorry, but I seem to have lost an entire day from my memory."

Her jaw dropped and she cried plaintively, "But, you seemed fine yesterday. How is that even possible?"

He started to shrug but winced again and sighed. "I woke up this morning thinking it was two days ago; the day after I drove you home and we argued, and you told me you didn't want to see me for a while. I can't remember anything about yesterday, or about the night before after I pulled into my driveway and Ralph shied at something."

"The mountain lion," she whispered.

"So they tell me. But I can't remember. And I don't know if there's any point going all through it again now. They ran some tests on my head today, and there's swelling in my brain. It's possible I could wake up again tomorrow morning and forget everything that happened today, including this conversation, again." He stared at her, unsmiling. She reached out and took one of his hands in hers.

"Sam, that's really scary. I hope that doesn't happen again. But if it does, I'll remind you what we talk about. And I'll tell you what I heard happened to you again if necessary. I'll tell you every morning until you remember for yourself. After what we've both gone through to finally find the courage to talk honestly with each other, and to share how we feel about each other, I'm not going to let us backslide just because a mountain lion scared your horse into kicking you in the head. That may sound callous, but I refuse to lose you again, Samuel Mast!" She grimaced as she realized her voice had risen steadily during this speech until she was nearly shouting. "Sorry," she whispered.

He reached out with his free hand and gently wiped her face, and she became aware that tears were rolling down her cheeks. "Oh, sis yuscht! I'm sorry to get emotional."

He chuckled. "Don't worry, I've been pretty emotional myself the last few days—I mean, as far as I can remember." He gave her his old, wry grin and she returned it in full.

"Sam, it's going to be oll recht. Gott will bring you through this, you'll see. So far you've only lost one day and one important conversation. We can have that conversation again when you feel better. And meanwhile, I'm not going anywhere. You just try to get rid of me!"

He looked a little less lost, she thought, as he reached out with his free hand and caught her other hand and then gave both hands a squeeze. "Denki, Jane. I don't deserve you."

She smiled impishly and returned his squeeze. "Oh, I think you do, Sam. And you may get sick of me and regret telling me you care for me."

He shook his head. "Never." He gave her another little grin. "Even if I only have your word for it that I told you that."

She gasped in mock outrage, and he managed a small laugh. He moved his thumbs over her hands, and she felt a huge upswelling of happiness. "I'll hold you to that."

Before they could say any more, the room was suddenly filled with people and noise as Lydia, Abram, Ben, and Eliza crowded inside. Jane released Sam's hands and stepped back, turning to look at their friends.

"We're back from dinner!" Eliza announced. "And we figured you'd be hungry after talking to Sam, so we brought you some food!"

Jane saw that each of her friends was holding something for her, and her eyes misted a bit at their thoughtfulness.

"Denki," she sniffed. "I am hungry. But before I eat, there's something you need to know."

Sam was grateful that Jane was there to tell their friends about his memory loss. His head still hurt, and he didn't think he had another explanation in him.

Jane's broken voice as she explained what had happened nearly undid him, as did the shocked expressions on the faces of Ben, Eliza, Abram, and Lydia.

"Ach, Samuel, that's no gut!" Ben sputtered, looking as if he wished he knew who to complain to about this latest twist in Sam's recent health journey.

"What are they doing about this?" Abram asked, putting a hand on Ben's arm and giving it a reassuring squeeze.

Sam took a sip of water and swallowed before answering. "They say I just have to go on and hope for the best. The swelling isn't life threatening, and as long as it doesn't get any worse, I should start to see improvement in a couple of days. Or a couple of weeks. They aren't sure."

"What if the swelling does get worse?" Lydia asked, sitting on the chair near the bed. "How will they know?"

"I would have symptoms," Sam told her. "Seizures, trouble breathing—noticeable things that would alert them."

"But what could they do about it?" Eliza whispered.

"There are things that could be done, if necessary, but I recommend against borrowing trouble," a voice said from the doorway where Dr. Reuben King had entered in time to hear the end of their conversation. He moved through the small crowd in Sam's room and smiled at Sam.

"So, how are you this evening, Sam?"

"About the same. I don't think I've forgotten anything I've been told today." He gave a tiny, helpless shrug. "But then, how would I know?"

Reuben gave him a smile in return. "You'll just have to sleep on it tonight and see what you remember in the morning. But even if you forget some things again, don't despair. That's normal with a brain injury like yours. You took a really hard hit to the head. Give it a little time."

Sam frowned as the phrase "Give it a little time" rang a bell somewhere in his head. But he couldn't retrieve it, and it made his head hurt to try to force it. So he let it go.

"Okay, I guess that's all I can do, then," he said. "So, since there's really nothing else that you guys can do for me here, can I go home soon?"

Reuben chuckled sympathetically. "I understand that it's boring in here and you'd rather be home. But you couldn't do any farmwork yet anyhow, or build buggies. You need rest for a couple weeks before you can get back to your normal life."

"But my business! My animals!" Sam sat up straighter, seriously worried about his livelihood.

Ben cleared his throat dramatically. "Ahem. I can't build buggies, but I promise you I know perfectly well how to care for a few horses and a herd of ugly sheep."

Everyone laughed at that, but Sam felt anxious. If a mountain lion had tried to get at his sheep, what was going to protect them if it came back? Or some other predator? Ben wasn't a farmer, not really.

"Ben, I know you are doing your best, but you don't know all their routines. And what if coyotes attack? Or a bear? Or a pack of dogs? Or another lion?"

"Sounds like you need a couple of herd protectors," Lydia said, sending a secret smile to Abram, who nodded and left the room saying he'd be right back.

Sam wondered what that was about, but he was too worried to pay much attention. "Ja, I know. But I can't look for one while I'm laid up in here." He squeezed his eyes shut against increasing pain and rubbed his forehead below the stitches.

"Time for more pain meds, I think," Reuben said. "I'll be right back. Oh, but first. . ." He went to the sink and got a clean washcloth, wet it with cold water, and handed it to Jane. "If you press this to his forehead, it'll help with the pain." He smiled at her and left the room. Jane turned to Sam and held out the cold, damp washcloth.

"Um, do you want me to do this? Or would you rather hold it yourself?"

"Oh, I think he's too weak to hold his arm up in the air for long, Jane," Ben said. Sam saw Eliza nod vigorously. "You'd better do it."

Jane bit her lip and moved to the side of the bed and leaned awkwardly over Sam to press the cloth to his forehead and eyes.

"I think you should sit on the side of the bed, Jane," Eliza opined. "It'll be more comfortable for both of you."

At Jane's look of doubt, Eliza and Ben nodded. Lydia smiled and said, "Go ahead, Jane. It'll be much easier. Hurry now before the cold wears off."

So Jane sat on the bed beside Sam, her hip pressing against his leg through the blankets, and placed the cool cloth over his eyes and forehead. Sam felt himself relaxing as the soothing coolness seeped into his skin and the pain in his head dwindled. After a couple of minutes the cloth wasn't cool anymore, and he was about to tell Jane she could remove it when he heard a commotion in the room.

At Eliza's, Lydia's, and Jane's gasps and cries of, "Oh, how cute!" and "Look at how adorable they are!" he pushed Jane's hand away so he could see what was going on.

Ruth and Jonas Hershberger, old friends of his and Jane's, stood in the door, a beaming Abram Troyer behind them. And they were each holding a small, squirming bundle of white fur, big smiles on their faces as they looked in at Sam.

"Hey, Sam!" Jonas said. "Is this a gut time? We brought you someone to meet!"

Sam's mouth fell open as he realized Jonas and Ruth were each holding a Great Pyrenees puppy. Lydia was shooing them into the room, and Jane got up and moved to stand on the other side of the bed, followed by Eliza and Ben.

"Oh, Ruth, they're so precious!" Jane cooed.

"Can I hold one?" Eliza begged, reaching for the puppy Ruth was holding. Ruth handed it over and looked at Sam while Eliza and Jane fussed over the puppy.

"I heard from a little birdie named Lydia that you needed some fierce protectors for your sheep herd," she said, smiling at Sam. "And the timing is gut, because my Heftig just became a mama again. As it happens, these two pups are available to the right home."

Sam's eyes felt as wide as saucers, as if he'd reverted to boyhood, when he'd desperately wanted a dog but couldn't have one as he'd been raised in town above his uncle's buggy shop after his parents died, and there wasn't room for a big dog in their cramped house.

"What qualifies as the right home?"

Ruth, lovely in a green dress that set off her red hair peeking from beneath her prayer kapp, tapped a finger to her chin. "Hmm. They'd do best on a farm, with animals to herd." She grinned at him. "I think you've got all that, ja?"

He nodded. "Ja, I do. They'd have plenty of room to roam, and I have a growing herd of Tunis sheep."

"And they need a person who will love them and take gut care of them. That means spending time and possibly money on seeing them properly trained, and on veterinary care. These pups are brother and sister. I'll require you to neuter them both, as you don't need to be breeding them. Would you agree to all that?"

He wondered if he'd lost his mind. Was he really going to agree to buy a pair of puppies he'd have to learn to train, that wouldn't be big enough to defend anything for a couple of years yet? He felt a smile breaking out on his face. Ja, you bet he was!

"I promise to do all that, Ruth. I've always wanted a big dog. And two are even better. I'll learn to train them, and keep up on their vet care. And I have no desire to breed dogs, so your stipulation about neutering is fine too."

"Well, then, I think we can come to an agreement."

"How much do you want for them?"

Jonas stepped forward, the pup he held squirming to get down. He handed it to Sam, who gasped as the little guy—he thought it was a guy—plopped his bum down on Sam's stomach and looked into Sam's face, tongue lolling and eyes full of mischief and friendliness.

"Oh, he's really cute," Sam murmured, stroking the small animal's head gently. He looked at Jonas and Ruth. "I'm not sure I can afford them, though."

"Sure you can!" Jonas beamed. "We want to barter with you for a discount on a new, bigger buggy. It turns out that we're going to need it soon." He gave his wife, Ruth, a loving look and she smiled softly back at him before looking around at her friends, all of whom looked delighted at the news.

"Well, then, I think we can work something out," Sam said. "But I'm going to need something else for now. These two won't be able to scare off any predators for a while."

"We have that covered too," Ben said. "We've rented a pair of llamas for you." He looked ridiculously pleased with himself. "They're already out at your place hanging with the sheep."

Sam blinked. "A pair of what?"

"Llamas! They're great herd protectors! And they'll just hang out with the sheep, going inside and outside with them and eating grass and—whatever else llamas eat." Ben shrugged.

"You got me some rental llamas?" Sam said, to be sure he hadn't misheard.

"Yep. And the best part is, they're rent to own. If you like them, you pay them off and keep them. And unlike the pups, you can breed these two, as they're a mated pair."

Sam sat back. "Huh. Rental llamas. I guess that works." He looked at the pups, growing sleepy now, and stroked the little male in his lap. "And I'm excited about these pups. When can they come live with me?"

"They're six weeks old now. They need to stay with mama for another four to six weeks, and then I recommend we send them to basic obedience school. You'll have to go for the last week, nightly, to learn how to keep up their training."

"I can do that."

"Oh, my goodness, what is going on in here?" Nurse Nancy came into the room and took in the scene with a quick sweep of her eyes. "Are those dogs in my hospital room? Is that a dog sitting on my patient? Are you trying to contaminate his wound?"

Ruth quickly swept the pup off Sam's lap, despite Sam's protest, and backed toward the door. "Sorry! We thought they would cheer him up. These are his puppies!"

The nurse pursed her lips, but Sam saw the twinkle in her eyes. "Okay, you've cheered him up. Now it's time for you all to go. He needs his meds and his rest. Come back tomorrow. Without the dogs." She crossed her arms and looked narrowly at each of Sam's visitors.

"Will do," Jonas said. "Gut to see you, Sam. Feel better!"

He and Ruth and the pups disappeared into the hallway, followed by Abram and Lydia. "We'll see you tomorrow, Sam!" Lydia called.

Ben smiled winningly at the nurse, who gave him a look that said she wasn't going to be charmed. He looked at Sam and waggled his eyebrows. "Well, I guess it's time for us to go. Eliza and I will just head on downstairs with Lydia and Abram. You can say good night to Jane and send her down. Don't take too long, Jane. I think the driver will be here pretty soon."

Sam couldn't believe their visit had passed so quickly. He looked at Jane and grabbed her hand. "Denki for the flower and chocolate, Jane. And. . .please come back tomorrow. Hopefully I'll remember . . ." He glanced at the nurse, who seemed to be busying herself with little tasks to give them a semblance of privacy. "Hopefully I'll remember everything! You can refresh my memory tomorrow, about our talk."

She squeezed his hand and smiled tenderly at him. "I'll be here." She stood and picked up her cape from the back of the chair. "Gut night!"

"Gut night!" He watched her leave and then sighed when she was out of sight.

"So, is that your sweetheart?" The nurse took his vitals, and he said, "I think so. We'll see if I remember that in the morning."

She smiled at him compassionately. "I'm praying for you, Sam. Don't lose hope. God has you covered. Now I need to go see where those pain meds are. I'll be back."

She bustled out, and Sam reflected on her words. "Gott does have me covered," he murmured.

"Vader," he prayed, "please let me remember everything that happened today when I wake up tomorrow. I really want to remember talking to Jane. And speaking of that, denki for Jane. And for all my friends. Rented llamas!" He chuckled. "And the pups are perfect. Denki for everything, Vader. This has been pretty hard, but I know You've got me covered, as the nurse said." He sat there for a few seconds, just feeling grateful that he wasn't alone in life, that he had friends who cared, and a Father in heaven who cared. "Vader, Your will be done."

CHAPTER SIXTEEN

"I can't believe Sam finally gets to go home today! I'm almost as excited as he is!" Jane peered impatiently out the window of the van they'd hired to pick Sam up from Pomerene Hospital. It was the following Sunday afternoon. There had been church services that morning, and after lunch Jane, Eliza, Ben, Lydia, and Abram had called Ned to take them to Millersburg to bring Sam home.

Jane sat back and huffed. "I feel like a little kid, wanting to ask my maem, 'Are we there yet?'"

"Ten more minutes, kid," Ned, their driver, answered from up front, making them all laugh.

"I think if he had to spend one more night he would have staged a breakout," Ben called from the back seat where he sat with Eliza.

Jane agreed and glanced back to exchange grins with Eliza while pretending not to notice that she and Ben were holding hands. She smiled to herself. *I bet there's going to be a wedding next fall!*

"It will be gut to get back to a normal routine," Jane said, facing front again. "All this running back and forth to Millersburg after work every day is cutting into my sleep!"

"Sam won't be able to do normal tasks for at least another week," Lydia reminded everyone from her seat beside Jane. "Ben, you're staying with him for another week, ain't so?"

"Ja, whether he likes it or not!"

"I know he's grateful for all you've done to take care of his farm and his animals this past week, Ben," Jane pointed out. "But you can't blame him for wanting to go home."

"It's not that he doesn't trust you," Abram put in from the front seat.

"He just trusts himself more!" Ben laughed.

"Ach, here we are!" Lydia said, gathering up her things. She leaned forward and asked Ned if he could just wait for them as they wouldn't be long.

"Sure, I figured since you're here to pick him up I'd just go park in the free lot, and someone can call or text when you're ready to go."

They all looked at each other blankly, and Ned asked, "Does anyone have a phone?"

"Nee, it seems not," Eliza said. "But we can call from the room phone before we head downstairs."

"Ja, that works!" Abram said. "I've got your card in my wallet, Ned. I'll call when we're ready."

"That works." Ned pulled up to the door and moseyed around to pull the little steps out of the back and set them by the van door to make it easier for Lydia in back, then Abram in front, to descend. The others didn't need them, so he stowed them in the back then waved and drove off.

Jane paused, looking up at the hospital windows gleaming in the chilly November sunshine. Sam was in there, waiting for them. Waiting for her. She shivered a bit from nerves and excitement. Eliza slipped her hand into Jane's. "*Naerfich*?"

Jane looked sheepishly at her friend and squeezed her hand. "I am a little nervous." She laughed at herself. "I don't know why."

"I have a feeling everything is going to be oll recht, Jane." Eliza squeezed her friend's hand back and got a grateful smile.

Abram glanced back at them from the door, which he was holding open. Lydia was already inside. "Coming?"

"Ja, denki," Jane said, hurrying forward, the breeze blowing her cape back to reveal her new red dress and crisp white apron. She'd somehow found the time to sew both during the past week between working at the bakery and visiting Sam every evening, so she'd have something extra nice to wear for his homecoming.

Ben followed the women, taking the door from Abram so the older man could go inside.

They all walked to the elevator and rode up to Sam's floor. When the elevator doors opened, Eliza cried, "Reuben! What are you doing here? We're here to bust Sam out!"

Reuben King had apparently been waiting for the elevator. He grinned and gave his little sister a hug. "I know. Sam told me. I've just seen him. He's dressed and ready to go, sitting in the chair in his room checking the time every two or three minutes and driving the nurses nuts."

"You've got that right!" Nancy called from the desk where she was busy charting another patient. "Take that man home and let him see that his precious endangered Tunis sheep are safe, please! I might just have to drive out there and see these miraculous sheep. And the watch-llamas I've heard tell about."

They all smiled at Nancy, who had become a friend during the past week and more that Sam had spent in the hospital.

"They're all safe and accounted for," Ben said. "He'll soon be able to see for himself."

"Well, thank heaven for that!"

"Denki for all you've done for Sam, and please pass our thanks to everyone else here," Jane said shyly.

The older woman smiled at her. "It's been a pleasure. I'll see you in a minute with a wheelchair. I know our boy isn't going to want to ride in it, but it's hospital rules."

They headed down the hall to Sam's room, and when they reached it, Sam jumped up from the chair by the window.

"Finally! I thought you'd never get here!" He started to gather up his things, but Nurse Nancy entered the room pushing a wheelchair, with an orderly following behind her with an empty cart.

He frowned fiercely at Nancy. "I can walk down on my own. I don't need a wheelchair."

She put her hands on her hips. "We talked about this, Sam. It's hospital policy. If you don't get in the chair, you don't leave."

"Come on, Sam, we've got a nice dinner ready for you," Eliza cajoled her friend, who looked at her suspiciously.

"I made lasagna, and Ben made a salad. Lydia and Jane both contributed things. It's going to be appenditlich! But if it gets cold, it gets yucky. So come on and get into the chair."

Sam groused, but he reluctantly sat in the wheelchair. The orderly with the cart loaded up his flower arrangements, backpack, books, and other odds and ends.

"Ready?" Nancy asked. Everyone was, so they all trooped to the elevator and rode down joking and laughing. Jane managed to stand next to Sam, and she gave him a special smile when nobody else was looking at them. She leaned down and whispered, "It's so gut that you're going home!"

He returned her smile. "Oh, ja. I'm more than ready!"

Sam hadn't suffered any further memory loss after that first day. A week later his tests had looked normal, and he was allowed to go home with strict instructions on what he could and could not do for the next week. Ben had promised to make sure Sam followed the doctor's orders with a gleeful expression in his eyes.

After a week, Sam would get checked out one more time, and assuming all was progressing well, he would be released from Dr. Seifer's care. And Jane knew it wasn't a minute too soon for Sam, who was very impatient to at least be back in his own home even if he wouldn't be permitted to do any real work yet. She figured he'd enjoy bossing Ben around. And Ben would enjoy reciprocating.

Soon they were out front and the van was already waiting. Nurse Nancy gave Sam and Ben some last-minute instructions and handed Sam a discharge packet. They loaded Sam's things into the back, and Ben and Eliza piled into the back of the van, followed by Lydia and Jane, leaving the seat by the door for Sam.

Nancy locked the wheels of the chair, and Sam stood to his full height, towering over the nurse. "All this time, I thought you were taller!" he joked, giving her a saucy grin.

"Ha! That's because you were usually looking up at me from your bed, lazy bones! Now give me a hug, and promise not to get kicked by any more horses."

He gave Nancy a big hug, and she waited while he climbed into the van and strapped his seat belt before turning to follow the orderly inside. Abram climbed into the front, and Ned closed the door, picked up the steps, and loaded them into the back. And they were on their way to Sam's farm.

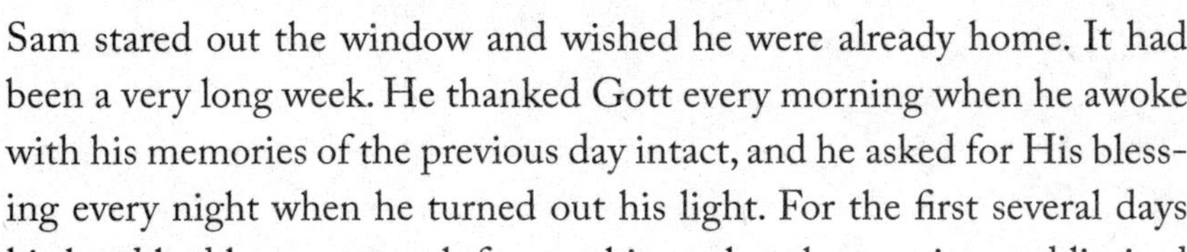

Sam stared out the window and wished he were already home. It had been a very long week. He thanked Gott every morning when he awoke with his memories of the previous day intact, and he asked for His blessing every night when he turned out his light. For the first several days his head had hurt too much for anything other than resting and limited talking with friends.

But after that, his headache got progressively better until he was able to spend a little time each night before bed reading from his Bible, searching for favorite scripture passages that reassured him that everything would be oll recht.

Toward the end of the week, he got so bored he began watching television, and he found that while he enjoyed a few of the programs, most were pretty silly.

When a nurse told him about the Hallmark Channel, he discovered he really liked the movies—all love stories with family-friendly plots that he and Jane had enjoyed together a couple of evenings when she visited. He found himself wishing for a happily-ever-after ending with Jane like the ones they watched on television. And he began planning to make it happen. Today she would see his place for the first time. He couldn't wait to see what she thought about it!

The farm finally came into view, and Sam felt himself practically vibrating with eagerness to be on his own land and to share it with Jane.

The van pulled up to his front door, and the driver went around to open the door, but Sam couldn't wait. He threw the door open and jumped out; then he just walked a few feet away, closed his eyes, and breathed the good country air. He offered Gott a silent prayer for bringing him home.

Seeing that their master had finally arrived home, the horses all ran to the fence of their paddock, whinnying their welcomes.

"Ach, it's so gut to be home!" Sam choked up then walked to the fence to pet his horses and give himself a minute to get his emotions under control.

Jane joined him at the fence and slipped her hand into his. He held on tight, struggling to get himself under control. She said nothing, just offered silent comfort for which he was grateful. Millie, Ralph, and the Belgians vied for his attention.

"Sorry, guys, I have no treats for you right now. But I'll come out later with some carrots." He scratched them all on the noses and then, feeling that he had mastered his emotions, squeezed Jane's hand before releasing it and turning to face his friends. The van was gone. He hadn't noticed it driving off. He wondered who had paid the fee, thinking he'd need to reimburse them.

"Denki for standing by me and helping me through this," he said. "You're the best friends a man could possibly have."

Everyone looked a tiny bit embarrassed, and Sam sort of wished he'd kept his heartfelt thanks to himself. He looked at Ben in desperation—*Do something to get us out of this!*

Ben and Eliza looked at each other and seemed to come to some kind of understanding. She nodded at him and Ben cleared his throat. "So, since it's true that we are all very gut friends, and gut friends share with each other, Eliza and I have something to share with all of you."

Sam's eyes widened as he heard his best friend's words; could it be? Could Ben and Eliza have found what everyone hopes in their secret heart to find one day?

Ben smiled at Sam and then looked at Eliza, holding his hand out to her. She took it and drew close to Ben's side, an incandescent glow of pure happiness radiating from her. They stared at each other for a few moments until Abram cleared his throat, awakening the young couple to the fact that there were others present.

"Ach!" Ben said. "Right, so Eliza and I want to share with you all that we've decided to marry next fall!"

Lydia and Jane exclaimed in delight, hurrying to hug the engaged couple, and Abram said something about not being blind. Ben's eyes met Sam's, and he tilted his head a bit, clearly asking for Sam's blessing.

Sam snapped himself out of his momentary jealousy spiral and allowed himself to feel Ben and Eliza's joy; his heart filled with it and his grin was authentic. He went forward and pulled Ben into a bear hug, thumping him on the back before turning to Eliza and giving her a gentler embrace. "I am completely overjoyed for both of you. You deserve each other and all the happiness in the world."

"Denki," Eliza sniffed. Ben handed her a handkerchief, and she blew her nose before saying, "See? He's so handy to have around! Of course I have to marry him!"

"My secret plan to win her heart included being a handy guy," Ben quipped.

"Well, you always say all your plans work out, so I guess I didn't stand a chance," Eliza joked back.

"Not all his plans work out!" Sam said. "Ask him about the pie thing sometime!"

"What's the pie thing?" Jane asked.

"I'll tell you about it sometime," Sam promised.

"Well, my plans usually work out, and the pie thing really doesn't count. It wasn't my fault."

"Tell us about the pie thing!" Eliza demanded.

"Another time, I promise," Ben said, throwing a mock scowl at Sam.

Lydia and Abram looked at each other, and Sam saw a private message passing between the two elders. Lydia beamed and said, "Well, not to steal your thunder, youngies, but Abram and I are also going to take the plunge!"

"She gave in! Just couldn't resist me!" Abram said, beaming around proudly at everyone.

They all laughed and congratulated the older couple, and Lydia gave him a mock scowl. "Gave in, my foot! I weighed my options and the pros and cons and made an informed decision."

She looked at the gathered group of friends. "Come, let's go sit on the porch for a spell, and I'll tell you about it. An old woman gets tired standing around for too long!"

Sam suspected Lydia's aim was actually for him to take a seat, and since he was getting a bit tired, he went along with it. The group moved to the porch and took seats, and Sam said, "I'll go in and get everyone some lemonade—if I have any, that is."

He frowned, realizing he had no idea what was currently in his refrigerator or pantry, and Ben said, "Aha! His first attempt at slipping past the doctor's orders. You all witnessed it! Nee, Sam. You sit down and Eliza and I will get lemonade."

Seeing no way out of it and realizing it was going to be a long week,

Sam complied. Eliza went inside followed by Ben, and soon they returned with glasses and a pitcher of icy lemonade, which they shared all around. When everyone had a drink, Eliza took a seat and Ben leaned on the porch rail.

"Let's hear your story," Jane asked, voicing what everyone wanted to hear, Sam suspected.

"Well then," Lydia said, "I agreed to marry Abram if he would agree to get the knee replacement he's been putting off for years now." Abram groused a bit, and Lydia patted him on the knee. "He'll stay with me in the dawdi haus at Ruth and Jonas' farm until we can build a new, larger dawdi haus on his farm so his son and his family can move into the big house. It should all work out very well."

She sat back, smiling approvingly at Abram, who shrugged and looked at Sam and Ben. "What choice do I have? The woman refused to marry me unless I get the knee replacement and agree to all her terms! And I realized that if I want to enjoy her cinnamon rolls for the rest of my life, I was going to have to give in."

"A limited supply of cinnamon rolls, Abram," Lydia said.

"We'll negotiate," Abram said, sending a twinkling look at Sam, which reminded him of their earlier conversation.

Huh. Abram was the first one to have gut news after all. Sam snuck a look at Jane, who was chatting animatedly with the other women, probably about wedding plans, and wondered whether the time was ripe to see if he could make it three for three—three couples planning weddings, that is.

"We're going to get married next month, before Christmas," Lydia confided. "What's the point of waiting at our age?"

Abram nodded. "Right. Someone recently told me I don't have time to waste."

He looked at Lydia. "Speaking of which, we'll need to announce our plans at the next church service Sunday. That gives us just enough time to plan."

She stood up and dusted off her skirt.

"I believe it's time for dinner, isn't it, Eliza and Jane?"

"Oh, ja!" Eliza hurried toward the door. "The lasagna is ready, and it'll only take a minute to get everything on the table." She hurried inside, followed by the other women.

Sam looked at Abram and Ben and shook his head. "You two certainly moved fast while I was laid up. Two weddings!"

Abram looked pleased with himself. "I was going to have the knee done anyway, but don't tell Lydia. She thinks she won that point. Might as well let her have her moment of triumph. I'll be laughing on the inside every time I bite into one of her scrumptious cinnamon rolls!"

Ben and Sam chuckled. Then Ben's expression sobered. "Reuben gave me permission to court his sister, and he approves of our marriage. But we have to travel to Lancaster so I can meet her family and ask her parents' permission to marry their daughter. I confess I'm a bit naerfich about it."

"You'll be fine," Sam said. "When will you go?"

"Right after Abram and Lydia's wedding. We'll spend Christmas week there. The mill closes down that week anyway, so it's perfect timing."

"Gut plan," Abram said. "I expect you'll be married there?"

Ben nodded. "Ja, it's her hometown and all. They actually live in Bird-in-Hand, a little town in Lancaster County. They have a hardware store. I believe her parents were hoping she would move back and marry a guy from their community."

"Oh, well, instead they get you!" Sam laughed. "I'm sure it'll be fine. You're a gut catch! You have a gut job and you're eventually going to inherit part of your dat's farm, right?"

"My bruder, Matt, is the farmer. He's going to inherit the farm and the family house," Ben said. "But they've said I can build a house on the property. There's a little parcel Dat and Maem are giving us with about ten acres secluded from the main part of the farm by a field and a small patch of woodland that will let us have a nice garden. Eliza likes to garden. We'll be close to family but have our privacy."

Sam thought he looked satisfied with the idea of moving out of his parents' house into his own place and starting a life with Eliza.

"We'll begin building in the spring. And honestly? I can hardly wait!" He looked at Sam. "I guess I've been a bachelor long enough!"

Sam was filled with happiness for Ben and Abram. He glanced at the door of the house, knowing Jane was inside puttering around in his kitchen, and that felt right. He wanted to show her the rest of the house—a house he hoped she would agree to share with him.

"Let's eat," he suggested, moving toward the door. "I'm starved. And

I need to talk to Jane after dinner."

Ben and Abram smiled.

"I thought you might," Ben said.

"Well! What an eventful day!" Lydia stood up from the table after they had enjoyed the delicious meal, including apple pie and coffee. "Denki for sharing dinner with us on your first evening home, Sam. You must be exhausted. I'm so glad Gott has granted all of our prayers and seen you safely home. Now it's time for this old woman and that old man to head home."

Jane smiled at Lydia's insistence on referring to herself as an old woman. She didn't think Abram liked it very much.

"If you're old, then I must have one foot in the grave. I'm at least three years older than you!" Abram grumped at Lydia as he helped her on with her wool cape and handed her the black bonnet that had been hanging on a peg in the kitchen since they'd all come inside to eat.

"Then it's a gut thing we're getting married so soon!" she teased. "We'll be newlyweds! Something I never thought I'd do again."

He winked at the others. "It's because she can't resist me!"

She chuckled. "Tomorrow you need to call your doctor and schedule your knee surgery, Mr. Irresistible. You don't want to end up like me and wait for it to just break in two! It's not fun, believe me!"

"I will, I will. Don't nag." He winked at Jane over Lydia's head, and Jane felt warm and happy for her elderly friends. She snuck a glance at Sam, who was looking back at her. Standing, she hurried over to the sink to begin the dishes. "Gut night, Lydia! Gut night, Abram! Talk to you soon!"

They waved, and Ben walked them out while Eliza walked over to help Jane with the dishes. They'd just finished when Ben walked back inside. He looked meaningfully at Sam and then said to Eliza, "Would you like to help me with the barn chores? Jane can keep Sam company and make sure he doesn't give in to temptation and try to help us."

"Hey, I promised Nurse Nancy I would be a gut boy," Sam protested, a twinkle in his eyes.

"Come on, Sam," Jane said. "We can take our coffee out on the porch, and you can supervise from there."

Ben and Eliza disappeared in the direction of the barn, and Sam and Jane went out and sat in the comfy Adirondack chairs on the porch.

"Should we let them spend time alone in the barn?" Sam wondered, peering toward the big building.

Jane laughed. "I think we can trust them. What are we going to do otherwise? Follow them around while they feed and muck out?"

He grimaced. "Ja, that was a dumm question." He stared toward the barn, and Jane wondered what he was thinking. She was sure it was not easy for Sam, who was used to being an active man in charge of his own life, to accept the limitations his injury had forced on him, even though only temporarily.

She was about to suggest they take a little stroll, even though the evening was quite chilly, when Sam turned and regarded her intently.

"What is it?" She asked, wondering whether something was wrong.

"I was wondering whether you like my house and land."

She looked around. "Ja, what I've seen. It's beautiful. I really like the way you've done the house too. Our tastes are very much alike."

She blushed a bit, wondering whether that had been too forward. "Gut. That's gut. I want you to like it here. This place is everything I've ever wanted." He took a deep breath. "My parents died when I was pretty young. My dat's much older bruder was the only family I had left. Our farm was sold off and the money put in trust for me, though I didn't know that at the time. My uncle took me in to live with him above his buggy shop in a big old barn in downtown Berlin. He taught me the business, and when he died, he left it all to me. That's when I found out about the trust. I had enough money to buy this place. I was outgrowing the old buggy business, so I sold it to my cousin, Jonathan Mast, who moved his farrier business into it. And I moved here."

She nodded silently, waiting for him to continue.

"Jane, all those talks we had in the hospital, about our dreams for the future, and our plans. Were you serious? Do you really dream about having a place of your own and settling down and raising a family?"

She blinked at him, wondering what was behind his question. "Of course, Sam. I said so, didn't I?"

He shifted in his seat and studied her face. "Well, ja. But you live such an independent life now. You've got the whole third floor of the bakery building to yourself. And you work full-time. Would you really want to give all that up?"

She let a smile slowly spread across her face as she realized where he was going with this. "Sam, for the right incentive, I'd give it all up in a heartbeat. Working in Lizzie's bakery is fun and satisfying. But in the end, it's Lizzie's dream, and Lizzie's business. Now she has John to help run it, and let's face it, eventually they'll probably need to expand to both floors of living space, as their family grows, fashtay?"

He looked at her very intently. "Ja, I understand what you're saying. But maybe you want a business of your own? A place of your own?"

She nodded. "Ja, I do."

His face registered disappointment, and she held up a hand. "Sam, I do want a place of my own but not in some business somewhere. Don't you get it? I want my place to be wherever you are! I want it to be with you!"

Hope lit his eyes and he reached for her hand. "Do you mean it? Even after everything?"

"Ja, Sam. Even after everything. I told you I forgave you for the narrish nickname. Will you please forgive yourself so we can get on with our lives already? I'm honestly getting tired of waiting!"

A beautiful smile spread over his face. "I can do that." His eyes locked with hers, and she found herself losing her ability to think as she sank into his hazel gaze. He leaned toward her, and she realized he was going to kiss her. But a sudden thought had her pressing a hand to his chest.

"Wait!"

He snapped back. "What?"

"What about Secret?"

He blinked in confusion. "What secret? Do you mean the secret admirer thing? I promise, no more mystery gifts or bad poems." He started to lean in again, and she pushed against his chest to stop him.

"Nee, not the secret admirer." She paused a minute. "Although, I kind of like getting cheesy gifts and poems, so you could maybe surprise me with that kind of thing from time to time."

"Then what secret did you mean?"

"My cat, Secret! Where I go, she goes. Is that oll recht?"

He stared at her a moment. "Do I need to ask her permission to marry you?"

Jane felt a huge surge of happiness roll over her senses. She gave a giddy little giggle. "Nee, probably my dat would be a better choice for that. I just want to be sure you will be oll recht living with a cat in your house."

"Our house, Jane. If you marry me, the house, the barns, the buggy business, the whole property—all of it—will all be ours, not just mine."

"Oh."

"In fact, I'd welcome your help with the business, if you're interested. You could take over the bookings and the accounting if you like that kind of thing."

She thought about that a minute and decided she wouldn't mind giving it a try. She nodded, and he beamed.

"So, will you do it?"

She found she'd lost the conversational track. "Do what?"

"Marry me, Jane. Will you please marry me? I love you. I've always loved you, even when I was just a dumm kid. And if you marry me, I'll even love your cat. You can have ten cats if you want!"

She gave him a beautiful smile and threw her arms around his neck. "Oh, ja, Samuel! It's all I've ever wanted! I've loved you since I was a little girl. I accept!"

"You do?"

"Ja! I do!"

"Denki, Jane! I promise to make you happy!"

"We'll make each other happy, Sam. And when unhappy things happen, which they're bound to, we'll weather them together."

"Ja, that's exactly it," he whispered. He started to lean in again then paused, looking into her eyes.

"What?" she asked breathlessly.

"I just wanted to make sure you didn't have any more questions."

She gave a tiny shake of her head, and he responded with a satisfied smile.

"Gut, then I can finally do this." He leaned in the rest of the way and kissed her gently and lingeringly, finally breaking off the kiss with a sigh and leaning his forehead against hers.

"Jane, *ich lieba dich*."

Her head spinning a bit from the lovely first kiss, she opened her eyes and dreamily replied, "I love you too, Sam. And fortunately for you, I don't want ten cats."

They laughed together and shared another kiss as twilight fell and a meteor streaked across the indigo November evening sky.

EPILOGUE

Two Weeks Later. . .

"Is everything ready?" Eliza hurried over to Jane, who was consulting a list on a clipboard. "Lizzie and John will be here any minute!"

Jane and Eliza had planned a surprise welcome home party for the newlyweds, whose train had arrived on time in Akron over an hour before. They should be walking through the front door of the bakery at any time.

"Ja, I believe so. Little Mouse and Secret are snoozing on the chairs in front of the fire over there. I know Lizzie will want to see Little Mouse as soon as she gets in. Is everyone in the kitchen?"

"Ja, I'm keeping them all happy with pastries and coffee until the guests of honor arrive."

"Perfect. Hopefully it won't be much longer."

The bells over the front door jingled, and Jane and Eliza spun to face the door, ready to welcome the travelers home. But it wasn't Lizzie and John who walked inside.

"Daniel Beechy?" Jane asked in astonishment. They hadn't seen Daniel since the night he'd returned Little Mouse to them, and to tell the truth, she'd almost forgotten about him.

He looked uncertainly from one woman to the other. "I hope you don't mind if I stop by? I won't stay long. I have something I want to show you. Well, someone really."

Jane noticed that Daniel was carrying two things—a large, flat, wrapped parcel and a cat carrier, from which emitted a plaintive meow. She saw two feline heads pop up above the backs of their chairs by the fireplace, checking out the intruder in their territory.

"Is that a cat?" Eliza asked, darting forward and peering into the openings in the carrier's top and sides.

"Ja." Daniel gave her a shy smile then looked at Jane. "I took your advice and went to the cat shelter last week. I checked out all the cats, but really, there was no contest. As soon as I saw my little Juniper, I was a goner." He bent over at the carrier and cooed to the angry cat inside, who responded with another yowl. Little Mouse and Secret abandoned their chairs and slunk closer to see the creature emitting the loud cries from inside the carrier.

Jane and Eliza exchanged disbelieving glances. Was this the same guy who had been so difficult before? Now he seemed like a different man.

"I really want you both to meet her. If you have a minute?"

The kitchen door opened, and Sam and Ben came through. Jane glanced at Sam and saw his eyes narrow when he noticed Daniel.

"Sam, Daniel has come by to show us his new cat!" she said. "Isn't that nice?"

"Oh, you brought her over?" Ben asked, peering into the carrier. "You mentioned that you were picking her up yesterday. Did she come through her spay okay?"

Daniel beamed at Ben. "Ja! She's gut. And she's the sweetest cat I've ever met. No offense, Jane, but I'm really glad you realized I had your friend's cat. If you hadn't, I'd never have found my little Juniper!" He leaned down and cooed into the carrier again, and Juniper answered with a yowl. Secret and Little Mouse yowled back challengingly, leaping up onto a nearby table to get a better view.

"I'd get her out, but she's recovering from surgery. I just picked her up today, a day later than planned, because she had some complications and they wanted to observe her longer. Anyway, denki so much for telling me about the shelter! I owe you for that!" He offered the wrapped parcel to Jane. "So I picked you up a gift." Catching Sam's frown, Daniel quickly added, "Nothing secret, ha ha! Just a thank-you for helping me find my cat, and really, for just being nice to me in spite of the fact that I was pretty much a jerk." He frowned. "I admit I was pretty lonely, and I behaved badly. I hope you can forgive me. All of you."

Jane nodded. "Of course we forgive you, Daniel. And you weren't that bad."

Sam cleared his throat, and Jane smiled. "Okay, you were. But now you can make a whole new start!"

Daniel laughed. "I plan to. I've accepted a job in Shipshewana, Indiana, as a journeyman carpenter. It's what I apprenticed in, and what I really want to do. I'll be leaving at the end of the month after I take care of some obligations here. So, anyway, here's your thank-you gift. I know you really like it, and I want you to have it."

He handed her the large, flat package, and she took it reluctantly. "Are you sure? You really don't have to give me anything."

"You really don't," Sam agreed and then shrugged when Jane and Eliza glared at him.

"I really do," Daniel said. "In friendship, nothing more. And before you open it, I'll tell you I worked out a deal with the gallery owner to build frames for him. I'm gut with wood and such." He shrugged. "Carpenter. So I didn't pay full price for it. Just so you don't feel awkward." He took a step back. "Don't try and return it—that would hurt my feelings!"

He turned and headed for the door. "Goodbye! See you all in gmay!"

He left with his cat, who emitted a final yowl on the way out the door, which was returned by both Little Mouse and Secret as they jumped up onto the windowsill to make sure the strange cat was truly leaving. Sam, Ben, and Eliza turned and stared at the package in Jane's hands.

"Well, you'd better go ahead and open it," Ben said.

Jane had a suspicion as to what was in the package. But he couldn't have, could he? She carefully pried the brown paper from the corner of the package and pulled it off. It fell away to reveal the beautiful painting depicting a quilting bee done by their friend Miriam.

"Ach, nee! This is too much! Catch him, Sam, I have to give this back!"

"He's gone," Ben said. "I saw him drive away. Besides, he wants you to have it. It's an apology for his behavior. I say keep it if you like it."

"I love it, but it's really expensive! Really, really expensive!"

Sam was frowning at the painting. "It's a very nice painting, though. I like it. And wouldn't it look gut hanging in our living room?"

She looked at him in surprise. "You wouldn't mind having something

Daniel gave me in our house?"

"Why should I mind? I'm the one you're marrying, not Daniel. And I have a feeling that Daniel has turned over a new leaf."

"Besides, you heard him. He didn't pay for it," Ben said. "He worked out a deal with the gallery manager in trade. And it sounds like this is something Daniel needs to do to clear the slate, so to speak."

"And he's moving away," Eliza pointed out. "Which closes that door!"

The door to the kitchen opened again, and Miriam Zook came out, along with Lydia and Abram. "Did we hear the door? Are Lizzie and John here?"

"Nee, it was someone else," Eliza said. "You'll never guess who!"

"Wait, is that my painting?" Miriam asked, bewildered. "What's it doing here?"

"Well, remember Daniel Beechy?" When Miriam nodded, Eliza said, "He worked a deal with the gallery owner to get the painting as an apology to Jane for behaving like a jerk. And also as a thank-you to her for telling him about the cat shelter. He brought his new kitty to show us. She's pretty cute, from what I could see through the cat carrier."

"He bought this painting? But it's, um, kind of pricey," Miriam said.

"I know!" Jane said. "But he said he's making frames to pay it off. And he insisted. The truth is, I really want it. I love this painting."

Miriam looked at her in surprise. "You do? Why didn't you say so? I'd have given it to you."

"Nee, you can't do that! You work hard, and this is how you earn your living!" Jane looked at the painting. "You know what? I'm going to accept it. Sam says it's fine, and I really want it." She laughed. "I'm so excited to hang this up in Sam's house!"

"Our house," he reminded her.

Her heart melted and she gave him a dopey smile. "Ja, our house. In a little under a year, anyway!"

The front door bells jingled again, and they all looked at the door, but instead of Lizzie and John, in walked one of the last people any of them expected. There was a gasp, and Miriam stepped forward, one hand slightly raised toward the man who had come through the door.

"David," Miriam whispered tremulously.

David Miller, Lizzie's cousin who had decided he wasn't ready to be baptized into the Amish faith six years before and had left to work as a carpenter in a Mennonite community near Indianapolis, stopped and stared back at Miriam.

"Miriam," he whispered. "You're here?" Then he cleared his throat and licked his lips. "Ah, wie ghets? It's been, um, a long time."

"It's going fine, denki," Miriam said, straightening her spine and glaring at the newcomer. "Ja, it's been a long time. So, you're back, I hear?"

"Ja, got back recently. I'm staying at my parents' place."

"So, are you staying for good? Are you getting baptized?"

He swallowed then shrugged. "Probably. I'm still deciding what I want to do. But I had to come home. My mudder is ill, and my vader needs my help."

"I. . .see. That's why you came home? No other reason?" She looked at him miserably, her heart on her sleeve, and he dropped his eyes.

"Ja, that's why."

Jane's heart was breaking for her friend, who had feelings for David Miller and had waited for him to come back to Willow Creek for six years, declining invitations from other men in the hopes that David would someday return. And now here he was, back again, but he'd as good as told her he wasn't there for her. Publicly.

As if recovering herself, Miriam pasted a brilliant smile on her face, and she turned to Jane. "Well, I'm so glad you like my painting! I'm happy it's going to someone who will cherish it. Now, I really need to go. My maem needs my help tonight with a sewing project."

"Oh, can't you stay?" Jane asked, taking hold of Miriam's hand and giving it a sympathetic little squeeze. "I don't get to see nearly enough of you."

Miriam's smile brightened even more, and she shook her head regretfully. "Nee, but denki for inviting me. Please tell Lizzie and John I'm sorry I had to leave before they got here. But they're running late, and I really have to go!"

Without another word, she rushed past David and out the door, the bells jingling merrily in her wake.

David stared after her. Everyone else stared at David.

"Well, that could have gone better," he muttered, turning to find his old friends looking at him in disbelief. "Well, it could have," he said, looking as miserable as Miriam had moments earlier.

Before anyone could comment, however, the bells again sounded, and this time it was Lizzie and John who came through the door, suitcases and bags in hand. "We're back!" Lizzie cried, dropping her luggage on the floor and hugging Jane, then Eliza. "Was that Miriam Zook I saw driving away in a buggy just now? She looked upset."

"Lizzie! Welcome home! It's so gut to see you!" Jane cried, handing the painting to Sam, who leaned it carefully against a wall where it would be safe.

"Ja, it was Miriam. She was upset at me, I guess," David said.

"David! You're back! Oh, welcome home, it's so gut to see you! What did you do to Miriam?" Lizzie gave her cousin a big hug and ruffled his hair, which was cut quite short in a style favored by Mennonite men. "Look at your hair! So short! It looks gut on you."

Forgetting her own question, she turned and took in her friends. "But what are you all doing here?"

At that moment, the kitchen door burst open, and people poured in, yelling, "Surprise!"

Someone handed Lizzie and John glasses of lemonade and plates of cake, and soon everyone was greeting them and welcoming them home and asking questions about their travels.

Lizzie looked at Jane with a raised eyebrow.

"Surprise!" Jane said and giggled. "I hope it's a gut one!"

Lizzie threw her head back and laughed. "Oh, ja! We're tired but not too tired to eat cake with our favorite people!"

"You see?" Ben said. "I told you this was a gut plan! All my plans work out!"

"Not the pie thing," Sam reminded him.

"Okay, that's that," Jane said. "We've heard about this pie thing for weeks now, and I, for one, want to know what it means!"

Abram and Lydia had joined their small group, seated at a table in the bakery's dining room. The room was full of people who had come to welcome the newlyweds home, but most of them were busy talking to each other and paying no attention to the small group of friends.

"Oh, I can tell you about the pie thing," Abram said, sending an amused glance at Ben over reading glasses that he'd donned to take a look at Jane's painting a few minutes ago and forgotten to remove.

"Uh-oh," Ben said. "I forgot you knew about that."

Abram smiled. "Oh, ja, and I'm not likely to forget, since it involved ten missing pies at a Sunday church lunch, and five Amish boys who ended up doing extra chores for several weeks to atone for the missing pie—after they got over how sick they all got from stuffing two whole pies each into their greedy gullets, that is!"

There were several moments of stunned silence as everyone turned to look at Ben. "Hey, it wasn't only me!"

"Ja, I was in on it," Sam said. "And so was David, there."

David nodded. "Yep. Afraid so. Which is why whenever I hear Benuel Fisher say he has an idea, and his ideas always work out, I head for the door before I get talked into eating two stolen pies and painting the inside of someone else's house." David grinned at Ben, who had the grace to smile back.

"Well, the pie thing didn't work out, it's true. But this party did!" He raised his glass of lemonade and called loudly, "Welcome home, Lizzie and John!"

Everyone in the room raised their glasses of lemonade or cups of coffee and echoed Ben. "Welcome home!"

"It's very gut to be home," Lizzie said, sharing a fond but tired glance with John and snuggling her cat in her lap. "So, did anything interesting happen while we were gone?"

It took the laughter that followed that question several minutes to peter out, after which Jane, snuggling her own precious cat in her arms, said, "About that..." And she, Sam, Ben, Eliza, Lydia, and Abram entertained the returned travelers with quite a tale!

Anne Blackburne lives and works in southeast Ohio as a newspaper editor and writer. She is the mother of five grown children and has one wonderful grandchild and a spoiled poodle named Millie. For fun, when she isn't working on Amish romance or sweet mysteries, Anne directs and acts in community theater productions and writes and directs original plays. She also enjoys reading, kayaking, swimming, searching for beach glass, and just sitting with a cup of coffee looking at large bodies of water. Her idea of the perfect vacation is cruising and seeing amazing new places with people she loves.

THE HEART OF THE AMISH

Full of faith, hope, and romance, this series takes you into the Heart of Amish country.

AVAILABLE NOW:

The Flower Quilter

By Mindy Steele

Barbara Schwartz struggles to find what brings her joy amidst traditional expectations. But while staying with her grandmother in Indiana, a chance to help landscaper Melvin Bontrager may lead to a unique expression of her artistry—and romance.

Paperback / 978-1-63609-642-1

Ruth's Ginger Snap Surprise

By Anne Blackburne

Ruth Helmuth learns that being independent doesn't necessarily mean you can't accept help—especially if it means saving what's most important to you and maybe realizing your dreams in the bargain!

Paperback / 978-1-63609-689-6

The Quilt Room Secret

By Lisa Jones Baker

Trini seems to have her life all lined up, owning her own quilt store before the age of thirty—but secret dreams pull her, despite her falling for a handsome farmer. And soon she will be faced with an agonizing choice for her future.

Paperback / 978-1-63609-775-6

Courting an Amish Bishop

By Mindy Steele

Simon, a dedicated bishop, and Stella, an herbalist, each have been so busy serving others that they have neglected romance—until now. Brought together to help the sick of the community, is it possible for them to have a second chance at love?

Paperback / 978-1-63609-815-9

Mary's Calico Hope
By Anne Blackburne

Mary Yoder is happy with her life despite her disability from a childhood accident, but then a Mennonite doctor comes into her life, challenging everything. Can Mary risk hoping for a future free of pain and a love outside the faith she has already been baptized into?

Paperback / 978-1-63609-855-5

Serenity's Secret
By Lisa Jones Baker

Serenity Miller, the flower shop owner of Arthur, Illinois, is content with her path in life. But a brush with danger and a taste of romance make her question the secrets she has always held close.

Paperback / 978-1-63609-958-3

A Stolen Kiss
by Mindy Steele

LeEtta Miller's daring impulse to kiss a stranger will lead to events neither she nor Benuel Ropp ever imagined.

Paperback / 978-1-63609-993-4

Lizzie's Little Mouse
by Anne Blackburne

Lizzie Miller is determined to open a French-inspired bakery. But even on opening day, threats of putting her out of business arrive, and it'll take all her strength and friends to help her overcome the opposition.

Paperback / 979-8-89151-068-5

Hunting for a Husband
by Mindy Steele

Leah Wickey moves to Kentucky with a strong desire to find a husband, but when she sets her sights on Joe, could his disabilities get in the way of romance?

Paperback / 979-8-89151-145-3

A Daughter's Choice

By Kelly Irvin

Henrietta Miller has one passion—animals. Dodging her aunt's matchmaking attempts, Hen expands her business of selling products from her farm animals.

Paperback / 979-8-89151-221-4

COMING SOON

A Heart on Consignment

By Mindy Steele

Despite knowing her parents' eagerness for grandchildren, Salina Stoltzfus takes a break from the disappointment of courting to help start a consignment shop for her community. Embarrassed by a failed engagement, Seth Weaver seeks respite in Indiana, and his uncle volunteers him to help the spunky girl in setting up a new store. When Salina's parents are caught meddling in her love life, she devises a crazy idea that might gain her some time and space. Could it be that the road to happiness is paved with good intentions and epic fails—until we cross paths when the one made especially for us?

Paperback / 979-8-89151-313-6

Christian Fiction for Women is your online home for the latest in Christian fiction.

Check us out online for:

- Giveaways
- Recipes
- Info About Upcoming Releases
- Book Trailers
- News and More!

Find Christian Fiction for Women at Your Favorite Social Media Site:

 Search "Christian Fiction for Women"

 @fictionforwomen

---